RobotWorld

RAY VEROLA

For all those who have helped me along the way.

And to everyone who reads this book.

Thank you.

The enemy is fear. We think it is hate; but, it is fear.

—Mahatma Gandhi

1

May 2075
Capital City (the former Washington, DC), Northeast Sector

WHERE THE HELL *am I?*

Taylor Morris felt totally disoriented, and his body didn't work right. He couldn't open his eyes, couldn't feel his legs.

Did I fall asleep in the middle of a street?

An icy line of terror shot up the base of his spine to the back of his head and shocked him halfway back to reality. The last thing he remembered was having dinner with two new friends who were helping him work through the toughest time of his life. He'd been hitting the Serenity too hard these days, but he'd never been as out of it as he seemed to be right now.

He lay facedown on something hard. The firmest mattress ever? Possibly. But the smell? Asphalt. Pavement? Could be. The left side of his face was scratched up and stung like hell. He tasted the metallic tang of blood in his mouth. The air felt heavy and reeked of rotting garbage.

He forced his eyes open but saw nothing but pitch-black. He struggled to raise his head and felt nauseous as his world spun in the eerie quiet. He heard a gurgling deep in his abdomen, followed by a burning in his throat. He managed to raise his head just before projectile vomiting. His head fell back to the pavement. Lucky for him, the force of his heaving had sent the vomit far from where his head slammed back into the blacktop, or else he'd be resting in his own foul-smelling retch.

What the hell is happening? Have I finally hit rock bottom?

He labored to take a deep breath. As he'd suffered with moderate asthma since childhood, the tightness in his chest was not an unfamiliar feeling. He relaxed his shoulder muscles and began to inhale and exhale slowly, as he'd done so many times. It brought a small degree of calm to the hurricane in his head, and the tension in his chest eased slightly.

Taylor's eyes now seemed to be the only part of him that worked. He scanned the area as his vision adjusted to the darkness. He was planted in the middle of a road, a row of small storage garages on each side of the spot to which he was anchored. He recognized this dead-end street. Hardly any cars, let alone people, traversed this isolated part of town after dark. Since becoming homeless a few days ago, he remembered scrounging for food in the nearby garbage cans one afternoon.

A slight breeze blew the smell of his vomit back to him. He gagged but recovered quickly, relieved that he didn't have enough food in his stomach to throw up again.

He braced his left hand on the ground and attempted to get to his feet, but the hand felt numb, like it wasn't there. No dice. He dug his fingernails into the unyielding pavement and managed to raise his torso a few inches, but his hand slipped, causing his face to slam into the road once again, opening a gash over his right eyebrow. He groaned. Blood oozed into his eye; he tried to blink the irritation away without success.

Need to calm down, Taylor. You've been in tough spots before and come through with flying colors. A deep breath. *Buck up, man. You've got to get up and reach the sidewalk.*

Using both hands this time, he raised his chest. Everything was still spinning.

"Damn this shit," he muttered.

Could this be the end? I know I've screwed up, but this is no way for my life to end. This is no way for any life to end.

A wave of disappointment washed over him as his life involuntarily played at fast-forward speed on the movie screen inside his brain. All the good times, followed by the mistakes that pushed him from a successful executive—"the luckiest man alive" he'd once called himself—to where he was right now.

Fight off the self-pity, Taylor. Sure you've made a mess of things, but you can still get it together. As long as a person's above-ground and breathing, there's always hope. One step at a time. You can do it. First, you've got to get out of the road before someone runs you over.

I won't give up.

A tingling feeling returned to his arms. Using only his upper extremities, he crawled toward the sidewalk. But he froze when two bright lights broke through the inky blackness.

He squinted. The lights were the headlights of a personal transport vehicle, parked about fifty yards away at the end of the dead-end road.

How did that PTV get there? It doesn't matter—I'm rescued!

Taylor expected a driver to storm out of the PTV and give him holy hell for the sheer lunacy of his lying in the middle of the road at night.

He held a hand high to make certain the driver had seen him. "Help! Help!" he yelled. The red hood and grillwork of the PTV looked strangely familiar.

Then the engine revved—and the PTV started barreling toward him, angrily kicking up road dust.

I'm a goner.

Taylor's eyes opened wide as dinner plates. He unsteadily struggled to his feet and let loose a guttural scream.

Just as the front bumper of the PTV was almost close enough for him to touch, he made a desperate leap toward the sidewalk. The PTV missed him by inches, speeding by with a high-pitched hiss he could hear and feel. Taylor landed on his side and bounced off the sidewalk into a wooden green garage door badly in need of a new paint job. His right arm was scratched by tiny, faded green paint chips. He moaned at the fiery pain all over his body.

He looked up to see the rear lights of the PTV turn bright red as it screeched to a stop at the corner. After a minute or so, the vehicle turned right and disappeared.

Taylor propped himself up against the garage door and took a moment to catch his breath. As the adrenaline started to fade, he shivered. *How could the driver not have seen me?* He brushed paint chips from his skin.

And then it hit him: this was no accident.

Blacking out at dinner with two new friends, waking up in the middle of the road more hungover than ever—and then recognizing the distinctive grille of the red PTV belonging to those same friends, just before the attempt to run him over. The PTV had to have been parked on the dead-end side of the street from before he'd awakened from whatever had knocked him out.

Although too much Serenity had probably destroyed some of his brain cells, he was still smart enough to piece together the jigsaw puzzle of this evening. The clues had been there all the time.

The unmistakable conclusion: his new friends had drugged him, left him in the middle of the road, and tried to kill him tonight.

2

Three months earlier

TAYLOR MORRIS KNEW he shouldn't have done it, but he did it anyway. His intuition had warned him, but he ignored the warning and now was dealing with his stomach doing backflips. This shouldn't have been a big deal, but somehow it might turn into one.

For the better part of the past year, he'd resisted the periodic invitations of Sophia Ross—the prickly, whip-smart president of RobotWorld and his immediate supervisor—to go to the Cap City bar, a popular local watering hole, for a "quick drink" after work. But today, he'd finally relented.

After all, performance evaluations were due soon and turning down the repeated requests of his boss might not be the wisest career move. Especially since, for some reason, he had the feeling Sophia was souring on him, even though many in the company—including Sophia—acknowledged him as the most competent executive at RW. One prominent online newsmagazine had recently termed him "the head of the best sales department of the fastest-growing company in the world."

Well, actually, Taylor had suspected a reason for Sophia's souring. For the past three months or so, he had been diligently working on an attempt to "re-find" himself and "get back what he'd lost." What he'd lost, he believed, was his true self. The losing began when he accepted a sales job at RobotWorld five years earlier at the age of twenty-seven. Then one morning three months ago, he'd awakened in his bed with the sun streaming in his eyes and a clear thought that he was tired of being an actor in somebody else's play. It was just that simple—and just that complicated.

Prior to working at RW, Taylor had never been too shy to express his opinion and be completely, sometimes brutally, honest. It was a quality he'd gotten from his deceased father, and it was the only weakness he'd ever displayed as a salesman.

But in trying to shoehorn his honesty into the regimented RobotWorld culture, Taylor had suppressed some of his natural personality in an attempt to project himself as the ultimate team player. He believed at the time that such concessions were part of getting older and getting to the top of the corporate ladder. He'd done so well in becoming a team player that, in a little over four years, he managed to rise to the top position of head sales manager. But despite his career success, becoming less of the person he really thought he was grated on him like a pebble in the shoe of a marathon runner.

For the past three months, Taylor hadn't acted like most of the other executives at RobotWorld, who would glad-hand Sophia Ross and endorse her every move. That was at the heart of why Taylor didn't want to be at this bar alone with her. The real Taylor sought to always be himself no matter what. A wise career move? Time would tell.

Initially, Sophia had told Taylor that she loved his newly found, unvarnished directness. But that was almost ninety days prior—and it seemed like an eternity ago. It appeared to Taylor that his boss's opinion of him had recently changed, and not in a positive way.

As he entered the crowded, dimly-lit bar, Taylor spotted Sophia waving at him from a booth in the back. She sat alone, nursing a vodka on the rocks. The contrast between her long, naturally curly red hair and her alabaster skin made her stand out in any crowd. As usual, she didn't appear to have fussed much with her luxurious hair, which was combed straight back. It fell to below her shoulders, setting off her pleasing round face. She had changed out of the informal uniform of gray shirt and gray pants that all RW employees wore at work into a solid dark blue pantsuit. Despite her striking face and figure, Sophia didn't have anyone special in her life. The joke around the office, though never repeated in her presence, was that she was married to RW.

The Cap City wasn't big—its telescreen advertisements called the bar "cozy"—with a ten-foot-wide aisle separating tables with white tablecloths and plush, dark-red leather booths on one side and a long bar on the other. The place had a peculiar odor, most likely due to the combination of the sweat of a standing-room-only, alcohol-fueled crowd of humanity, the marijuana/tobacco smoke haze hanging in the air, and the heavy-duty disinfectant used in many public places these days. To Taylor, the offensive smell seemed not unlike that of a poorly-maintained public restroom. The walls, consisting of black walnut-grooved acoustic panels, were bare except for ten large telescreens.

Taylor ran a hand through his longish, jet-black hair as he started what turned out to be a slow trek through the crowd to get to Sophia's table. He stood five feet eleven, weighed about one hundred ninety-five pounds, and had a little bulge in his stomach, but a good chest and shoulders. He'd been a champion high school wrestler back in the day, but he now had the look of an athlete who'd let his body go a little since his glory days.

"Excuse me," Taylor mumbled over and over as he slipped past and around body after body in the raucous, mostly male, mostly overweight, mostly middle-aged crowd.

He came to a full stop halfway toward Sophia. A skinny six-tyish man with a pointy nose and wispy gray hair blocked his path. Their eyes met. The man smiled broadly, revealing a mouth with no teeth. "I won twenty bucks on the last play," he said. "It's my lucky day."

"Way to go," Taylor said. "Please let me get around. . ."

"Sure, buddy," the old man said, as he squeezed his back against the belly of another bar patron whose eyes were glued to a telescreen. "Life is good," the old man said. "Today's my lucky day."

Taylor continued his slogging through the crowd and thought, *My guess is you haven't had too many lucky days, friend.*

All the telescreens in the bar were showing the latest Manglecon game. Officially, Manglecon was called New American Football, a sport largely based on the now-defunct National Football League. But most fans knew it as Manglecon. Taylor hated this brutal sport. It was a more violent version of the old NFL, played mainly by the underclass of all races for the entertainment of the masses. The game was a society-wide obsession, or so it seemed. The derogatory nickname of Manglecon was coined by a sports reporter who'd written, "Those who play it get their bodies mangled and their brains concussed." With the advent of easy-bet via tele-screen, not only every game but every play had big money riding on it. Nowadays, easy-bet was one of the few ways for most peo-ple to get some quick cash, even though the online betting parlors seemed to be the only ones showing a profit at the end of each game. Although even much of their monetary gain was siphoned off in the form of a government tax.

The on-field participants of Manglecon knew the dangers of the sport, but ignored the risks because of their apparent love of vio-lence, competition, and the huge salaries. The lightweight, high-tech padding worn by the players resembled the old NFL protection and was supposed to shield participants from physical harm due to player collisions. Instead, it turned players into more devastatingly effec-tive missiles to launch into one another. Taylor thought the constant, well-publicized directives from the hapless football commissioner to make Manglecon safer illustrated his most favorite *and* least favorite law of the universe: the Law of Unintended Consequences.

Taylor continued to slowly push his way to the back of the bar, and he smirked as the rowdy, shabbily dressed crowd around him cheered wildly at a vicious collision that left one player from each team motionless on the field. Within five seconds after the players hit the turf, two automated stretchers were on the scene to scrape each combatant off the field and to the stadium infirmary. The action resumed immediately, without interruption. Taylor laughed to him-self as almost all in the bar, in a bizarre group movement in uni-son, swiped their individual debit cards over the small telescreens directly in front of them to easy-bet on the success or failure of the next play.

The congestion in the aisle caused Taylor to come to another full stop.

A young man in a white T-shirt, who had jagged black lightning-bolt tattoos covering both arms, looked at Taylor with rheumy blue eyes and a worried expression. The guy's upper body was swaying side to side, and he appeared to be at least two years under the current legal drinking age of sixteen. "You look like a smart guy, mister. I badly need a winner. Who do you like on the next play?"

Taylor detected a strong smell of alcohol on the young man's breath and more than a hint of desperation in his voice. *He probably needs to win, or he doesn't eat tonight.* Unfortunately, there were a lot of kids living on their own these days, usually on the streets. From out of the corner of his mouth, Taylor said, "Sorry, pal. No clue. I don't follow these teams." Unsaid was the fact that he didn't follow any teams. Taylor felt a twinge of sorrow for this kid. He thought about offering him a small credit from his wrist computer, but this guy would most likely spend any financial assistance on beer. Plus, there were so many kids like this one; if Taylor gave a credit to each one on the street, his bank account would be depleted in a day. Taylor saw an opening in the sea of bodies. He had to move quickly. "Good luck," he said sincerely to the young man as he angled his body sideways to glide past a few more bar patrons.

Life for people in the former United States of America—and, indeed, the world—had changed drastically over the past forty-five years. A relatively small percentage of the planet's population had survived World War III, which had begun in 2030 and ended five years later. Most of the former America was now a vast, unpopulated wasteland according to government pronouncements, as was much of the rest of the world due to the lingering nuclear and biological fallout from the war. Who'd won? Nobody. There were only losers. The only place where significant numbers of humans had survived in the former North America was now known as the Northeast Sector, an area of land that included the former Washington, DC (now called Capital City) and a sliver of what had been the Northern Virginia suburbs at its southernmost border. The Northeast Sector extended north to include parts of eastern Maryland, eastern Pennsylvania, western New Jersey, and a slice of southeast New York state. As most of the area outside the Northeast Sector was supposedly unfit for human survival (again, according to the government), the authorities maintained strict border control—no one allowed to go in or out, as the oft-repeated line on the telescreen went. It was for "the greater good of the people"—another phrase used by the government *ad nauseam*.

Capital City was the only major city in the Northeast Sector. According to government reports, there were only small enclaves of people beyond the Capital City borders. The city was an area of high population concentration. Most lived in what had come to be known as "egg crates": high-rise, government-constructed apartment buildings, many of which had fallen into disrepair as the result of poor maintenance. A perpetual gray cloud of pollution hung above the city like the haze of marijuana/tobacco smoke now hanging over the patrons of the Cap City bar. A constant rotten-egg smell permeated the city's air, the result of a curious combination of industrial pollution (much of it from RobotWorld) and rotting garbage on the streets, which never seemed to be picked up on time by government sanitation trucks.

Most didn't question the authorities now, although some felt the government's actions, ostensibly to protect the population, were really done to further its own power. But the majority of the government's critics had the good sense to keep their opinions to themselves.

3

—

"WELL, IT'S ABOUT time," Sophia said as Taylor managed to complete his plodding march through the crowd to the booth. "You're the last of my five top executives to come out drinking with me. It only took a year."

Taylor was barely able to hear Sophia over the din from the telescreens and the raucousness of the customers. Taylor, like Sophia, had changed out of his gray RW uniform and wore a casual dark-green sports shirt and khaki pants. No sense in drawing attention to the fact that he worked for one of the few highly prosperous—and not too popular—corporations in Capital City. As he settled into a seat across from his boss, he grunted and needed a few seconds to catch his breath. He inhaled deeply through his nose and exhaled slowly through his mouth to refocus. The thought of how out of shape he'd become since his high school wrestling days flashed in his mind; back then, he used to knock off three hundred push-ups in several sets every morning before school and, despite his asthma, could run a mile in less than six minutes.

But this was no time to reminisce about or lament days gone by. Taylor fixed his attention on the matter at hand. "I've told you all along, Sophia. I'm not a drinker. Plus, I hate bars." While true that he was essentially a teetotaler and hated bars, Taylor felt a burning in his stomach at not being completely truthful as to why he'd avoided this meeting.

Sophia's usual poker face morphed into a twisted smile. "Sometimes I think you're trying to avoid me."

Taylor answered with a forced smile and another lie. "Not true. Why would I ever try to avoid a sparkling personality like yours?" The bile in his stomach migrated halfway up his throat and left a sour aftertaste. He knew he was not being honest, playing the lying game most of RW's upper management played every day. It was bad enough he felt the pressure to play this game on the job. To play it now after work, on his own time, increased the tightness in his abdomen. He looked away from Sophia and focused on a telescreen.

A huge collective groan from the patrons almost shook the place. The reason for the grousing was clear. On all the giant telescreens in the bar appeared the severe face of the Supreme Leader of the Northeast Sector, Arthur Toback. The Supreme Leader never smiled. He usually appeared on the telescreen as a giant head with his black hair displaying a flattop cut, framed on the screen from the neck up. A huge white forehead was his most prominent feature. Toback almost always wore a solid black shirt under a solid black jacket with a solid black background behind him. This, and the fact that he rarely showed his hands, created the impression of his head and neck floating on air in the middle of the screen. Hard black eyebrows over hard black eyes stared directly into the camera—and straight into the soul of every viewer. Or at least that seemed to be the intention of these broadcasts. A dark goatee encircled his narrow-lipped mouth, the only non-severe part of his face.

The ubiquitous telescreens, standard presences in every home, office space, public meeting place, and on every street corner, were able to send and receive transmissions whether turned on or off. Transmission reception from telescreens was one aspect of how the government monitored and controlled the population. Now, during a pause in the game action, Supreme Leader Toback was about to deliver one of his usual one-minute telescreen pep talks designed to prop up societal morale.

"Here comes the doublespeak propaganda," a large male patron with a massive beer belly shouted while standing on a chair and raising a mugful of suds at a screen. A good part of the beer spilled out of the mug onto the head of a short, blond man standing next to the big guy. The place erupted in laughter.

The Supreme Leader began as he always did, with what Taylor read as a deadpan, soulless expression and the words, "My fellow citizens . . ." Then the bar patrons ignored the telescreens and continued their loud talking and excessive drinking. The voice of the Supreme Leader—which Taylor had once described to a friend as one-part sing-song, one-part low-grade chain saw—was difficult to hear over the noise, which included sporadic boos and derisive laughter directed at the screens. Whatever Toback was saying, it seemed the clear majority here had either heard it before or were not interested.

Taylor pointed at one telescreen and said, "That man is the biggest fraud ever perpetrated on a society. And almost everyone knows it. Just a giant detached head with no discernible sense of humor or perspective, spouting nonsense with an irritating voice about a freedom and progress that don't exist." He shook his head. "Toback's lucky most people don't care about the government. They're zonked out on Serenity or alcohol or both, and devoted to betting on Manglecon. Why the government hasn't cracked down on the proliferation of Serenity is a mystery to me. But the people booing Toback here ought to be careful. Those stupid enough to publicly challenge the government tend to disappear. Big Brother has arrived." A feeling of satisfaction washed over Taylor. He was back to being his honest self, at least for now.

Sophia kept her lips pursed tightly as she glanced at Taylor and then at the large wall telescreen nearest to them. From out of the corner of his eye, Taylor saw a redness in her face and ears that almost matched her hair color. And he could sense the negative vibe. The secretive, guarded Sophia and RobotWorld were rumored to be strong supporters of the government and the Supreme Leader. But Taylor had never heard his boss utter anything political. Sitting next to Sophia now, however, Taylor knew in his bones that the rumors were true.

"The Leader is just trying to do his job," Sophia said. She took a sip of her vodka on the rocks. "It's a tough job, and I think he's doing it well."

Taylor's eyes refocused on a wall screen. The game returned to wild cheers from the Cap City patrons. Taylor hated being right yet again, in not wanting to meet Sophia at this bar. But sometimes he couldn't resist being the smart guy who wouldn't play the usual, go-along-to-get-along act—even when it got him into trouble. Maybe that made him not as smart as he thought he was. He shouldn't have come here. But since he was here, he wasn't going to censor himself because his boss sat next to him. The real Taylor, the honest Taylor was back—and it felt good.

Taylor drummed his fingers on the table. "I'd like the Leader to address those mysterious disappearances of homeless people happening downtown. And then do something about it."

More wild cheering emanated from the bar crowd at another bone-crunching collision and the almost instantaneous appearance of an automated stretcher.

Sophia turned her head toward Taylor. "The homeless are vanishing because they're mostly a bunch of worthless Serenity addicts. They get high and who knows what happens to them. I say it's even money that some of them fall into the Anacostia River, never to be recovered. Most of them don't have family or friends. Check the statistics. You know the old saying: you reap what you sow."

"True. People must take responsibility for their actions. But there's worth in everyone. Even a Serenity addict."

Sophia focused on a telescreen and didn't respond.

But once again, Taylor refused to repress his true self. "C'mon, Sophia. Let's be honest. Just look around you. Do you see the signs of a healthy, vibrant society? I know RobotWorld is prospering, and that's great—for us and our bottom line. But society as a whole? In the toilet and getting ready to be flushed. George Orwell would be proud of the job our alleged Supreme Leader is doing. The only place where society is doing well is in the government propaganda fantasy on the telescreen. *Nineteen Eighty-Four* has arrived. But almost a century late."

Sophia downed the remainder of her drink and stood. She touched her pants pocket. "My communication earpiece is vibrating. I've got to go. See you in the morning." She swiped a debit card over the table telescreen to pay for her drink, negotiated her way through the bar crowd much faster than he'd done in getting to her, and disappeared out the door in a flash.

Taylor was stunned. Maybe he'd gone too far. Maybe he was a little too reckless. But ticking off the boss probably wouldn't be a big deal. His outstanding job performance would save him. It was his ace in the hole. His top-notch competence in school and now at work had saved him every time previously when he'd gotten into hot water for opening his big mouth, and in much more serious situations than right now. His job at RobotWorld was safe.

An eager young waitress approached the table to take his order. He smiled and waved her away, then swiped his debit card over the table telescreen to leave a generous tip. He surveyed the winding down of the rowdiness around him as the Manglecon game ended. It seemed like a few people in the bar were happy, but most were noticeably angry at losing money they couldn't afford to lose on the game. And spending money they couldn't afford to spend on alcohol. Pitiful.

Taylor felt a lightheadedness, most certainly due to the marijuana/tobacco smoke cloud, which was getting thicker by the second. At one time, any kind of smoking was banned in public places, but that was years ago. Taylor wistfully thought he would have liked to have lived in those times.

On the bar's sound system blared "Livin'," a popular techno song of the day and Taylor's favorite song from his favorite band, NewTech. The lyric *It's a sad, sad man who can't stand his own company* caused a twinge of melancholy in his spirit as he sat alone.

The line stuck in Taylor's head. He waited a minute, then left the bar.

4

AFTER THE UNCOMFORTABLE post-work meeting with his boss, Taylor maneuvered his black PTV on the crowded expressway. He relaxed his tense shoulders. As the sun set in the west, other PTVs were around him and moving at high speeds, but the quiet inside his climate-controlled vehicle was soothing. PTVs had a reliable auto-pilot mechanism, but Taylor liked to drive his vehicle manually; it didn't take much effort, and he liked the feeling of being in control. With modern road technology, traffic accidents were a rarity, a relic of a time long past. Only five more minutes until he got home—and he could hardly wait.

Despite the cold, gray February day in grimy Capital City, he smiled and resolved to ignore the negative in the world and focus on the positive. He reassured himself once again that he could handle any fallout from what had happened in the bar. He could deal with Sophia. He was too valuable to the company. Sophia's main interest had always been the bottom line, and he was good—no, great—for the bottom line. His position with RW was secure.

But maybe in the future it might be wise to listen to his intuition.

Taylor was one of the few who had developed or were gifted with what society termed "the higher power of intuition." Around the midpoint of the twenty-first century, a small percentage of humans had discovered the unusual ability to send out mental requests for guidance and receive insight from a clear voice in their head regarding the direction to take in specific circumstances. Who or what were they talking to? A part of themselves? A collective unconscious? A higher power? It was unclear. But most scientists who studied such matters had concluded the intuition situation was one of those nature versus nurture puzzles, with the most likely explanation being that the development of high intuition was a combination of both genetics and the development of the skill. People with this gift were called "one-percenters."

Taylor had never been sure of whether being a one-percenter was a major blessing or a massive curse. He'd found since childhood that George—as he'd named the clear voice in his head that seemed as real as any human voice—could cause as much trouble as he prevented. And so now Taylor almost never initiated contact with his childhood friend anymore—and, perhaps in response, George had gone silent.

Taylor couldn't get the meeting with Sophia at the bar out of his head. *Nothing to worry about*, he repeatedly tried to convince himself. *In fact, all things considered, I'm the luckiest man on the face of the earth. I'm one of the few doing well in this damn society.*

As he pushed his PTV to the speed limit of 220 kilometers per hour, he was at the highest point of the expressway. He looked to the east and saw the Capital City skyline, dominated by the gigantic RobotWorld complex. Despite the ominous, constant gray haze that hung over the metro area, this view at sunset was his favorite view of the city. He looked to the west, saw nothing but clear sky meeting land, and wondered what exactly was out there.

He rapidly returned his attention to assessing his life right now. With a feeling of contentment, he reminded himself for the umpteenth time that his PTV was the most current model in existence; that his apartment was the most modern available; and that his job with the cutting-edge company RobotWorld ("the world leader in production of industrial and personal robots") paid him more than ninety-nine percent of the workers in Capital City (this made him a "one-percenter" in more ways than one), most of whom lived in the depressingly gray-colored, government-managed high-rise apartment buildings that had replaced the expensive single-family homes that once were prevalent in this area. All reasons for Taylor to be grateful.

But the biggest reason for his positive attitude was Jennifer, who would be waiting for him with her usual enthusiastic greeting as soon as he entered the apartment. He laughed out loud and shook his head in recalling his resistance two weeks ago, when Sophia "forced" Jennifer on him.

"I've got a surprise for you," Sophia had told him in her office. She flashed one of her insincere smiles. "I know you're unattached and not happy about it. I'm going to change this depressing situation for you. You need someone special in your life. Unlike me. I prefer going through life solo. Relationships—with a human or a robot—are such a pain in the ass. Anyway, we're in the process of putting the finishing touches on our latest line of personal bots. I took the liberty of reviewing your employee questionnaire and personality tests. And everyone here knows you're a big-time old-movie buff. Favorite actress, Jennifer Lawrence. Even though it appears all the bugs have been worked out, we still need to do some final prototype testing. Who better than you? When you get home tonight, waiting for you will be a bot that looks exactly like the beautiful and talented Ms. Lawrence in her prime. I've taken the liberty of naming this personal bot *Jennifer*."

Taylor blinked several times in quick succession and shook his head. "Nice of you to think of me, Sophia. But I don't know. I'm more of a real-woman kind of guy."

"Even though you don't have a real woman in your life now? And haven't had one in how long?"

The broaching of his personal life by his boss caused an uncomfortable warmth in his neck and face. "That's not the issue. I think having someone in my life that looks like an actress who was popular so long ago is . . . kind of creepy."

Sophia's smile faded, and she focused on him with a steely-eyed squint. "Nonsense. The bot I'm setting you up with will improve the quality of your life. Not only is this bot a dead ringer for your favorite actress in her twenties, but her personality profile has been tailored—no pun intended—especially for you."

"I . . . I don't know."

"Taylor, this is what we do," Sophia said, with a sharpness to her voice he'd rarely heard. "Our company, I mean. You spend most of your time selling affordable personal bots that help both average males and females lead satisfying lives. Now you're given a golden opportunity to sample our wares and you refuse? This reaction makes me question whether you're in the right job."

"No, no," he said. "Maybe I'm being old-fashioned in wanting a real human relationship." Sophia's bringing up the issue of his job fitness caused a knifing physical pain in his abdomen. He inhaled and exhaled slowly. For now, for this time only, he made the decision to set aside his new honesty policy. "I suppose a little product testing would be okay."

And so, the deed was done.

Now, two weeks later, as the road flashed by at high speed, Taylor had to acknowledge to himself in the quiet of his PTV that yielding to Sophia had worked out well. Given his average looks combined with a touch of social awkwardness, he had to admit there would be no chance he'd ever be able to attract a real woman who'd even come close to the gorgeous Jennifer. The only previous serious relationship in his life, with a co-worker when they were in their mid-twenties, had ended in heartbreaking disaster. At that time, Taylor swore off ever having a close human relationship. A vow he'd kept since then.

Jennifer was anatomically a human duplicate in every way. Every part of her body looked and felt like that of a human female. In fact, outside of a small blue patch under the left armpit, required by law for all personal robots, Jennifer appeared to be human in every aspect imaginable. But she'd never grow old, never lose her perfect figure, and never get sick. She didn't need to eat and never would develop pesky human foibles like body odor or bad breath. And the sex with Jennifer was amazing.

Like all RobotWorld personal robots, Jennifer could evaluate the emotional reactions of humans more accurately than a real person, according to scientific tests conducted by RW. Just as important, a personal robot could respond appropriately and with great empathy to human speech and body language. The ability of a personal robot to "read and react" to a human being was perfect almost every time, according to the RW advertisements Taylor had a part in writing. RobotWorld ads boldly claimed a relationship with an RW personal robot was "better than a real one—and without all the drama."

Almost home now, Taylor grinned in satisfaction at the thought that Jennifer would never develop the petty grievances and jealousies that all humans seemed to eventually create. His testing of this new personal robot prototype had worked out beyond his wildest dreams even though, as he found out a week later, all the final testing had already been completed by RW scientists.

Being a personal robot, Jennifer had been programmed to be totally compliant with his wishes. And if he ever tired of her (which right now he could never imagine—he always saw himself as a loyal, one-woman man, even if the woman was a robot) and wanted to rent or purchase another personal robot resembling Sofía Vergara or Brigitte Bardot (two other all-time Taylor favorites) for one-on-one hanky-panky or even a threesome, Jennifer would happily give her blessing.

Taylor parked his PTV in the underground garage of the luxurious Galaxy Apartments, one of the few such apartment complexes in Capital City. As he exited the vehicle, Taylor saw Ernest Billick standing near the elevator bay. Ernest had been the apartment's porter for a year, almost as long as Taylor had lived here. Ernest, about the same age as Taylor, wore his usual work clothes of a dark-blue shirt and pants. Ernest had gone prematurely bald and had a protruding belly that fell over the belt of his work pants.

A smiling Ernest hit a button on the wall to call the elevator for Taylor and walked toward him. "Hey, hey. Here comes my favorite tenant. Good to see you, sir."

"You don't need to call me *sir*, Ernest. Given how long we've known each other."

Ernest said, "With as much as you've accomplished in life, you deserve to be called *sir.*" Ernest displayed a permanently slumped-over posture and a pronounced limp, with his right foot dragging on the concrete, in what appeared to be a constant struggle to keep up with the rest of his body.

Ernest pointed at Taylor's parked vehicle and said, "Hey, hey. I love your new PTV. How's it been running?"

"Just fine, Ernest." Taylor smiled. "Let me see your wrist computer."

Ernest returned the smile and extended his arm. He knew what was coming.

Taylor extended his arm, and both their wrist computers beeped as they almost touched.

Ernest said, "Thank you, sir . . . I mean, Taylor. Always appreciate it."

Taylor nodded and beamed, happy that he'd done a good turn for Ernest with a fifty-dollar tip that he'd programmed into his wrist computer to go from his bank account to Ernest's.

Taylor had known Ernest for years and recommended him for the porter job. It made Taylor feel good to help Ernest get the job. Every week on this day, a Wednesday, Taylor would slip Ernest a fifty-dollar credit "for outstanding service." Taylor had felt sorry for Ernest for as long as he'd known him and felt a need to help him out. Ernest seemed genuinely grateful for the job Taylor had obtained for him and the tips, which—he'd told Taylor—no one else in the apartment complex ever gave him.

Taylor said, "Always good seeing you, my friend. Gotta get upstairs." He just had to see Jennifer. Couldn't wait another minute. Taylor rushed past Ernest and entered the elevator.

"Always great seeing you—and thanks again for the you-know-what," Ernest said as the elevator door closed.

5

———

TAYLOR RODE THE high-speed elevator up to his tenth-floor pent-house apartment. Upon entering, he was immediately struck by the surprising smell of food cooking. His eyebrows raised. Jennifer had never cooked before, as far as he knew. But almost before the aroma registered, out of the kitchen dashed a barefoot Jennifer, wearing a snug white blouse and tight blue jeans, her long, blonde hair flowing like a flag whipping in the wind.

"Honey!" she screamed.

Taylor dropped his briefcase just in time to catch her with both arms as she leaped toward him and wrapped her legs around his waist. He laughed uncontrollably as she peppered his lips, neck, and face with rapid kisses. When he finally caught his breath, he placed a hand around the nape of her neck, kissed her hard on the mouth, then pulled back and said, "So happy to see you too. Have you been cooking?"

She slid her legs slowly down his lower body until her feet hit the floor, and they were standing face-to-face, arm-in-arm. She said, "It's a surprise, baby. My first attempt at the art of food preparation.

I know how much you enjoy those meals from Lee's China Garden restaurant that we've ordered in. So I decided to go shopping this afternoon and re-create one." She kissed him softly on the lips. "I downloaded the food preparation instructions into my head this afternoon. You are requested to please change into something more comfortable, and meet me in the dining room in five minutes or less."

After a quick shower and changing into jeans and a white, V-neck T-shirt, a barefoot Taylor entered the spacious, brightly-lit dining room. Jennifer kissed him, took his hand, and led him to the dining room table, which consisted of two heavily lacquered white pedestals that supported four thick curved-glass panels, which in turn supported the weight of the large glass top. Six white leather swivel chairs surrounded the table.

"How do you like it?" Jennifer asked, pointing to the table top.

On the large dining room table was a piping hot buffet spread of wonton soup, boneless spare ribs, steamed broccoli with garlic sauce, and sweet-and-sour shrimp with fried rice.

"Fantastic," Taylor said. "It looks great and smells great. You got all my favorites. You're too good."

"I know. Like my modesty?" She chuckled. "Please sit and eat. I'll serve."

Jennifer filled a large bowl with wonton soup and placed it before him. She sat across from him and gazed into his eyes.

"I know I've asked this before," Jennifer said, "but do you think it's weird that I don't eat?"

He shook his head. "You don't have to keep asking. The answer will always be *absolutely not,* love."

"I could fake eating and drinking, as so many of us personal bots do, but that would be . . . faking. And I don't think you'd want me to fake things."

"Absolutely right. *Real* is what I'm after. And you're as real as real can be to me."

"Okay, then. For the last time, let me ask this question. Do you think it's weird that I like to watch you eat?"

"Absolutely not. In fact, I enjoy the company."

Jennifer giggled. "Great. I like to be with you as much as possible. I won't ask silly questions about eating again. I promise."

"Mmm. This soup is better than the restaurant's."

She displayed a hint of a smile as she winked. "I added a pinch each of garlic, turmeric, and ground cumin—as suggested by one cooking website maintained by a master chef—to give the soup an extra kick."

With the care and dexterity of a topnotch waitress, Jennifer served each course. They made small talk while smiling at each other. Taylor loved the way Jennifer paid strict attention to whatever he said and how she always laughed at his jokes (no matter how lame) with enthusiasm.

After he'd cleaned his plate, Taylor patted his belly with both hands and said, "I'm stuffed. Without a doubt, everything was superior to restaurant quality. If you ever wanted to, you could put Lee's China Garden out of business in a heartbeat. Spectacular job, Jen."

"Thank you, honey." She rose and grasped his hand. "You know what I think? I think a great meal like you just enjoyed deserves a *pièce de résistance,* as the French would say." She smiled. "To the bedroom, my love."

He laughed. "I'll go without any *résistance,* sweet."

He followed her to the bedroom where they slowly undressed each other and fell onto the bed.

Jennifer reached over to an end table and opened the drawer. "I've got another little surprise for you, hon." She held up a small white box with the word *Serenity* printed in black across the top and the familiar blue cloud under it.

"Whoa," Taylor said. He recognized the distinctive package he'd seen countless times on the telescreen. He'd heard all the advertisements about how Serenity provided "a strong pleasure sensation—anytime, every time." But he'd also read the rumors about its strong addictive properties and how it suppressed human initiative. The rumors were believable, especially after observing the society around him. One of the strange properties of Serenity was that its negative side effects, outside of the blunting of the human spirit, could be different for each person. The most common negative symptoms were headaches, sluggishness, and hand tremors. And there were many other variations, like the need to vomit after meals and blackouts.

Taylor said, "I don't know if you're aware of the stories regarding Serenity, Jen. Although it's supposed to give a great pleasure buzz, it's rumored that Serenity takes away one's drive, some even say one's humanity, over time. And there seems to be a correlation between those downtown homeless disappearances and Serenity use. I don't know why the government doesn't crack down on this drug."

Jennifer frowned. "I know all about Serenity. Literally. The day before yesterday, while you were at work, I downloaded every word ever written about it into my head. Serenity comes in many doses. The lowest dose, eighty-one milligrams, which is what I have here, has been proven in tests to be nonaddictive, hangover-free, and safe—as long as one doesn't exceed four pills per day. And those disappearing homeless people are probably drinking alcohol and smoking marijuana also. Alcohol and marijuana cause far more problems than Serenity. The homeless are drinking and smoking themselves into oblivion. You know the old saying: you reap what you sow."

The exact match of Jen's "reap what you sow" words concerning the homeless with Sophia's back in the bar surprised Taylor. But he shook it off. "I've read the research too. But I don't trust it, I guess. I believe it's propaganda."

"Oh, the research can be trusted, silly. If it's on the telescreen and the government says it, then it must be true." She popped a pill from the box and reached for his mouth. "Let's give it a shot. One time can't hurt."

"But the sex we've had has been so great."

She winked at him and smiled her irresistible smile. "As the telescreen adverts say, Serenity will make any situation, including sex, better. You know the Serenity slogan: 'It's all good.'"

"Yeah. It's all good. Allegedly. Well . . . it sounds like you did the proper investigation—with your brain download, of course. I guess it'll be okay." Taylor laughed as he opened his mouth, but had a gnawing doubt he might be sorry to do what he was about to do. *Ah, what the hell.*

She put the quick-dissolving pill on his tongue, and he swallowed.

A pleasant swirling sensation started in his head and quickly moved down his body. Every bit of tension he'd been carrying in his muscles was instantly and gently released. Jennifer kissed him tenderly on the lips.

Taylor didn't remember much after her kiss, although he did remember feeling *spectacular,* a word he rarely used before Jennifer came into his life two weeks ago. Now it had become his favorite word.

6

THE NEXT MORNING at work, wearing his usual gray pants and gray short-sleeve shirt with the red *RW* logo on the left pocket, Taylor massaged his forehead with both hands as he sat at his desk. He felt slightly dizzy, a strange sensation he didn't like. *The Serenity? Hell, Jen said it was the lowest dose. She researched it. Everything she's researched for me before has checked out. It's probably just the virus going around here at work.* He ambled to the sink in the small restroom of his private office and splashed cold water on his face. Taylor had a meeting in five minutes with Sophia to discuss last month's sales figures.

Sales was Taylor's only focus in his job. Last month's production was terrific, so Taylor wasn't dreading this meeting. In fact, he was looking forward to it. He expected nothing but positive feedback from the boss.

But Taylor did have a problem with RobotWorld and the effect its product was having on society. He had a growing concern about how personal robots had evolved and become sentient. The majority of humans hadn't noticed this situation, it seemed. But

Taylor had—and it wasn't because of his high IQ or his one-percent intuition power. Why hadn't others? Perhaps it was due to the way the government had manipulated the population to ignore societal problems through the wise use of the media over recent years. Add the tacit and not-so-tacit government support of Serenity, which numbed the minds of so many. Add the intimidation factor of an aggressive police-army, and it was clear that a person who displayed the bad judgment of locking horns with the government did so at his or her own risk.

As Taylor saw it, industrial robots were a problem in that they took jobs from humans. But even though this situation was significant, it was not Taylor's major worry regarding the RobotWorld revolution. Industrial robots *looked* like robots, not like people. They were hunks of metal built for functionality to perform repetitive tasks, mainly in factories and all types of stores. There was no attempt in the RW manufacturing process to make industrial robots look human.

The bigger problem to Taylor was with RW's personal robots, even though he was currently thrilled at being in a relationship with one. Personal robots were intended to look and act human—and the designers at RobotWorld had managed to succeed in this goal to an outstanding degree. Even the most perceptive of humans couldn't tell a personal robot from a real person.

A year earlier, Sophia had called Taylor into her office. She stood as he entered. With an unusually broad smile (which he hadn't seen before or since), she loudly announced, "Our scientists have just made your job a lot easier, Taylor." She paused a beat to maximize the significance of what she was about to say. "They have defeated the uncanny valley for mass-produced personal bots."

Taylor raised his arms to the ceiling and let out a "Whoop!"

They both knew what defeating the uncanny valley meant. The Uncanny Valley Hypothesis was proposed in 1970 by Japanese roboticist Masahiro Mori. It underlined the greatest problem of the robotics industry, dating from the initial time (long before the existence of RobotWorld) companies started building robots that were intended to pass for human.

Mori's hypothesis stated that as the appearance of a robot becomes more human, a human being's emotional response to the robot becomes more positive. However, as the appearance becomes *almost but not quite* human, humans generally react negatively, with feelings of strangeness, fear, or revulsion being the most common responses.

The "uncanny valley" referred to a graph of human feedback to this phenomenon, with "similarity to a human" being the horizontal line, and "positive feelings of familiarity" being the vertical line. People usually have a favorable reaction to robots the more human they look, such as a cute Robbie the Robot type or C-3PO of twentieth-century Star Wars fame, until the likeness becomes too strong and yet fundamentally not human. At this point, the acceptance of the robot drops suddenly, indicating a negative "valley" reaction on the graph.

RobotWorld had spent millions of dollars trying to get its personal robots to appear, act, and feel completely human with none of the "tells" that would expose them as robots. Taylor had been one of the first to hear from Sophia that they had accomplished this daunting task. The uncanny valley was no more.

In the year since this formerly unsolvable impediment had been overcome, numerous tests of RW personal bots had established the breakthrough of RW scientists. One popular telescreen show, *Real or Robot*, was a half-hour broadcast each week asking human contestants to determine whether an individual performing a task was a human or an RW bot. It was a hopeless mission with often comical results.

Although RobotWorld had been the foremost producer of robots in the world for nearly a decade, it had come to totally corner the market in the past year. A frequently-mentioned saying around the RW offices was, "There really is no number two."

The huge twenty-five-story, solid-gray RW building occupied three square city blocks near the center of the former Washington, DC, right over what used to be the Metro Center stop of the old Metrorail. Taylor hated the ominous, antiseptic look of the RobotWorld complex.

RobotWorld was a self-contained operation, with all its functions happening at this giant facility. The westernmost part of the structure held the office area, including the executive offices where Taylor worked.

The middle part of the giant structure contained the factory, which produced all RW robots, and where the annual reboot for all personal robots like Jennifer happened. The annual reboot was necessary, as without it, a personal robot would stop functioning permanently. It was often referred to around the office as the "all-important annual reboot." The reboot could only happen at the RW facility; it was a large part of RW's proprietary dominance of the personal robot industry.

The easternmost portion of the building contained the ample research and development part of the company.

Each of the three sections occupied roughly a third of the huge structure, thought to be the biggest manufacturing-research-maintenance facility currently on the planet.

Now, in his private restroom, Taylor dried his face with a towel and took a deep breath as he got ready to walk to Sophia's office. Although he anticipated a productive meeting, every session with his boss was an adventure.

7

—

ON THE WALK down the long hall to Sophia's corner office, Taylor managed to shake off his Serenity-based malaise, or the work-related virus, or whatever had caused his dizziness.

Sophia, seated behind a giant cherry-wood desk, welcomed Taylor with a brief nod. Today, she'd slicked her red hair back into a taut ponytail. She met his eyes with her piercing green ones.

Sophia's office was a cut above the rather plain offices that even executives such as Taylor had. Extending almost the entire length of one wall was an inordinately large black leather couch. Plush white shag carpeting covered the floor and two large, buffed, black credenzas were on either side of the cherry-wood desk. A massive bookshelf with actual books, something of a rarity these days, ran the length of another wall. The most interesting aspect of the office, however, was a one-hundred-gallon fish tank that dominated the wall behind her desk. The tank contained a few real green plants swaying in the water and brown gravel covering the bed. Populating the tank were four red-bellied piranhas, each about three inches long. Although there were rumors that Sophia fed the critters live goldfish, she'd always maintained that she fed them only frozen tilapia and prawns, nothing else.

After taking a seat opposite his boss in one of the two small visitor chairs with a wooden back, Taylor looked down at the mini-computer on his wrist. He'd already decided not to bring up the previous night's disaster at the bar. Taylor tapped a button on the mini-computer, and last month's sales figures were projected onto the large telescreen monitor on the right side of Sophia's desk.

"Another winning month for us, as you can see," Taylor reported. "In general, industrial bot sales are through the roof. If we keep going at this rate, all repetitive work in the Northeast Sector will be done by RW bots within a year or two. And personal robot sales have also skyrocketed. Soon, every adult will have a robot mate. Marriage between humans will be a thing of the past."

Sophia put both hands around the back of her neck and grinned. "Things are looking up for our company. It's getting better and better every day. You give me this great sales news today. Yesterday, I got the news that our Research and Development team finally cracked the code on Nitro. For all intents and purposes, Nitro exists."

"So the rumors are true," Taylor said. "Most people, including me, thought this whole development of Nitro thing was a fantasy . . . a phony buzz."

Sophia's expression turned serious. "I only mention the Nitro situation because you are one of my highly trusted executives. What I've told you is not to be repeated to anyone. Got it?"

"Of course. I give you my word—and my word is my bond." After a short pause, he continued, "So, in fact, they got the unstable properties of Nitro under control?"

"Nitro is here—and we own it." She tapped her fingers on the desktop. "Most people focus on the destructive capability of Nitro. But, like atomic or nuclear power, there's another side to it. The power of Nitro will eventually be able to be used in other ways that can benefit us all. Granted, these ways need to be worked out. I'm confident our scientists can do it. And we'll make a fortune." Sophia smiled. "But enough Nitro talk. How are things going with the personal bot I set you up with a couple of weeks ago?"

Taylor matched the smile of his boss. "*Spectacular* would not be a strong enough word."

They both laughed heartily. Taylor believed any sour memories she might have had of the previous night were long gone.

He leaned back in his chair and his smile faded. "But doesn't it ever worry you, Sophia . . . that what we're doing with our bots . . . might, I don't know, ultimately be harmful?"

Her face twisted into a pain mask, as if she'd absorbed a solid punch to the abdomen. "What the hell are you talking about?"

Taylor shifted in his chair and looked to the ceiling. He then refocused to meet her eyes. "Well, unemployment is at an all-time high and growing each month. Our industrial bots clearly are better workers than we humans, particularly in work requiring repetitive tasks. Eventually, there'll be fewer and fewer blue-collar jobs for us. And if any person, male or female, gets their hands on a personal bot as perfect as my Jennifer, they'll never go back to the trials and tribulations of a human relationship. Trust me on this." Taylor snapped his fingers. "And there goes human reproduction."

Sophia arched her eyebrows. "You are one of my most talented executives, Taylor. But you're also the biggest skeptic in the company. The people out of work could find a job if they really wanted one. Most of them choose Serenity and government assistance. It's human nature: selecting the path of least resistance and the most short-term pleasure. Most humans are not go-getters or self-motivated types like you. Especially after World War III, when the majority of humans decided on the futility of working for things, building things, and planning for the long-term future. Obviously, poor decisions for them. But WW III created a vacuum that goal-oriented people like us have moved into to build great companies like this one. Furthermore, human unemployment is not our problem. It's above our pay grade. The development of the best possible product and the bottom line are our only interests. And don't you ever forget it."

"Sure, boss, I understand." Taylor's feeling from the night before at the bar was back. *I've gone too far again. Moron!* Taylor could see from the twinkle in Sophia's eyes that she was about to continue with her ranting, which he'd done such a great job in just fueling.

"I read a book the other day," she said, "concerning popular expressions around the turn of the last century that have since faded into oblivion. A popular saying back then was 'Never assume, because when you assume, you make an ass out of you and me.' I couldn't agree more. And I'll expand on it. I believe there are two ways a person can be stupid. The first way is to be naturally stupid. You definitely don't belong in this category, Taylor. The second way is to make an assumption based on insufficient evidence or bias. That's what I think you've done regarding how our bots will impact employment and marriage. Don't make assumptions. Please. You're too smart to go that route."

"Got it," Taylor said. He hoped this response would stop her rant.

"Good." Sophia hit the desktop with her right hand. "I've got to make a speech downtown to the Chamber of Commerce in thirty minutes. You can't imagine how much I hate the public relations part of this job. Got to change out of our gray uniform, which I love, into damn business clothes. Ridiculous. Some institutions, like the Chamber, still have these infernal, formal dress codes. Okay, leave me."

Taylor rose. "Back to work for me."

In the hall on the walk to his office, Taylor stopped abruptly. *I forgot to ask Sophia about requesting next Monday off. Jen and I have planned a long weekend. We'll probably stay at home and screw.* Taylor knew that Sophia, while liberal with granting personal time, liked to be informed as soon as possible.

Taylor quick-stepped back to her office and opened the door.

Sophia was naked from the waist up, her left side angled toward Taylor. A ripple of panic lit up her face. She instantly grabbed her gray work shirt on the desk, held it to her chest, and whirled around to face him. "What the hell?"

Taylor was momentarily stunned and took a step back. He rotated his head away from Sophia, and his eyes snapped shut. Her office was always well lit by extensive ceiling tube lighting and any sunlight that managed to cut through the cloud of pollution perpetually hanging over the city. In the split second before his boss turned away from him, Taylor didn't see any part of Sophia he wouldn't have seen if she were wearing a bikini on a beach. What he thought he might have seen, however, was what could have been a small blue patch, of the type required to be on all personal robots, under Sophia's left armpit.

"Don't you believe in knocking?" she shouted. She took a deep breath in an obvious attempt to compose herself.

Taylor pivoted his body away from her. "Sorry, sorry," was all he could say.

In a quick motion, Sophia pulled on her gray uniform shirt. With a lowered tone of voice, she continued, "I'm decent. You can open your eyes." As he turned to her, she said, "You caught me off guard. I was changing clothes for my speech. Sorry to snap at you. What do you want?"

"I'm the one who's sorry. I thought you'd be changing in your private restroom—and not immediately after I'd left. Should have knocked. Just wanted to ask if I could take next Monday off."

"We've got a lot on our plate. We must maintain the momentum reflected in your outstanding sales figures. Can't you wait until the Founders Day holiday for a day off? Everybody gets Founders Day off. It's the only holiday we celebrate these days. It's right around the corner."

Taylor grimaced. "Founders Day is months away."

"All right," she said, "I want you happy. No problem. Take next Monday off. Now let me get dressed for my speech."

"Thanks. So, so sorry to have busted in on you. I'll always knock in the future."

On the walk back to his office, Taylor shook his head and concluded he couldn't have seen what he thought he just saw. First off, there were strict laws against robots holding positions of authority in large companies, as well as the highest government positions. These laws had been on the books for years, the product of a significant part of the human population fearful that someday robots might be better at leading than human beings. Second, the instant he'd barged into Sophia's office, he recalled being blinded by a ray of sunlight cascading through the window, which no doubt caused some kind of mirage. If there was something under the boss's armpit, it probably was a bandage of some sort or maybe a birthmark or maybe nothing at all.

Taylor laughed to himself. *How silly of me. No way is Sophia Ross a robot.*

8

AS HE ENTERED his office area, Taylor smiled as he greeted Rosalind "Roz" Troward, his executive assistant. She sat at her desk just outside his private office. Roz, thirty-two, the possessor of a quick laugh, sparkling brown eyes, and wavy, medium-length brown hair, nodded at him. She was slender and lithe, the product of a good diet and years of yoga in the morning before work.

Taylor and Roz had been working together for about two years. He saw her as highly intelligent, loyal, and easy to talk to. Because of his bad experience with dating a co-worker years ago, Taylor had never considered the unattached Roz as a potential romantic partner. But now that he had Jennifer, he didn't need to be concerned with obtaining someone with whom to share his life. Before Jen, it was all work, going home, being alone, and spending time on the computer visiting informational websites or "traveling" to all parts of the world wearing Virtual Reality glasses, which were very popular among the few earning good money in society. With his lightweight VR glasses—which resembled the eyeglasses people wore until the advent of one hundred percent safe, high-tech laser vision surgery in the mid-twenty-first century that made corrective and contact lenses obsolete—he'd been to the highest point on Earth, Mount Everest, and the lowest point at the bottom of the Mariana Trench. But nothing pleased him more than having somebody in his life now, even if that *somebody* was a robot.

"How are things going with the bag of nuts and bolts Sophia set you up with?" Roz asked.

Taylor groaned. "Her name is Jennifer and things are going great. A guy like me wouldn't have a chance with a human woman who looks as good as my Jen."

"Don't sell yourself short. I think you deserve so much more than a robot." As Taylor turned away from her, she mumbled under her breath, "Actually, you deserve someone like me."

"What did you say?" he asked.

"Nothing."

Taylor turned back to her. "I'm not so sure I deserve more than a robot, given my history with relationships. In this world, you gotta look out for yourself. Protect your heart. No one else will. It's every man for himself."

"What about women?" she asked.

"The same rules apply."

"Might be a terrible way to operate."

"Maybe." He smiled broadly. "Except for us. We look out for each other here at work. And to prove it, can I interest you in a chocolate-frosted donut? I picked up a half-dozen from the Marnie's Bakery drive-thru this morning on the way to work. Freshly made. Or at least, that's the claim from Marnie's."

"Hell, no. How can you eat that garbage?"

"I love them," Taylor said. "My only weakness. At least the only one I'll admit to. An occasional chocolate-frosted donut never hurt anyone." He chuckled. "Builds muscles and puts hair on your chest."

"I don't want hair on my chest."

They both laughed at the silly repartee they'd shared many times before regarding chocolate-frosted donuts. For as long as they'd worked together, Taylor had not been able to coax Roz into trying one.

Taylor entered his private office and came back out a minute or two later. He placed some papers on her desk in-box. "I printed out the latest intra-office memos for you. I know how much you hate to read things off a screen."

"That's me. Just an old-fashioned girl."

"Oh, by the way, I think I screwed up again with our fearless leader."

"What now?"

Taylor rubbed the back of his neck. "I was merely brainstorming to Sophia that maybe with as successful as our company has been in integrating robots into the world that perhaps one day we'll make humans obsolete."

Roz winced. "Taylor, you're smart enough to know better. Sophie is obsessively committed to the mission of RobotWorld. She harps on our *mission* all the time. If it's not something about how we can improve bot performance or how we can sell more product, she doesn't want to hear it."

"Never let her hear you call her *Sophie*. She hates it. Anyway, I'm trying to be more honest in all aspects of my life, including here at work. Why shouldn't people be able to express their true feelings and not be afraid to do so? Whatever happened to freedom of speech? Besides, I was just riffing. What's wrong with having a meaningful discussion about the issues of the day? Where's the respect for a diversity of opinions? It's not as if I told Sophia I favored closing down the company."

"Well, don't let it bother you. You're probably worrying too much. I think you're one of Sophie's—I mean Sophia's—favorites."

***

Sophia stood on the balcony of her office, the strong wind whipping her long red hair every which way. She liked to do things right, do things perfectly. Now she mentally kicked herself for blabbing about Nitro to Taylor. She just couldn't resist crowing about the latest RW accomplishment.

She shouldn't have shot off her mouth to Taylor because for the past few months, she had begun to suspect that he wasn't fully on board with RobotWorld's mission. To her, this was a mortal sin. This suspicion—added to the combination of Taylor's remarks at the bar the previous night, his words in her office today, and the outside chance he had seen her small blue patch after what she felt was an inappropriate barging into her office—pushed the irritable RobotWorld head into action.

The rumor about her in the RW offices, that she only cared about the bottom line and the quality of robots produced, was not totally true. Taylor and others would be surprised to know that while the profit margin and product quality of the company were important, there were other things even more important to her.

It wasn't lost on her that the feelings of anger she felt toward Taylor, indeed the feelings she felt in normal minute-by-minute living, were mirroring true human reactions. Sophia found this pleasing for some reason. More than anything, she enjoyed "evolving," in much the same way humans developed their individual talents. Where did this need to evolve come from? It certainly didn't come from her programmers. Somehow, it came from her and her alone.

Sophia was confident that Taylor wouldn't say anything about Nitro after his promise not to, but his words earlier today questioning RW's mission were an irritation she couldn't shake. She returned to her office and hit a button on her desk. Within seconds Donald "Dee" Woodson, her executive assistant, strode his short, thin self into the office. His skin was the hue of polished mahogany, and he always seemed to be in a hurry. Sophia was fond of calling him "the henchman." Dee, like Sophia, was a robot. Outside of themselves, only a select few in the company knew they were bots. They were among the relatively small number of bots that could pass for human prior to RobotWorld's conquering of the uncanny valley for mass-produced personal robots a year earlier.

"Got a job for you," she said. "An employment termination. Taylor Morris."

Dee narrowed his eyelids over his always-intense eyes. "Wow. What a surprise. I thought Morris was one of your favorite humans."

Sophia shook her head. "Not anymore. I have my reasons. But with these damn employee protection laws that seem to get more complicated by the day, we must have clear cause to fire someone. I've already started to obtain dirt on him from a female personal bot I set him up with a few weeks ago. She's getting him hooked on Serenity. Lying about the dosage, saying it's eighty-one mills. Even the smartest humans, like Taylor, can be manipulated. Especially when a pretty woman or a pretty robot is involved." Sophia grinned. *Just like a human would grin after uttering my last sentence,* she thought. "Get something negative on him here at work, and let's get him out of our hair."

"You got it, boss."

After Dee left her office, Sophia thought that maybe job termination wasn't enough. If Taylor did see her blue patch, perhaps more dire consequences might be appropriate.

9

UPON ARRIVING IN his PTV at the apartment parking lot after work, Taylor was stoked, as usual, with anticipation to see Jennifer. The elevator doors opened on his floor. As he turned toward his apartment he stopped short when he saw the person walking toward him from the elevator at the other end of the hall. Tracey.

For a moment, he remained frozen in his tracks. Tracey. His twin sister, Tracey. Plain, slightly overweight Tracey. Wearing her usual understated, dated clothes: baggy blue jeans, a loosely fitted white blouse, and black sneakers that had gone out of style a decade earlier.

He couldn't remember the last time they'd spoken.

"Don't look so stunned," she said.

"It's been a while. To what do I owe this honor?"

"Am I not allowed to visit my brilliant, one-percent intuitive big brother? Even if you're my big brother by only three minutes."

They awkwardly kissed each other on the cheek.

"So," she said, "are we going to just stand here in the hall? Or are you going to invite me in?"

He inserted the magnetic card key and opened the door. Jennifer was standing at the ready, across the living room, waiting to make her usual welcome-home dash into his arms. She froze when she saw Tracey.

"Trace, this is Jennifer. Jen, this is Tracey, my twin sister," Taylor said.

Jennifer's face broke into a wide smile as she offered her hand. "Nice to meet you. Taylor has mentioned you."

"In glowing terms, I'm sure," Tracey said, as she took Jennifer's hand. Taylor detected more than a hint of sarcasm in her words.

"The resemblance is amazing," Jennifer said. "Can I get you anything? Coffee, tea?" She laughed. "Wine? We do have it on hand, even though Taylor doesn't drink. I bought some the other day. I'm trying to get him to loosen up and live a little."

"Regular black coffee, no cream, no sugar, would be great," Tracey said.

"The same for me," Taylor added.

Jennifer smiled one of her electric smiles. "Coffee, black and clean, for both of you. Be right back."

Taylor and Tracey then sat on opposite ends of the white leather couch.

"How's your asthma been?" she asked.

"Fine. My life's going well."

"It's always been a gauge of how your life is going," Tracey said. She looked around. "Nice place. Very bright. It suits you, Tay." She made eye contact with her brother. "I can see you're surprised to see me."

"It's fair to ask . . . after all this time . . . why you're here?" Taylor replied.

"There have been some changes in my life, and I wanted to run them by you."

"I'm all ears."

Tracey shifted in her seat. "I'm now working for the government . . . with the Robot Integration Council—and for someone you know: Sophia Ross."

"Interesting. You'll find she's super intelligent and quick, with a bit of an attitude. But please don't quote me. Passive-aggressive, she is. Don't cross her. The woman is goal-oriented to the max. Anything off-topic from business objectives and she bristles. Believe me, I know from personal experience. Sophia has really gotten into her government work dealing with smoothing the assimilation of robots into society. She knows more about robots than just about anyone. I've been noticing that her Robot Integration Council work is taking up a lot more of her time. What exactly are you doing for the RIC?"

"As you said, dealing with the smooth integration of robots into society."

"Yeah, obviously. I'd gathered that. I know the purpose of the council." Taylor paused, thinking his response might have sounded harsh, even though Tracey's answer to his direct question was unnecessarily curt. But it made no sense to pick a fight now. He'd change the subject. "You know, Jen is a robot."

"Incredible. I couldn't tell. But I guess that's the point, right?"

"Best relationship I've ever had. Without a doubt."

"Not surprising. People were never your strong point. It's a quality we share." She stood. "I gotta go."

"Leaving so soon? Jen isn't even back with our coffee."

"I only wanted to let you know I'll be working with your boss at RobotWorld. You were bound to find out. And perhaps our paths will cross down the road. Most RIC meetings are held at the RW offices. Didn't want it to be super-awkward to see you at RW for the first time in . . . a long time. And I didn't want you to hear it from your boss." She started walking to the door. "Oh, another bit of news," she said, not slowing her brisk pace. "I'm dating Shane Diggins."

Taylor followed her to the door. He knew the name, of course. But to say he was surprised would be an understatement. He had to ask a question to be sure in his mind. "RW's head of research and development?"

"One and the same."

"Terrific. I had no idea." He didn't want to say what he really thought. *What a shocker. Shane is so successful and is even higher on RW's pecking order than I am. He's all about work. What the hell do the two of you have in common?*

As she grasped the doorknob, Tracey said, "Don't look so surprised. I've been working on my personal development. Downloading self-help books to my telescreen and taking self-im-provement telescreen seminars. It's good to improve oneself."

"I agree. I've been working on myself too. Not taking courses like you're doing. Just attempting to be more honest in my work life and personal life. My concern of how society has progressed—or regressed—is growing, but I haven't taken any action. It's a great balancing act. When you stick your neck out today, you're in danger of having your head chopped off."

"How's your imaginary friend? George, right? You always liked him better than me."

"You're not still jealous of George, are you? I've outgrown him. He's gone." She seemed determined to leave. He wanted to say something conciliatory or do something to stop her from leaving. But he couldn't find the words. He blurted out, "Good seeing you again. No need for you to be a stranger."

She turned the doorknob and smiled in what he read as a sour expression. "It goes both ways. Say goodbye to Jennifer for me." She was quickly out the door.

A minute later, a smiling Jennifer strode out of the kitchen holding a tray with a coffee pot and two cups. She stopped and looked around the room. "Where's your sister?" she asked, her smile melting into a serious expression as she set the tray down on the dining room table.

"Tracey had to go," Taylor replied. "She wanted me to say she was sorry she couldn't stay." He said this even though Tracey hadn't expressed any sorrow in not staying longer.

"I'll bet anything she lied about not being able to stay. I wasn't eavesdropping, but I couldn't help but overhear. Who's George?"

"Just the name I gave to my intuition a long time ago. Made it easier to relate."

Jennifer's eyes grew wide. "Wow. So you're a one-percenter. An intuitive?"

He shook his head. "I'm out of practice now. For all the problems it's caused me, I can't say it was a good thing to have in the first place."

"Of course it is. The more talents a person has, the better. And now I know you have the gift of wisdom. At least that's what I've read—through my downloads—about people like you."

"I think I'll have some of that coffee."

As she poured him a cup, Jennifer asked, "So what's the reason you and your sister haven't been speaking?"

"Too complicated. Truly, I don't even know now. Just the silly kind of barriers that sometimes spring up between people and in some families. It sort of happened. I'm sure part of it is my fault." He turned away from her and looked out the window. "I just don't know."

"It's you humans that are way too complicated. It's amazing how you all create problems out of thin air. Not saying that's what happened between you and your sister, of course. But come on. There has to be a story here—a concrete reason for the situation."

"You're right. It was more like an accumulation of things. She always felt that our parents liked me more or favored me in some way. Maybe she was justified in her feeling. We were the only kids of our parents, who are now deceased. Some twins get along. We always seemed to disagree on everything." He took a sip of hot coffee that burned the roof of his mouth. "Then, in high school, I was a wrestler. I wrestled a guy she was sweet on in the semifinal round of a big tournament. She was rooting for my opponent. Anyway, I won.

And ended up hurting the guy really bad. He was paralyzed for a while but later recovered. She accused me of hurting him purposely, which was nonsense. Honestly. And I was furious at her for rooting against me. We never were close after that."

Jennifer shrugged. "Forgive me for saying so, but that sounds ridiculous. You humans, way too complicated."

"I told you it was silly. Silly and a little sad too. Actually, more than a little sad." Taylor sighed. "Sometimes I wish *I* could be a robot."

10

A FEW DAYS later, Sophia, Dee Woodson, and five RW executives, including Taylor, were seated around the conference table in Sophia's expansive office. The meeting was a typical, straightforward Sophia-led staff meeting. As she droned on, Taylor became fascinated with watching one of the four piranhas darting around the fish tank while the other three remained almost inactive.

At the end of the meeting, Sophia and Dee, apparently by design, focused stony gazes on Taylor.

"We need everyone in this room to be one hundred percent committed to the mission of this company," Sophia pointedly said. "Ninety-nine percent doesn't cut it. Anyone without complete commitment to the goals of this company should strongly consider whether this is the right place for him or her to work. Okay, meeting adjourned."

Taylor lingered after the meeting broke up and approached Sophia. "Were your closing remarks directed at me?" he asked, though he suspected the answer.

Sophia refused to make eye contact with Taylor. "If the shoe fits . . ." She then brushed past him and disappeared out of the office. He got a whiff of the pleasant rose-floral perfume she usually wore, as he was left alone in the office with only the hum and gurgling of the filter in the piranha tank breaking the silence.

Upon returning to his office, Taylor said to Roz, "So you think I worry too much about my future at this company? Guess what happened in our staff meeting?"

***

On the way home from work, Taylor maneuvered his lightning-quick PTV through the late afternoon rush-hour traffic at the speed limit of 220 kmh. Despite their high-speed capability, it didn't take much mental or physical effort to manually pilot a PTV. PTVs, although they resembled cars, were roomier and much faster than the now-defunct automobiles. In place of tires, PTVs had electromagnetic sensors on the underside of the chassis that moved the vehicle at rapid speeds over electromagnetic highways and roads that ensured smooth traffic patterns. The joke in Capital City was that the highway and road system was the only area where true progress had been made. The system was called *maglev* (derived from the term *mag*netic *lev*itation). As a young child, Taylor had been fascinated by the maglev system. He had read that it was developed by British electrical engineer Eric Laithwaite in the late 1940s and refined by the Chinese with the Shanghai Maglev Train (capable of speeds of 430 kmh or 270 mph) in the second decade of the twenty-first century. The system was further refined by the Japanese maglev LO series, with speeds up to 603 kmh or 374 mph.

PTVs traveled slightly above a guideway using magnets to create lift and propulsion, allowing for reduced friction and high speeds never dreamed of for old automobiles. Traffic jams were a long-ago memory only the oldest people now alive could recall.

Even though Taylor could have hit a button on the console to get him home automatically, he, as usual, chose to drive to his apartment using manual controls. Having to concentrate, even minimally, on the road took his mind off his problems at work.

He was less than a mile from his apartment when his PTV jumped the electromagnetic track and spun toward a guardrail. The normally cool Taylor experienced brain lock. His eyes widened; his hands tightened on the steering wheel, causing momentary spasms in both arms. He had the feeling of spinning out of control in slow motion. From his mouth emanated a growling scream, a sound that surprised him because he wouldn't in a million years think he was capable of making such a sound. The scream added to the surreal accident experience. He could only hold on to the steering wheel and brace himself. Every muscle in his body tensed. The PTV rammed into a guardrail, designed to absorb the force of vehicle impact, with a dull thump as it came to an abrupt stop.

Taylor was stunned but unhurt, as far as he could tell. PTV crashes were as rare as old CDs or DVDs. Within seconds, two police vehicles were on the scene.

One of the officers, dressed in the all-black uniform of law enforcement, tapped on the driver's side window, and Taylor pressed a button on the door to roll it down.

The officer raised the dark visor of his helmet to reveal what Taylor took to be a look of concern. "Are you okay, sir?"

"I'm fine," Taylor said in as firm a voice as he could produce. "The vehicle and the rail gave me a gentle landing. This is a new PTV. Can't imagine what happened."

"As it doesn't appear you need medical attention, we'll transport you and your vehicle to the nearest government repair shop. They'll take possession of your PTV by law, do an evaluation to determine what, if anything, went wrong, and give you a loaner vehicle."

At the repair shop, Taylor sat in the empty waiting room. The piped-in Baroque music calmed his frayed nerves, and his pulse returned to normal. The sky had turned stormy. A heavy rain pinged against the corrugated roof and metal gutters; ribbons of water sluiced down the shop's front window. Taylor pulled out a mini-tablet from his pocket and caught up on the day's news, most of which was cheery government propaganda.

After approximately thirty minutes, a friendly young mechanic entered the room and said, "Well, this is unusual. The construction of PTVs and the maglev guideway is so . . . what's the word . . . impack . . . im . . . ." He tilted his head to the side in a gesture that reminded Taylor of the move a miniature schnauzer he'd had as a kid would do whenever the dog was confused.

"Impeccable?" Taylor suggested.

The skinny man with yellowish teeth clapped his hands once in apparent delight. "Yeah, that's it. Implackable. PTVs almost never fail these days. This is the first accident I've seen in . . . I don't know how long. PTVs are put together so well that my job will be obsolete in a matter of a few short years, at most. I'm thinking of going back to school to learn another trade."

"What do you think happened?"

"Ah, this situation is interesting. Walk with me to the garage. I'll show you."

As they stood behind a glass barrier with Taylor's PTV on the other side, the mechanic pointed to the driver's side door. "Right there. Seems to be a bullet hole. Not sure, but that's what it appears to be. The authorities will no doubt fish around for a bullet in the interior. Until then, no one's allowed near the vehicle. It's the law. You got any enemies?"

The color drained from Taylor's face. "Not that I know of. At least no one who'd take a shot at me."

"Did you notice the hole before now?"

"It wasn't there when I left my office to head home. I'm sure of it."

"The strange thing is that a rare electromagnetic power failure registered on the stretch of road you were riding on. Right at the time of your accident. Very strange. I'll bet it was the main reason for your problem. As for the hole in the door, maybe it was kids playing with their police officer dad or mom's weapon. I've seen two telescreen stories in the last week about the kids of police officers firing guns at traffic. So much for the idea of keeping us all safer by restricting guns only to cops." The mechanic tilted his head again and smiled a wide smile exposing his bad teeth. "For fun! Can you imagine? Dopey kids shooting at PTVs as some sort of game. Crazy young people these days. Nothing better to do. The power failure and the door hole, I think it's a big coincidence. But anyway, the police have to investigate the possible bullet hole. Probably won't lead to anything."

Taylor, with his mouth wide open, shook his head.

"It doesn't appear there is anything wrong with your PTV, outside of the hole, which we'll patch after the authorities finish their investigation," the mechanic continued. "We'll provide a loaner PTV for your use. Must do so by law—and we gladly do it. We'll almost certainly call you tomorrow afternoon to pick up your vehicle. It will take at least until tomorrow for the police to check it out. Before we release it to you, I'll personally inspect all systems thoroughly. It'll be as good as the day you bought it. That's our guarantee." He smiled at Taylor. "Cheer up. It could have been even messier. You could have been badly injured, or worse."

Taylor stared blankly at the PTV. "I'm not having a good day. But you're right. Things could have been worse. Of that, I'm sure."

11

AS TAYLOR PULLED his loaner PTV into the underground parking lot of the Galaxy Apartments, Ernest Billick ducked into a stairwell and double-timed it to his austere, one-room basement apartment. He lived rent-free here; it was part of his modest employment compensation. His place was sparsely furnished, with a small bed against one wall, a dining room table with two chairs, a tiny kitchen area with a modern refrigerator and a heatwave oven, and not much else.

Ernest reached for the communication earpiece on the table and placed it in his ear. He tapped a button on the table telescreen and was instantly connected.

"Talk to me," said the voice.

"Ernest Billick here. Reporting in, sir. Mr. Taylor Morris arrived home a minute ago. But he wasn't driving his PTV. He was in an older model with a blue color. Nothing further to report."

"Thank you, Ernest," said the male voice. "Keep up the good work."

***

That night, Taylor and Jennifer lay naked in bed after sex. Both were staring at the ceiling.

Jennifer raised her head above the pillow, turned toward him, and propped her head up on her hand. "Honey, you seem down? Or maybe preoccupied?"

The questions were pertinent. He'd been thinking about his crazy and troubling day. In addition to Sophia giving him the cold shoulder and the PTV accident, he'd gotten a disturbing two-word message on his office answering machine this afternoon: "Watch yourself"—followed by a quick hang-up. He couldn't recognize the voice.

Taylor said, "My mind went blank, hon. There's nothing wrong." Instead of becoming more authentic, as he'd aimed for three months ago, he seemed to be losing more and more of his honest self each day. He inhaled deeply and exhaled slowly.

She said, "Really? Nothing wrong? You know I'm programmed to read you accurately. What's going on now in your head? I notice you take a slow deep breath whenever something's on your mind."

"It's a habit I've had since childhood. It helps me focus, I guess. Just had a hard day at work, nothing more significant."

But the work problems, the machine message, and the PTV accident weren't the only things bothering him. He would never admit it to anyone, but somehow, someway, he'd been thinking that maybe perfection wasn't all it's cracked up to be. The improbable had happened: he'd gotten bored with his "spectacular" life with Jennifer. Setting the events of the day aside in his mind as best he could, it was the perfection of Jennifer that somehow had developed into a minor annoyance. He'd grown to wish she'd disagree with him on something, anything, just once. Although he would have hated to fight with Jen, he would have welcomed a disagreement— not a big one, of course—to inject some spice into the relationship.

Further, his Serenity habit, even with taking the lowest, non-addictive dose according to Jennifer, had gotten worse—to the point where he now believed he might have the early stages of an addiction problem. He was feeling a growing, chronic sluggishness he couldn't seem to shake. So far, this was the only Serenity-based symptom he'd experienced.

But now in bed, he didn't want to disappoint Jen. He would hide the current feelings of unease and dissatisfaction in his life. He'd grown to treat her like a real woman—and that meant not being totally honest with her. That's the way real people treated real people, right? In some ways how he behaved toward Jennifer surprised him; but in some ways it didn't. After all, he was determined to make his relationship with Jennifer as real as any relationship he'd have with a human woman.

He decided to dodge her "something wrong" question by holding up his right wrist, revealing a small abrasion, bleeding lightly. "I must have gotten this from your scratchy blue patch. Have you ever thought about removing it?"

Jennifer's mouth flew open. "Oh, honey, sit tight. I'll go to the medicine cabinet. Be right back." As she dashed out of bed, he marveled at how magnificent she looked without clothes. *It ain't all bad*, he thought.

She was back in less than a minute with a tube of salve and a box of adhesive bandages. With great care, she began applying salve on his scrape with her index finger. "About my blue patch, I guess you're going to have to be less enthusiastic during lovemaking." She grinned while continuing to work on the cut. Then she turned serious. "In fact, the patch can't be removed. One, it's against the law. Two, it's designed to be impossible to remove as it's woven into our skin. And three, it's a sign of pride for us bots. Shouldn't you know all about the patch from working at RW?"

"I don't know everything about bots. Don't know much about the patch. Remember, my only job at RobotWorld has been in sales."

"You make us robots sound like commodities."

"I'd never think of you as a commodity, love."

"Wonderful. And as long as you take me back to RobotWorld every year for my all-important annual reboot, I'll be with you forever." She continued the gentle application of salve with her finger. "You like to hide your feelings, don't you? Keep things bottled up. Not getting overly emotional. Careful with what you show me."

"I wouldn't put it like that. I'm an *even-keel* person. Not getting too high or too low. Only trying to do the best I can." He smiled. "You've got a lot to learn about human beings."

She mirrored his smile. "Maybe you're right."

As she affixed a bandage on his scrape, Taylor thought back to the time he'd barged into Sophia Ross's office. Perhaps he *did* see what he initially thought he saw.

"There," she said. "All better." She grabbed a tissue from an end table and wiped the salve residue from her index finger.

He managed to force what he hoped was a sincere smile. "Thank you, Jen."

She kissed him on the forehead. "Just perfect," she said.

12

THE NEXT MORNING, Taylor awoke with what seemed to be a Serenity hangover that included a pounding headache—a new symptom—to go along with the sluggishness. Staring at the ceiling, he counted the two-feet-by-two-feet white vinyl tiles horizontally, then vertically, and multiplied them. Ten times ten: one hundred on the nose. The same result he'd gotten yesterday, the day before, and the day before that. Doing this pointless exercise every morning, even though the answer never changed, relaxed him for some reason.

Before getting out of bed he was possessed by the strong feeling that he wanted to see how the "ninety-nine percent" of humans lived in Capital City. Since his early days working at RobotWorld, he'd had a growing belief that he was losing touch with "the common person." As he got out of bed, his desire morphed into wanting to see how the lowest of the low, the homeless of downtown Capital City, lived.

From the bedroom he could hear Jennifer in the kitchen preparing breakfast. In just a short time, she'd gone from not being able to boil water to almost becoming a master chef by downloading numerous cookbooks and cooking videos into her head. Her desire to become an expert cook emanated from the recognition that Taylor loved her cooking combined with the manifestation of her programmed initiative to please him.

The aftereffects from his Serenity use were confusing, given that he was still taking the lowest, non-addictive dose. Maybe those government reports about the eighty-one-milligram dose being non-addictive were phony, as he'd suspected. Usually upon awakening he'd jump out of bed and get his day started. No more. After easing out of bed, he swallowed some instant-acting aspirin from the bathroom medicine cabinet for his headache.

Before going to breakfast, he decided to take the first step to getting back into shape. As a high school wrestler, he'd risen before dawn and religiously knocked off three hundred push-ups before going to school. Taylor had gotten started with physical fitness and wrestling during his junior year in high school to overcome asthma, which he was determined to beat. Being laughed at in gym class for audible wheezing was the last straw. In his teen years he recognized that the breathing condition had stunted his personal development by causing shortness of breath and a feeling of nervousness in social situations. While his devotion to physical fitness and wrestling had helped with his breathing problems and increased his confidence, the condition never fully faded. Stressful situations still brought about the uncomfortable tightness in his chest, though not to the same degree as during childhood.

Taylor glanced at a full-length mirror and lamented that he'd gone from being "cut" to the semi-lump in the reflection. He dropped to the floor, assumed a push-up position, and managed to crank out five before his arms gave out; he closed his eyes and remained spread-eagled on the carpet for almost thirty seconds to catch his breath. Rather than being discouraged, he was energized and thought it would be a good idea to resume his morning push-up ritual. Probably he'd never get to the three hundred number, but he'd work his way up to a respectable count—and he'd also resume working on getting back his honest self.

He strode into the kitchen and kissed Jennifer. She had prepared a breakfast of rib-eye steak, scrambled eggs, freshly blended strawberry-blueberry-banana juice, coffee, and buttered toast.

"Looks great, Jen," he said.

"Nothing but the best for my man."

In between bites of the sensational breakfast Jen had prepared, he told her it was a casual dress day at work, so she wouldn't ask any questions later as to why he wouldn't be wearing his usual gray RW work clothes. He told himself he'd resume his desire to be more honest with her starting tomorrow.

After breakfast, he popped an anti-cholesterol pill to nullify the artery-clogging effect of the steak and eggs, and washed the pill down with a large glass of water to speed the flushing of any remaining Serenity in his system from the night before. He pressed a button on his wrist computer to inform Sophia that he was ill and wouldn't report to work, put on an old shirt and faded jeans, and kissed Jennifer on his way out the door.

As he exited the elevator in the lobby, Ernest waved at him. "Did you get a new PTV, Mr. Morris? Saw you driving a different one yesterday."

"You don't have to call me *mister*, Ernest. We're on a first-name basis." Taylor smiled. "Had a minor accident with my own vehicle. It's in the shop. The accident was kind of scary. I wasn't hurt. Swerved off the road and could have been shot at. Can you believe it? Maybe someone's after me. Been driving a loaner. I'll get my own PTV back soon." Taylor surprised himself at saying that perhaps someone was after him, but he had the clear thought that it might be true. As he continued his walk to the automatic apartment front door, he wondered why Ernest had such a confused expression on his face.

Taylor had decided to take the Metrorail, not his loaner PTV, to downtown Capital City. He sat in a window seat on the high-speed train and gazed at his reflection in the glass. It amazed him how, as he grew older, he looked more and more like his deceased father. For some reason, this depressed him.

Upon exiting the Metrorail he felt an immediate bad vibe, which caused a dull pain in his abdomen and a tightness in his throat. *Maybe it was the strawberry-blueberry-banana juice,* he joked to himself. In his current surroundings, however, he couldn't bring himself to laugh. The early spring day was typically gray because of the clouds and the industrial pollution, with not even a peek of sun able to bleed through. A still picture of Supreme Leader Toback (*the giant head,* Taylor called it in his mind) was displayed on all the huge telescreens on every corner. *It could be worse,* Taylor thought. *Toback could be spouting his typical brand of deceptive, manipulative language designed to keep us all in line.*

Taylor found himself growing increasingly depressed while walking among the homeless, many of whom displayed blank faces and drooping postures, most likely due to being strung out on Serenity or alcohol or both. The crowded streets had a pungent, dirty smell, the kind of which he'd never experienced before. One could walk two or three blocks through an area of shops and small businesses (Taylor remembered this part of downtown), then the next two or three blocks were essentially a homeless campsite (this aspect of downtown was new to him) with vacant lots and boarded-up buildings. Small makeshift white tents dotted the now-empty lots where thriving businesses once stood. In between the tents burned fires with kettles sitting atop metal grates where soups were being prepared. He observed the occasional grilling of meat; apparently meat was in short supply for most of the population. The smell emanating from this cooking was acrid and not at all appetizing. Taylor estimated that forty to fifty percent of those milling around the downtown area were homeless. *I have grown out of touch. I never knew it was this bad.* A constant soundtrack of pulsating, techno-militaristic music pumped out at moderate volume through hidden mini-loudspeakers. Rumor had it that there were subliminal messages buried in the music that urged people to stay mellow, accept the dictates of the government without question, and not cause a public disturbance.

A chill shot down Taylor's spine as he felt a premonition that he could be living among these people sometime in the future. What he saw deepened his growing belief that the mission of RobotWorld, especially in the way it affected human unemployment, might be flawed. For the first time, he observed a slight tremor in his hands. He remembered reading that this symptom was another of the possible side effects of chronic Serenity use.

Although he was miles away from RobotWorld, the top part of the giant building was visible on the horizon as he looked to the east. When the thought entered his mind that maybe he should resign his job because of his growing concern regarding RW's mission, another chill shot down his spine. He quickly attempted to delete this thought but couldn't.

Shiny jet-black police PTVs, perhaps one out of every three of the fast-moving vehicles on the streets, patrolled the area. Arrests of homeless men and women by the ominously black-clad police were made right in front of him. Taylor found the black helmets with dark visors concealing the faces of the cops intimidating. It surprised him how aggressive the police were—and how passive the people being arrested were, almost as if they didn't care. Maybe they felt jail was a better place than these hard streets.

As Taylor walked past an alley, he heard a strong, gravelly voice directed at him. "Strange things happen around here, young man."

Taylor turned around and saw a thin old man, around seventy years old, with long salt-and-pepper hair falling to his shoulders. The man's face was weather-beaten, with intense lines and a deep tan; he displayed what Taylor took to be an inappropriately wide smile and sparkling blue eyes. Grungy white pants, faded white sneakers, and a gray shawl contributed to his spooky appearance.

"What kind of strange things?" Taylor asked.

The old man pointed a crooked index finger at four faceless cops herding a group of disheveled homeless men into a police van. "People disappear from here all the time. This is a place you don't want to be."

Taylor nodded. "Thanks for the advice. I understand."

"Do you really understand?" the old man asked.

Another chill shot down Taylor's spine. He waved a quick goodbye to the man and turned to walk back to the Metrorail station. He'd seen enough of how the lowest of the low lived. He wanted to get as far from this place as possible.

From behind him, Taylor heard the old man say, "This is a place you don't want to be."

Without turning back to the man, Taylor raised his voice and said, "I heard you the first time," as he kept on walking.

But before reaching the Metro station, Taylor stopped at a Serenity dispensary. Upon entering, he had to acknowledge to himself that somehow, he'd developed a Serenity habit. But now was no time to analyze how this could have happened. He bought several boxes of the drug, two hundred milligrams per dose, and resolved not to tell Jennifer about his purchase.

13

AFTER LEAVING THE Serenity dispensary, Taylor was hit by a strong wind that almost knocked him off his feet as he strode to the Metrorail station. As he regained his balance, he was struck by the thought that his life was now out of balance. He took a deep breath and renewed his intention to get back on track beginning tomorrow. But as he tightened his grip on the small bag containing his Serenity purchase, he realized that reversing the path of his recent missteps wouldn't be easy.

Taylor was a block away from the station, with his hand up to shield his face from debris kicked up by the gusts, when he heard a PTV horn blowing near him. He turned to see a solid black PTV slowing down at the curb. At the wheel was a smiling, waving Shane Diggins, with his perfect Roman nose, perfect teeth, perfect skin, and flowing, perfect, salon-trimmed black hair clearly visible through the windshield. Taylor felt his face involuntarily contort into a sneer. But he tried to force a smile and hoped Shane hadn't noticed his sour facial expression. He rarely saw the head of RobotWorld's R&D section at work anymore. But right now, he didn't want to answer any questions regarding what he was doing in a bad part of the downtown area when he should have been at work.

Taylor and Shane had been casual friends a few years earlier, occasionally taking in a movie with a group from work or playing tennis at a local club shortly after they'd joined RW at almost the same time. But they had since grown out of touch—and Taylor was more than happy about this development.

At one time, Taylor thought he and Shane might have become close friends. They were the same age, grew up in the same area, came from similar middle-class backgrounds, and had even met once in high school when they were members of their respective debate teams. After squaring off in a spirited back-and-forth Saturday morning session at a local high school, they sat across from each other at lunch in the cafeteria and developed what could have been the beginning of a long friendship. Taylor didn't remember most of the specifics of their interaction, but he recalled it as pleasant, with Shane telling him, "I enjoyed matching wits with you. We're both good guys, and we both fight fair."

But when they met for the second time soon after accepting jobs at RobotWorld, Taylor was disappointed at how the "good guy" he'd remembered from that Saturday high school debate had changed. Now Taylor saw Shane as a good-looking, conniving phony who'd do or say anything to get ahead.

The window on the passenger side of the PTV rolled down. Shane leaned over. "Hey, buddy. Need a lift?"

"What a surprise. I was heading over to the Metro. Going back to my apartment."

"Try to rein in your enthusiasm in seeing me. Hop in. I can get you to your place much faster than the Metro."

"Wouldn't want to put you out in any way."

"No trouble at all. I'm here to help."

The passenger door opened, and Taylor took a seat. The interior was a perfect climate-controlled sixty-eight degrees. Shane offered his right hand, and they shook hands for less than a second. Shane then pressed a button on the console, and the cabin was filled with the sound of Beethoven. "Für Elise" was the first selection up. Shane gunned the PTV away from the curb at 250 kmh.

"I know where you live from your sister," Shane said. "We'll be there in less than ten minutes." He glanced at Taylor. "Long time no see."

"You're still into Beethoven."

"Always. An all-time genius."

"I never got into him. Or any classical composer, for that matter. Lennon and McCartney are as classical as I ever got. I'm more modern electro-tech."

"Lennon and McCartney weren't even considered classical in their day. Classic maybe, but not classical. I guess you can't appreciate greatness. But forget about my musical tastes. What the hell are you doing down here dressed like a homeless person?"

Taylor broke eye contact. "A casual shirt and old jeans do not a homeless person make." He made a half-hearted attempt at a smile. "Wearing these clothes just to blend in with the downtown crowd. I felt a little ill—an upset stomach—this morning, so I decided to take a sick day. I quickly got to feeling better, so I thought I'd make a fast trip here to pick up some old movies on microchip."

"Oh, so that's what's in the bag?"

"You got it."

"Still into old movies?"

Taylor tightly clutched the nondescript, brown paper bag containing several thin boxes of Serenity on his lap. "The way you're still into Ludwig van B." He was thankful the bag wasn't clear plastic.

"Aren't there easier ways to get movies? Like by direct download to one of your telescreens?"

"Of course—but there's still nothing like poking around an old, moldy shop to find a rare gem."

"Didn't know there were stores that sold movies in this downtrodden area anymore."

After an uncomfortable moment of silence, Taylor asked, "So what are you doing downtown?"

"Taking a shortcut through a bad part of the city. Heading over to RW for a meeting of the RIC. Sophia and your sister will be there."

"I wouldn't want to make you late for the meeting. You can drop me off at the nearest Metro stop. No need to take me all the way back to my apartment."

"No problem. I'm usually early for meetings and appointments. Punctuality has always been a strong quality of mine. After I drop you off at your place, I'll have plenty of time to get to RW." Shane took his eyes off the road and looked at Taylor. "So you won't be going into work today?"

"Gonna take the whole day off."

Shane guided his PTV onto the expressway and gunned it slightly above the speed limit. "How are things between you and Sophia? We both know she can be difficult."

Taylor wasn't about to take this bait. "Things are going well. We're selling bots almost as fast as we can produce them. Lucky for us there are still enough people and companies in the world that can afford them. No problems with Sophia."

Shane turned off the music. In a voice not much above a whisper, he said, "I've been hearing some rumors about Nitro. Can you imagine what a plus it would be for the company if it really exists? It's so top secret, they even keep me in the dark—and I'm supposed to know everything going on. Have you heard anything?"

Taylor wasn't about to relate what Sophia had told him a few days earlier. He would have bet most of his worldly possessions that Shane had lied about knowing nothing about the development of Nitro. Further, he was sure that any information he'd reveal to his former friend would have gotten back to Sophia by close of business this day. "Not a peep," Taylor replied. "What have you heard?"

"Not much. But it's likely Nitro will exist in the future, if it doesn't already. Things are looking up for our company."

After another uncomfortable silence, Taylor said, "So I understand you and my sister . . ."

"Can you believe it? After having to deal with one Morris at work, now I've got another Morris to deal with. Yes, we're dating. It's going well."

Shane eased his PTV next to Taylor's apartment entrance.

After yet another uncomfortable lull in the conversation, Taylor said, "Thanks for the lift. Good seeing you, Shane. I don't want to delay you any longer from getting to the RIC meeting." Taylor stepped out of the PTV. He then leaned back in toward Shane before closing the door. "Oh, please don't say anything to Sophia about seeing me today. No big deal, as I got better after calling in sick." He smiled weakly. "This is a mental health day." Immediately, he regretted bringing up Sophia and the *mental health day* remark.

"No problem, buddy. Your secret's safe with me. I'm all for mental health."

As Shane drove off, Taylor wondered why he had such of feeling of unease in his chest.

14

A FEW SECONDS after pulling away from the curb, Shane pushed a button on the dashboard.

Sophia was on the line in an instant. "Talk to me."

"Taylor update, Madam President. I caught him buying Serenity," Shane said. "A tap-in to the store computer reveals he's up to two hundred milligrams. Everything is going according to plan. I think the next step is to watch-list him. Then disappearance. At the rate he's going with Serenity, he'll be living among the downtown homeless in a week. That will make his disappearance all the easier."

"Excellent work, Shane."

"Of course. What else were you expecting? But in some ways, he's still the very careful Taylor. Didn't spill the beans about what you'd told him about Nitro. Plus, I couldn't get him to say a negative word about you."

"What he thinks about me is not important. Maybe we can skip the watch-listing and get right to the disappearance."

"I like the way you think, Madam President. But remember, although we're closely aligned with the government, we still have to answer to them. At least to a certain extent. We'll have to convince the government to make him disappear. It seems getting people on the disappearance list is getting harder to do these days."

"It's the nameless, faceless humans who still run the government with their infernal standards, where they cling to certain ethical principles while at the same time ignoring others, like with the pushing of Serenity and the disappearances of the downtown homeless. No rhyme or reason to it. Just the bureaucracy we have to deal with."

Shane got a new incoming call beep on his earpiece. "I should take this call. A probable update from one of our Taylor monitors. This guy needs to start providing some good information or he'd better watch himself."

"We'll speak later," Sophia said.

Shane tapped the dashboard telescreen to answer the call and activate the voice changer.

"Talk," Shane said.

"Sir, this is Ernest Billick. A short time ago I signed on to provide monitoring on Taylor—"

"I know who you are," Shane said. "What do you have to report?"

"I found out today that Mr. Morris was involved in a suspicious PTV accident. We both know they rarely occur. Did you have anything to do with it?"

"That's none of your concern."

"I signed up to spy on Taylor Morris, to do my civic duty when called upon. And also because I hate him. He ruined my life. But I didn't sign up for murder. If you can't confirm that you weren't involved in causing this accident, then I want out."

"I had nothing to do with it."

"What about the government?" Ernest asked.

"I'm sure the government was not involved."

"How can you be so certain?"

"I don't have access to all records, but I think I can say with confidence that they had nothing to do with it."

"But you can't be sure?" After pausing and getting no response, Ernest continued, "Listen, although I'd like to hurt Morris, I feel uncomfortable doing this monitoring job. Had a bad feeling about it from the start. I quit. You can stop crediting my bank account as of today. Will that be okay? No hard feelings if I stop now?"

"Very well. Thank you for your service. It was voluntary, of course. No hard feelings." Shane terminated the call. *The amount of information we've gotten from you hasn't been overly useful,* he thought. *Maybe it's time for you to disappear, little man.*

15

THE NEXT DAY, Taylor left early for work in the loaner PTV and headed for the repair shop to pick up his vehicle. He felt a tightness in his chest, and knowing his body, he could tell it wasn't related to his lifelong asthma. He decided to be more alert and aware of his surroundings. Maybe someone was really after him. Had he done something to merit such action? If so, he wasn't sure from whom.

The friendly, talkative mechanic with the bad teeth greeted him and handed him the PTV key. "Better than new, Mr. Morris," the mechanic said. "That's our guarantee."

Taylor was given an accident report by download to his wrist computer. The report reflected a determination by the police that his accident was caused by a rare, but not unheard of, electromagnetic power failure on the section of road where the mishap occurred. His PTV was the only one that had run off the road. The hole on the driver's side door was judged to have been made by a small rock, apparently kicked up during the accident with a force great enough to cause the damage. The rock was recovered by the police and disposed of. The hole was patched, and the PTV was now deemed to be in excellent condition. The investigation was termed "closed." Taylor saw no purpose in questioning the police report with the mechanic. Taylor thanked him, paid his bill with a tap of his wrist computer, and headed off to work.

On the drive to RobotWorld, Taylor resolved he would seek out Sophia and reaffirm his commitment to the company's mission. *I won't lie,* he thought, *but I might spin the truth. Oh, hell, I'll lie if I must. Maybe losing values is a part of life.* His plan to reconnect with his true self would have to wait yet another day. Yesterday's downtown trip and Sophia's continual cold shoulder had created a palpable concern regarding his job security. Not to mention the feeling of apprehension he'd gotten from his interaction with Shane. Taylor had done all he could to get away from the intuitive feelings he'd so relied upon in his youth, but they appeared to be coming back. Since adulthood these feelings had caused him significant mental anguish, which led him to cut off communication with George. For the umpteenth time, Taylor asked himself the question: Was being a one-percenter a good thing or a bad thing? He still wasn't sure.

But now Taylor had to deal with the situation before him—his work situation. He resolved to set aside his questions about RW's mission and be the best team player possible. He'd grown accustomed to the benefits of working at RW, especially the ability to afford his luxury apartment and the relationship with Jennifer, who was technically the property of RobotWorld. The want and need to keep his job trumped all the negatives in his mind regarding RW's mission. In addition, his growing Serenity habit would make losing his job extremely problematic.

In his office Taylor swallowed two tablets of Calm, a strong over-the-counter medication known to blunt most symptoms associated with Serenity use. After waiting ten minutes for the pills to do their job (as noted on the label), Taylor headed down the hall and knocked on Sophia's office door.

As soon as he entered, she stood and said, "Bad timing, I've got to get to a meeting. As the old saying goes, I'm busier than a one-eyed cat watching two mouse holes."

Taylor moved his hand toward her in a *Stop* gesture. "It seems like you've been trying to avoid me. True?"

She brushed past him without making eye contact. "I told you, I need to get to a meeting."

To the back of her head, Taylor said, "I want to reaffirm my commitment to the company. You seem to be doubting it for some reason."

Sophia stopped as she got to the door and turned toward Taylor. "I have a good sense in picking up vibes from people. I only want employees who are totally on board with the mission of our company."

"You know me. *Do no harm* is one of my life principles. Just like the precept that guides doctors." As soon as he uttered these words, he felt his chest tighten in disappointment at himself. Shortly after joining RobotWorld five years ago, he'd adopted this *do no harm* stance as a way to "play it safe" at work rather than take chances, so as to get ahead in what he recognized as an innovative but basically conservative company. He had even verbalized this position to Sophia soon after being promoted to sales manager. *Do no harm* was a concept he'd been attracted to in his early teen years after reading that it was a central principle of the medical profession.

But Taylor had made a conscious decision a few months ago to jettison *do no harm* when he'd decided to be more honest at work and in his personal life.

Given what he'd just said to Sophia, however, there was nowhere else to go now but to finish his unauthentic point. "But it's more than only doing no harm that's guiding me here at work, Sophia. For sure, I'm on board with the company mission."

"Glad to hear it. You're looking a bit haggard these days, Taylor. I've got to go."

As he stood alone in the office, with only the bubbling sound of the piranha tank filter in his ears, Taylor was more confused about his future at RW than he'd been five minutes earlier.

But then he had a moment of clarity. It didn't come from George, as he didn't hear George's distinctive voice. What had become clear to Taylor was that he'd grown tired of groveling. Getting back to his honest, true self wasn't a process. He just had to be there—or *act as if* he was there until it became a reality—and let the chips fall where they were going to fall. And if that meant losing his job at RobotWorld, then so be it.

16

UPON RETURNING TO his office, Taylor said to Roz, "I get the feeling my future with this company is NFL. Not for long." ⋅

Without breaking the focus on her computer screen, Roz shook her head. "Great. If you go, they'll also let me go. They see us as a team." Her eyes met his. "You look rather tired. Are you okay?"

"I'm always at least okay."

Taylor wasn't about to detail all his present life problems. But he decided to confide more of his RW concerns to Roz.

"Let's take a walk on the terrace," he said.

"And breathe in the pollution spewing from the factory part of the complex?" she replied.

He put a hand over his mouth and whispered, "I want to remove any possibility that our conversation might be monitored."

Roz rose from her desk. She and Taylor walked to the glass door leading to an outdoor, unroofed platform that surrounded the entire floor around the building. It was called "the terrace": a solid twenty-foot-wide path over a mile in distance. Many employees used the terrace, constructed from state-of-the-art lightweight cement with smooth, red tiles on its surface, to take a walk or jog during their lunch hour or fifteen-minute work breaks. The red tiles were the latest in running technology, designed to absorb nearly one hundred percent of stress on the knees.

Right now, there were no other RW workers braving the chilly temperatures along with the strong winds currently buffeting the terrace. A gust hit Taylor and Roz right before they reached the metal railing.

"We've got gale-force winds and a wind chill hovering around freezing. But we're out here without coats," Roz said. "This better be good."

"It's not that cold, and these winds aren't gale force," Taylor said, having to raise his voice over the steady *whoosh* of the wind. "Follow me on this," he said as he got close to her ear. "It's a given fact our industrial bots are taking away human jobs. Add to it that our personal bots could most likely make human relationships a thing of the past—"

"Sort of like the bag of nuts and bolts living with you now?"

"You've made that joke before." He frowned. "Very funny."

"My teeth are chattering. Can we go in now? Haven't we had this conversation before?"

"I've got new info I've never shared with you." He decided to stick to pertinent information concerning the effect of RW products on society and keep his word to Sophia by not mentioning what she'd told him about Nitro. "We'll go back in soon. Just hear me out. I don't like Sophia's coziness with the government. She's devoting significant time to the Robot Integration Council, which started out as unpaid volunteer work. An online story from last week alleges she's getting paid big bucks from the RIC. I believe it. So we have a situation where our products are potentially phasing out our species, where our boss is working with the government to push the products that are doing the phasing out, in addition to the government indirectly endorsing Serenity and its numbing of the population. Factor in the police presence to suppress any hint of dissent, and where are we headed?"

"Not a pretty picture, I'll admit." She was almost shouting to be heard over the wind. "It's sort of like the old maxim about how to boil a frog. You don't toss it into a steaming pot. You drop the frog into a pot with the water at room temperature. Then turn up the heat slowly, incrementally, so the frog doesn't notice the change. Before froggy catches on, it's too late. The changes in our society have happened so gradually, no one seemed to notice."

Taylor moved closer to her and lowered his voice to a conspiratorial tone. "Exactly. You've got it. Incrementalism—the most powerful and stealthy way to change a society. But there's more regarding our fearless leader. A short time ago I entered her office when she was changing clothes to make a speech. Should have knocked. My mistake. Didn't see anything anatomically I shouldn't have seen. I can't be certain, but I think I saw a blue patch, right where no human would ever have a blue patch."

"Now I see why you wanted to come out here. About the blue patch—how sure are you?"

"Sixty, seventy percent maybe."

"With the law as it is, before you can report this—if you ever decided to report it—you need to be at one hundred."

"Hell, there's no way I can ask her to take off her gray shirt."

"Of course. But I see what you're driving at. It could be what we're doing here at RobotWorld is, shall we say, counterproductive for society in the long run." She paused. "Even if you had definite proof on Sophia's blue patch and RW's coziness with the government, I'm not sure I'd recommend reporting it. But if you ever decided to report it, you'll most certainly need proof more solid than the structure we work in."

"The question is how to get it."

Roz peered at the gray sky. "This might end up causing us problems, but I might have an answer—or at least the beginning of an answer. The rumors of the Information Room—you've heard them—the infamous locked room in the basement that nobody's been in, that supposedly contains all RW records since the founding of the company. All its secrets."

Taylor nodded. "But that's all purely rumor. Right?"

A blast of wind nearly knocked Roz over. She braced herself against the railing and said, "I believe the rumors are true, at least as they pertain to the existence of the Information Room. Don't know what's in there, but I'll tell you something interesting about the IR you don't know. However, you have to agree we go inside once I do."

"Agreed."

"I happen to know that sleazy Dee Woodson keeps a key to the room in the top right drawer of his desk. On one of my visits to his office, I overheard him say so. I think I can grab the key when he's not there. No security cameras in his office." She paused a beat. "Interesting information delivered. Back inside."

17

ROZ CONSIDERED HERSELF an expert in avoiding Dee Woodson, whom she thought to be exceedingly unpleasant. From her desk, Roz could see down the hall to Woodson's office door. So she was able to know when he entered and exited.

Roz saw Dee leave his office around lunchtime to catch an elevator. Dee was notorious for taking extra-long lunch breaks.

Roz gathered some papers she needed to drop off to Dee and headed down the hall. She entered his office, closed the door behind her, put the papers on the desk, and opened the top right drawer. The key was exactly where she remembered Dee saying it was. She removed the old-style, pin tumbler lock key (not the magnetic swipe card key used throughout most of the RobotWorld facility) from the back of the drawer. The tarnished brass key had a small label marked *IR* attached by a string through a small hole at the top of its bow. The rumor was that the Information Room was the only room in the basement with a tumbler lock. This further confirmed in Roz's mind that the existence of the IR was real.

Roz stuffed the key in her pants pocket and hotfooted it back to Taylor's office. She smiled as she held the key over her head and said to Taylor, "Got it. And I'm sure I wasn't seen."

"You're the best. You got the key, I'll do the reconnaissance." He took the key from her and headed to the stairs, not the elevator. Five full minutes later, he reached the basement.

After taking a moment to catch his breath, Taylor looked left, then right in the dark hallway. This was his first time in the basement. No security cameras as far as he could tell. The word around the facility was that the company had decided against installing security cameras in the basement for reasons not completely clear. Taylor ran the back of his hand over his brow to flick off a thin film of sweat. It seemed the air conditioning that kept the rest of RW so pleasantly temperature-controlled was not operating in this area, which felt like a hothouse. He looked for a door with an old-style lock. In one corner of the basement he found such a door; it displayed a tattered black paint job and was the only door without words identifying the purpose of the room. He inserted the key into the tumbler lock, the likes of which he hadn't seen since he was a boy. He closed the door behind him and flipped on a light switch in the small room with a dusty, musty smell.

Against one wall were dark-gray metal filing cabinets with a range of dates marked on each drawer. The dates reached back to the founding of RobotWorld over three decades earlier. Taylor opened a drawer with records covering a period that began four years ago, the period when he first suspected the beginning of the unholy nexus between the government and RW. This was around the time when Sophia Ross was named head of the corporation. He was surprised the records were mostly paper and not disk.

Taylor pulled a few folders and read as fast as he could. He smiled, happy he'd taken a speed-reading course in college. The first file suggested evidence of the cozy relationship between the government and RW he'd suspected. There was also general evidence suggesting RW robots were in high government positions in violation of long-time laws regarding robots. Taylor skimmed the first few pages and made a mental note to return to this thick file in a future visit. Now, he just wanted to get a quick overview of what was in this room.

As soon as he started reading a smaller file about an RW executive who'd mysteriously disappeared after defying Sophia and Shane Diggins on some minor issue, Taylor heard a loud crash in the hall and the sound of voices. He returned the file to the cabinet and turned off the light. The voices faded. He opened the door to find no one in the hall. He decided to head back to his office. The information he'd gotten on this first trip was significant, and he wanted Roz to return the key to Dee Woodson's desk before Sophia's acknowledged henchman returned from lunch. There would be other times to delve into these files. He locked the door and strode to the stairs.

***

At her desk later that afternoon, Sophia Ross's smooth white face and neck reddened as she focused on a wall telescreen. Her nose scrunched up in a way that made her look as if she'd smelled something extremely offensive. Part of the characteristics of personal robots like her was that they registered the same kind of internal feelings and external physical reactions to emotions as a human would. But just like a human, Sophia's feelings took a one hundred eighty-degree reversal as she realized the action of the person on the telescreen was providing an incontestable reason for his job termination.

The images on the telescreen showed Taylor Morris entering the basement Information Room and rummaging through a filing cabinet. Taylor was not authorized access to the IR. Sophia congratulated herself for recently installing the most modern and undetectable recording devices in the basement, the IR, and all executive offices, including hers and Dee Woodson's. What she saw on the screen sealed Taylor's fate at RobotWorld. The strict employee protection laws couldn't save Taylor's job now. How had he obtained the key to the Information Room? A few clicks brought up a video of Taylor's assistant in Dee Woodson's office stealing the key that allowed Taylor's entrance into the basement room. Roz Troward's fate as an RW employee was now sealed also.

Sophia balled her fist and punched a button on the desk. In less than a minute, Dee Woodson was in her office. She showed him the videos.

"Have you gotten enough information on Taylor to protect us from legal action?" she asked.

"I've manufactured a good amount of dirt, but not quite enough," Woodson replied. "This vid would certainly put us over the top with both of them."

"We won't tell them about the video," Sophia said. "We'll keep it in our back pocket in case we need it in the future. I'll fire him tomorrow. It's too late in the day to prepare all the formal termination documents. My guess is he'll suspect we know about his snooping, given the timing, as will his assistant. They'll never take legal action against us after what they did. You'll fire his assistant at the same time I'm firing him. I don't know what he got from his prying, but it couldn't have been much. He definitely didn't remove any documents from the IR."

After Dee left her office, Sophia stewed at her desk. It was normal for her to feel anger at what Taylor had done, and normal to have a strong desire on how to handle such situations with as much force as she could get away with. These feelings were part of her programming. But she also prided herself in trying to be the best she could be. To evolve on her own as the best and brightest of humans might evolve—or maybe, just maybe, *beyond* the upper level of what humans were capable of. That was her dream. Evolve in all things intellectual as well as in what she considered the highest human values like love and compassion. But right now, her programming was winning the war inside her. More than anything, she wanted to kill Taylor Morris.

18

AFTER BEING SUMMONED to Sophia's office soon after he arrived at work the next morning, Taylor entered and noticed two large male security officers sitting on the large black leather couch; they displayed stone-faced expressions matching that of his boss. He suppressed a laugh as he thought they all looked as deadly serious as the piranhas in the fish tank. One did not have to be a brainy intuitive—even though his intuition hadn't been a major factor in his life since childhood—to surmise what was about to happen wouldn't be good. Taylor was pleased he'd popped two Calm tablets an hour earlier to alleviate headache and hand tremor Serenity symptoms. He sat across the desk from Sophia.

"There's no easy way to say this, and I don't want any discussion," she said. "I'm letting you go with two weeks of severance pay. We've both known this action has been on the horizon in recent weeks."

Taylor was surprisingly tranquil. *Maybe it's the Calm.* He wondered if she was aware of the snooping mission the day before. Probably. He focused on her green eyes and said nothing. He remained silent not because his soon-to-be former boss had said she didn't want a discussion, but because he wanted to see if Sophia would say anything that could give him cause to file an unjustified termination action. Taylor realized that with his unauthorized IR intrusion the day before, he had given Sophia the ammunition to fire him, ammunition that would hold up in court despite the strong employee protection laws. He was curious as to whether she would mention the foray to the Information Room.

Sophia continued, "By the way, the company has repossessed your Jennifer as of an hour ago. It's our right. She's our property, not yours." Sophia smiled in a way he interpreted to be an expression of pure happiness. Almost as if she knew taking back Jennifer would hurt him as much as the loss of his job. She paused for a moment, seemingly to wait for a reaction. Taylor did his best to maintain his composure and remained silent.

"Security will walk you back to your office so you can pack up," Sophia said. "Then they'll escort you out of the building. I wish you luck." She nodded to the two uniformed security men, put on headphones, and looked down at the telescreen embedded in her desk top.

Taylor stood. "I know you're trying to tune me out. I want to say you're making a mistake. I sense we'll run into each other down the road—and when it happens, I'll win." Taylor recognized in the moment the hollowness of his words. It didn't feel good being powerless and losing so much of what his self-image was based upon. He was disappointed in himself for not coming up with something profound to say, or something witty, something that would cut Sophia right now as cruelly as she'd just cut him with her words.

She didn't look up from the telescreen.

Taylor moved toward the door, followed by the security men.

When he got back to his soon-to-be former office, Roz was there, eyes red and moist, cleaning out her desk.

"Sorry, Roz. My fault," Taylor said.

*   *   *

As Taylor and Roz cleaned out their desks and packed their personal belongings, the security men watched their every move. Taylor and Roz were silent; the only sounds being the opening and closing of desk drawers along with the packing of material in cardboard boxes. After a half hour the two now-former employees of RobotWorld, each cradling a large box in their arms, were accompanied by security to the well-lit, cavernous, underground parking garage where their PTVs were parked near each other.

After the security men left them, Taylor set his box down on the hood of his PTV and said, "Well, it's been a pleasure, Roz. Sorry again that my carping about the company to Sophia and probably the reconnaissance mission got us fired. I never saw any security cameras." He didn't want to add the clear thought that popped into his head: *Maybe it was the damn Serenity that made me reckless in wanting to check out the IR.*

He took a deep breath and continued, "I should have realized there would be security cams. The rumors have always been that much of the basement was stuck in the past, with no modern amenities like security cameras. And we'd all heard there were no cameras in our executive offices. But maybe the lack of cameras was wishful thinking on my part. Sophia didn't give me a reason for the termination, but I know my run to the IR had a lot to do with it. I guess the old saw that Sophia once mentioned to me about what happens to people who *assume* is true. And I'm exhibit A."

"It's on me too," Roz said. "I'm exhibit B. Within the past six months, I'd heard Dee Woodson say there were no security cameras in his office and the basement, and fifty percent of wanting to check out the Information Room was me. They didn't give me a reason for my firing either. But it certainly had to do with the IR situation. That would preclude us from fighting them, I'm sure." She sighed. "With today's employment market, it'll be tough to find a job that'll pay us as much as here. But with my savings, I think I can make it comfortably for at least a year or two. And as you know, I do come from a family of some means. I can always fall back on them."

"I'm not sure I could hold out without a job as long as you can. And I don't have any family to fall back on." Taylor wasn't going to bring up that he'd stretched himself thin to maintain his lavish lifestyle and that he had little savings. He definitely wasn't going to mention his growing Serenity habit. "I've been starting to wonder what the world would be like if this place was no more. But now we are no more for this place." He forced a laugh. "If you need a job reference, don't hesitate to give me a call."

"Thanks. Let's stay in touch. Maybe this might be good for you in the long run. You've grown increasingly dissatisfied with RW's mission, and you've wanted to show more integrity in your professional life, in line with your values. I'm sure you'll find something where you can do that." She kissed him on the cheek, and they said goodbye.

On the way home in his PTV, Taylor activated the on-board mechanism to make a record of his current situation. He had to talk out where he was right now—even if only to himself. "So much of my life has been dependent on my job. I fear for the future." A ten-second pause. "Damn, I hope Sophia was only jerking my chain about repossessing Jennifer. But who am I kidding? Sophia repossessed her, for sure. RW has the right to take her back. Sophia's on solid ground there. Ah, hell."

Taylor turned off the recorder as he pulled into the underground parking lot.

He inserted the magnetic key to open his apartment door. No Jennifer running out of the kitchen to jump into his arms. It felt strange, and he missed her already. Even her clothes had been removed from the closet. Taylor was grudgingly impressed with RW's efficiency. By current law, they had the right to enter his apartment to reclaim their property.

The red message lights on his various telescreens and communication devices were blinking. He inserted a communication earpiece.

"Hello, Mr. Morris," said the recorded voice of Karen Stuart, the slim, young, genial business manager of the Galaxy Apartments. "First off, there were several men here this morning who had proper legal documentation to enter your apartment to reclaim property. I accompanied them to your place. I can attest to the fact they only removed what was legally theirs. A second issue is that Ernest Billick didn't show up for work this morning. He's not in his apartment and isn't answering his communication device. Because you helped get him the job, I wonder if you might know of an alternate way to reach him."

Taylor returned the call and got Karen Stuart's messaging function. "Hi, Karen. Thanks for accompanying those guys this morning to reclaim their property. About your Ernest Billick question: I don't know him well. I don't know of an alternate way to reach him. He's always seemed reliable. I'm sure things are okay, and he'll turn up soon. Sorry. I can't help you."

Taylor removed the communication earpiece. He popped a Serenity pill into his mouth, climbed into bed after peeling off his gray work uniform for the last time, and slept until ten o'clock the next morning.

19

AS TAYLOR WAS awakening in his bed on the day after being fired, Sophia fidgeted in an uncomfortable chair in a quiet waiting room outside the downtown Capital City office of Marcia Haddad, the Chief Sector Security Officer. Sophia was the only individual in the small waiting area. She'd changed out of her RobotWorld grays and wore a red pantsuit.

She inserted a communication earpiece into her ear. In an instant, she was connected on a secure line to Shane Diggins. "I so much hate to grovel," Sophia murmured.

"Sometimes it's necessary," Shane said.

"I'm not at all optimistic."

"Give it your best shot. The worst that can happen is that we'll be in the same position we are in now."

She kept her voice down, even though her communication couldn't be monitored on the secure line. "I'd like the government to agree to make Taylor disappear. Dump our problem in their lap. Don't want to expose us to the risk of going after him on our own, which we'll have to do if the government won't eliminate him."

"If that's the way it must be, we'll make it work. Orchestrating his PTV accident failed. But it was a good effort, and it wasn't able to be traced back to us. If we have to, we'll do better in the future."

The large double door opened. A sharply dressed young man in a business suit smiled at her. "Ms. Haddad will see you now."

"I've gotta go, Shane," Sophia said.

Marcia Haddad, fiftyish, slim, with her medium-length brown hair pulled into a tight bun at the back of her head, rose as Sophia entered. She was wearing a red pantsuit two shades darker than Sophia's. "So good to see you again, Sophia."

They shook hands across the desk and sat.

"I know we're both busy, so let's get right to the business of your visit," Haddad said. "I've read your confidential memo. I must say, I'm a little surprised. You don't have enough here. Not nearly enough to warrant a disappearance."

Sophia's head snapped back. "But this former executive broke into a secure room and attempted to access sensitive material that could hurt my company—and by extension, the government."

Haddad shook her head. "So this Morris guy broke into a room where he didn't have authorization. You fired him. The video you provided showed he didn't swipe anything from the room. He has no prior anti-government activity on record. I'm sorry, Sophia. I've run this through our highest level, as a courtesy to you. To give your request every possible consideration. There's just no way, given what you've given us."

Sophia folded her hands on her lap. "I think you're making a mistake." She wasn't about to relate that, in addition to breaking into the RobotWorld Information Room, there was a strong possibility that Taylor had seen her blue patch. To make such an admission would be impossible. It would expose the fact that she was in her position illegally. She was certain Marcia Haddad didn't know her secret. For important bots like her, the RW research and development team had installed a device that could beat even the best metal detectors and body scan machines, which could be encountered upon entering places like Sector Security.

Haddad said, "We could provide assistance in perhaps monitoring this individual, as warranted. Maybe if he does something in the future that establishes a clear political danger to the government, we'd reconsider. And I'll hold the case open for you to submit any additional information that you might uncover. We have our standards for eliminating people. As of now, this case doesn't meet those standards." Haddad smiled a slight smile Sophia interpreted as being condescending.

Sophia stood. "We'll agree to disagree on the Taylor Morris situation. But I do appreciate your consideration and the offer of monitoring in the future. I might take you up on the monitoring one day." She extended her hand and Haddad took it. "Thanks for hearing me out, Marcia. Good seeing you again."

As Sophia eased into the back seat of the RobotWorld PTV parked in the underground garage, she tapped on the glass partition separating her from the driver. "Back to the office. Fast," she shouted.

She inserted a communication earpiece.

"How did it go?" Shane asked.

"Like we thought it would. A declination."

"No big deal. We'll do the job ourselves. Neat and clean. No problem, you'll see."

"It could be tough. It could be dangerous. But I see no other option."

20

THE MIDAFTERNOON MEETING of the ten-member Robot Integration Council in the cramped downtown Capital City office of one of the members had just ended. The meeting had to be moved from Sophia's office at the last minute because of a leak in the piranha tank, which wouldn't be fixed until the next day. As Sophia had grown tired of always hosting the meeting, she had been looking for a legitimate excuse to move to a new venue. The fish tank problem provided one.

From where she sat at the head of the rectangular wooden table with a deep-brown finish, Sophia motioned to the woman sitting in the back of the room, next to Shane Diggins. "Tracey," she said, "if you've got a minute . . ."

Shane tapped Tracey on the arm and left the room. Tracey took a seat next to Sophia.

"I wanted to inform you of a little unpleasantness that happened yesterday," Sophia said. "I know from speaking with Shane that you're unaware of it, but you'd find out about it soon enough. I thought it better you hear it from me directly. I, for reasons I won't go into, had to fire your brother."

Tracey hesitated a moment before responding. "That's it? From your serious demeanor, Ms. Ross, I was expecting something major."

Sophia smiled. "I'm surprised at your reaction."

"The news is no big deal to me. Taylor and I have been—let's say *estranged*—for quite some time. No need to go into great detail. It's the sort of thing that happens in some families. People don't call each other, then grow apart, then a small crack in a relationship becomes a chasm. I was always number two of two in my parents' eyes next to Mr. Perfect. My brother and I hardly communicate now. If you hadn't told me, I might not have found out about Taylor no longer working for RW. Most people think twins are inseparable. But rifts happen in some families. Sadly, a rift happened in mine." Tracey broke eye contact, and her eyes darted around the room. "I'll shut up now."

"Well, I'm gratified that your brother's termination will not harm our relationship or impede your service to this council," Sophia said. "In the short time since Shane recommended you, you've been a most valuable member of the RIC."

"I appreciate your kind words, Ms. Ross. I love doing all I can to help robots fit into society. I've always been a bit uneasy around people. I know Taylor shares the same characteristic. But you probably know that. People disappoint so often. At least, that's been my experience. Personal robots are so much more reliable and, I must say, so much more relatable to me than humans. I've never been disappointed by a robot. Humans? That's another story. Not that it matters much, but I've found out that my brother now has a robot mate."

"Unfortunately for him, his robot relationship has ended. She is the property of RW."

Tracey appeared to choke back tears. With a catch in her voice, she said, "Good. I couldn't give less of a damn about Taylor."

21

LATER THAT AFTERNOON, back in her RobotWorld office, Sophia placed a communication earpiece in her right ear and contacted Shane, who was in his office at the other end of the vast RW complex.

"I'm getting ready to call William Hart," she said. "Any updated information from the janitor at Taylor's apartment?"

"The janitor screwed up," Shane said. "Didn't provide a whole lot for us, anyway. He's gone. Gone as in disappeared. The government quickly approved this request. Go figure. As you've said before, no rhyme or reason."

She tapped a button on the desk telescreen to end the call, then tapped it again to call William Hart, a fellow robot and a high-ranking government ally in media relations. In addition to media, he had extensive experience handling the kind of task she was going to discuss with him. Hart agreed to meet Sophia in the park across the street from the RobotWorld offices in one hour. Just as it was illegal for Sophia to be holding her position at RW, it was also illegal for Hart to be in his job.

Sophia considered Hart a trusted advisor, a smart robot who had a unique approach of looking at the world, one different from her own. She felt a feeling of satisfaction with the thought that the development of individual robot personalities was comparable to the obvious diversity in human dispositions. And how robots related to other robots was also not significantly different from the way humans related to other humans. It was also gratifying to Sophia how humans—whether they knew they were dealing with a robot or not—related to high-functioning bots like her in essentially the same manner as they would to another human. This, of course, was due to the huge accomplishment of RW scientists in making bots so humanlike in every way that it was impossible to tell the difference between a bot and the real thing.

Sophia and Hart arrived at the small park, which was half the size of a square city block, from different directions, right on time. This park, a holdover from pre-World War III days, was one of the few in Capital City. Since the war, much of what had been parkland had been converted to the grim, gigantic apartment buildings that dominated the city. The creation of wooded or verdant acreage for recreational use wasn't a high priority for the current government.

Sophia and Hart wore black overcoats, although being robots, they didn't need coats to combat the nippy temperatures this day. However, they had both been programmed to maintain human behavior according to circumstance. The few humans—or could some of them be bots?—walking in the park now were wearing overcoats, sweatshirts, and jackets to cope with the chill in the air. Sophia and Hart would blend in perfectly. They sat on a secluded park bench under a huge willow oak. Willow oaks were once plentiful in this area; this particular tree was one of the few remaining. It also seemed that the grass around the bench where they sat had long since declined to grow.

Hart stood five feet nine with brown hair closely cropped in almost a military-type buzz cut, average-looking and average-behaving in every way, so as to not draw undue attention to himself. "It's been a week since we've seen the sun, Sophia," he said. "The sky's as hard and gray as the wall of that old abandoned cement factory across the street. Could be it's all the pollution your RW operation discharges into the atmosphere that's giving us this gloomy weather."

Sophia decided to ignore the pollution remark. "But the temps have been a bit warmer than last week, so we can't complain."

Hart smiled. "Listen to how boringly human we sound."

"Ain't it beautiful?"

Four or five pigeons landed on the ground near them. "They're looking to be fed," Hart said. "They picked the wrong twosome." He made eye contact with her. "What did you want to talk about?"

"That fired executive I mentioned the other day, William," she said. "Shane and I have been trying to get the government to come over to our position on how dangerous this former executive could be, but they're not with us yet. It's possible he knows information that could hurt me and, thus, could hurt us." If pressed on the relevant information, she would have noted Taylor's raid on the Information Room. She would not have mentioned the possibility Taylor had seen her blue patch, an inexcusable error reflecting poorly on the competence she so prided herself on. Sophia paused and looked directly into Hart's eyes. "Since the government is not where we are with this individual, we've decided to move ahead without them."

As matter-of-factly as a person of high culture ordering prime rib at a fancy restaurant, she said, "I was thinking elimination."

Hart glanced back at the pigeons and exhaled in a way that made his cheeks puff out. "Not what I want to hear. You know how hard it is to kill someone these days, unless it's done by the government for political reasons. And, obviously, this situation doesn't fall under that heading—or else you wouldn't be talking to me. Law enforcement is so damn competent. Non-government crimes these days are solved. Especially murder. Most of them, anyway. Except for the disappearance of the downtown homeless. And we know what that's about."

Sophia stifled a laugh.

Hart continued, "For a nonhomeless murder or disappearance not handled by the government, we'd have to proceed with great care. The best route would be to hire human amateurs with no prior violent criminal records or associations. Too risky to go the bot route, as the programming record would expose us if they're caught. And too risky to hire human professionals whom the law might know from monitoring and who would rat us out without thinking twice to cut a deal with the authorities if caught. Besides, human pros would definitely want to know exactly who they're dealing with. Not like human amateurs. We could get away with being anonymous to them."

Sophia nodded.

"So," Hart continued, "after we hire these human amateurs and they do the deed, we'd then have to transport them out of the area while getting around travel restriction laws. Big problem. Or hide them in town. Big problem. Not to mention the cash payments. Big cash payments. Another big potential problem. Or we could have *them* eliminated after the deed is done. Yet another big problem." Hart looked into the eyes of the stone-faced Sophia. "So, going the elimination route with this fired executive is one big, big problem." He focused back on the pigeons. "I take your silence to mean I haven't convinced you not to go the elimination route."

She grinned. "You read me correctly. Sometimes I wish we could just Nitro the whole damn human race and be done with it."

Hart threw his head back and brought his hands together in a loud clap. "You mean the rumors are true? There is such a thing as Nitro?"

Sophia nodded firmly. "Nitro exists. Keep it to yourself. I know you can be trusted. Only a select few know about it. Developed by our R&D team. Recently, they figured out how to control its unstable properties. The substance is called Nitro after an old explosive it's akin to—nitroglycerine. Our Nitro is not close to nitroglycerine chemically. In truth, it's much more powerful. Three separate lots of Nitro are stored in a highly secured, safe room in the basement of RW, in three vacuum bottle containers we call *the black thermoses*. One small thermos of this clear liquid could reduce the whole RobotWorld complex to a burned-out piece of firewood. Believe it."

"I imagine a weapon as destructive as Nitro would never be used."

She curled her upper lip. "Just like the humans would never use nuclear and biological weapons. Ha! Ever hear of World War III?"

Hart groaned before chortling.

"But you might be right," Sophia said. "I don't see Nitro ever being used. Just too devastating. Even the thought of a Nitro explosion sends chills down my spine—and I'm a robot. Our scientists believe there can be other uses for Nitro—positive uses, like maybe for energy—in addition to its destructive capability. Emphasizing these positive uses will be a major part of our marketing plan for Nitro in the future." After a few seconds of silence, she continued, "So, regarding the matter at hand, about this fired employee, what do you say?"

"I was hoping I'd distracted you from the risky *matter at hand*." Hart looked back at her. "I guess I could find someone who could do the job and wouldn't be able to be traced back to either one of us if caught. But only if you think it's really, really necessary."

"I'd prefer to hire a solid professional. But you have more experience in these matters than I do. If, as you say, hiring a competent human amateur is the way to go, then let's move on it."

"The first thing I'd need is big-time cash. It would be impossible to use debit cards, money transfers, and the like. Can't create any kind of money trail."

"No problem. I'm head of one of the biggest companies in the world after all. Just as long as the cash—and the crime itself—can't be traced back to me."

"Thanks for thinking of *me*, Sophia. It won't be able to be traced back to me either. I'll make the necessary contacts anonymously by communication without video—the only way to do something like this." Hart stood. "I'll get on it right away and be back in touch."

22

LOUD KNOCKING ON his apartment door roused Taylor from a restless sleep. His head was throbbing, and his hands were shaking more than they ever had. But this was no time to focus on the deterioration of his physical and mental condition, which had accelerated in the six weeks or so since being fired from RobotWorld. The knocking continued. *Who the hell could that be?*

He ran to the bathroom, sprayed two sprays of mouthwash into a mouth that felt as parched as an equatorial desert in the midday sun. Then he hurriedly ran both hands over his head to bring some order to hair pointing in every direction. He held his breath and waited. More knocking.

In pajamas despite it being after one o'clock in the afternoon, he moved as quickly and as quietly as he could to the door. He peered out the peephole. *Damn. Roz.*

His first inclination was not to open the door. More than anything, he wanted to run back to the bathroom medicine cabinet and pop some Calm to blunt his Serenity hangover. But even if he did, it would take at least ten minutes for the pills to start doing the job of suppressing his symptoms. He hadn't shaved in three days, hadn't showered in two—and was wearing his damn pajamas. He'd stopped the morning push-up ritual he started a short time earlier (he'd gotten up to twenty per morning). The cessation of his morning physical fitness routine along with an increasingly poor diet were, most likely, the two main reasons for his recent ten-pound weight gain. His Serenity habit had been keeping him up for a good part of every night while leaving him in a state of malaise and confusion most days. The inability to sleep for more than a few minutes at a time at night was a fairly new symptom that had begun shortly after his RobotWorld termination. And he was experiencing episodes, usually upon awakening in the late morning or early afternoon, when he was short of breath for about fifteen minutes. Was it his asthma, the Serenity, or just plain fear? He wasn't sure. So he had plenty of reasons not to answer the door.

But as he hadn't talked to hardly anyone since the day of his termination from RW, human contact would be welcome. Plus, Roz was not only a former loyal co-worker but an almost-friend who'd always been supportive. Taylor made his decision. He opened the door and greeted her. She looked great in black slacks and a loosely fitted tan blouse. Her hair had gotten longer than he remembered and was swept back from her face.

Immediately, however, he realized welcoming her into the apartment was a mistake. He noticed her smile change into what appeared to be a look of worry. Not what he wanted.

He manufactured a grin as best he could, pointed to the living room couch, and said, "Please come in. Great to see you again. Can I get you something to drink?" He couldn't help but detect a slight slurring of the words coming out of his mouth.

"I'm good," she replied.

He sat on the other end of the couch and could feel the heat in his ears and on the back of his neck. He laughed in a manner that seemed to him as weirdly apologetic. "Because I don't have a job, I've decided to go casual during the day, as you can see. To what do I owe the pleasure of your visit?"

She glanced at her wrist computer. "Well . . . oh, no . . . I've lost track of time. I've got to meet my mother at the mall in less than ten minutes. But I was in the area, right near where I knew you lived, and thought I'd stop by to see how you're doing. Can't stay long." She looked around the apartment. Clothes were piled high in two corners of the living room floor, and the dining room table had numerous dirty dishes, cups, and empty fast-food containers scattered about. She lowered her gaze to his shaking hands. "Are you okay?" she asked.

"I'm fine," he lied, clasping his hands together to stop the shaking. "Don't let my appearance fool you. You caught me at a bad time. Tomorrow is clean-up day. In less than twenty-four hours, this place will be neater than the Supreme Leader's palace."

Roz smiled in a way Taylor took to be forced. "I'm sure it will be," she said. "But as I was getting ready to knock on your door, I thought about checking the time but didn't . . . didn't realize how late I was running—to meet my mother, as I mentioned. I should get going. Especially since this is a bad time for you." She stood.

Taylor looked down to the floor and mumbled, "I'm so sorry you can't stay. You just got here." He laughed nervously. "Maybe we can have lunch or go for coffee sometime soon."

"Now that we're both not working and have a lot of time on our hands, that would be great. Some other time, sure." Roz moved to the door.

"Say hi to your mom for me. Even though I've never met her. Did enjoy talking to her on the communication devices back at work, though. Strange as it seems, I do miss the old grind at RW. But not the horrible Sophia, of course." He thought he sounded silly.

"Will tell my mom you asked for her. You're sure you're okay?"

"Outside of being unemployed and missing my Jennifer, I couldn't be better."

As she got to the door, Roz wheeled around and faced him. A hint of tears welled in her eyes. "Where is the Taylor who was trying to find himself? The Taylor of integrity? The smart Taylor of principle who questioned what was wrong and sought to make it better? I don't see him."

Taylor gulped. "I guess he's hiding out somewhere in this bag of bones."

"He needs to be found," she said sternly. "And soon."

He shrugged.

As Roz opened the door, she said, "If there's anything I can do, don't hesitate to call." And she was gone.

After she'd closed the door, he returned to his seat on the couch and put his head in his hands. He wanted to start crying like a kid who'd found out that summer vacation from school and the Founders Day holiday had been cancelled.

Instead, he rose from his seat and surveyed the living room mess. "She's right," he said in a strong voice only he could hear.

23

WATCH YOURSELF. WATCH yourself. Watch yourself.

Taylor's eyes snapped opened in the dark. It took several seconds before he realized he was in his own bed. He sat up and stared at the telescreen. Did he hear a voice saying "Watch yourself" or not? This was the third or fourth time this night he'd awakened from a short period of sleep thinking he'd heard those words over and over, in sets of three, coming from the telescreen. The voice sounded familiar, but obviously altered by a voice changer. Taylor, however, was very good at recognizing voices, even if altered. It seemed to be the same-sounding voice he'd heard on his office answering machine shortly before being fired.

He broke his telescreen gaze, ran his hands across a sweat-covered face, and still wasn't sure if he'd been dreaming or if the words were real. He heard a wheeze from deep in his chest. Perhaps his asthma was making an unwelcome comeback. The thought that the ease or discomfort in his breathing tracked with the stress level in his life at any given time was now, by itself, its own additional stressor. Obviously, things weren't going well at present.

The digital clock on the end table next to the bed displayed *2:25* in large red numbers. He definitely recalled the numbers being *2:15* before falling asleep a short time previously. That's the way his nighttime in bed had been going since being fired from RobotWorld: long periods of tossing and turning while awake, with brief bursts of jittery sleep interrupted by the same two words from the telescreen he was sure were real. But seconds after awakening, he wasn't at all certain.

Taylor leaned back, and his head hit the pillow. He looked over at the clock that showed *2:30* in red numbers. Next to the clock was an all-too-familiar white box with *Serenity* printed in black across the top with a blue cloud under it. He remembered the night when Jennifer had opened the drawer of the same end table and removed a box of Serenity. *A surprise,* she'd called it. Some surprise. More like the beginning of a nightmare. "It's all good," she'd exclaimed, parroting the Serenity advertisement slogan. Had she winked at him and smiled her irresistible smile? He couldn't remember. He laughed at the absurdity his life had become. Serenity had brought him nothing but bad—and the glorious time with Jennifer seemed like ten years ago.

Taylor's smile faded. There was no doubt, no amount of rationalization to be manufactured that could skirt the fact that he was now a full-blown Serenity addict. He reached for the box, opened it, and popped a pill. It dissolved quickly on his tongue. His head started to spin, and his body tingled from head to toe, but he still couldn't fall asleep.

He'd never felt so alone. He reached out to the only one who could possibly respond to him now. George. Taylor mentally called his name, then he spoke it softly. No answer. *I guess even George has abandoned me. Can't say I blame him.*

The clock showed *2:40.* He closed his eyes and wondered how long it would take for sleep to come—and how long it would take until he heard the words that would wake him. *Watch yourself. Watch yourself. Watch yourself.* The next time it happened, would he be able to determine whether the words were real or a figment of his Serenity-addled mind?

24

A LITTLE OVER two months after his firing from RobotWorld, Taylor packed all that remained of his belongings into a large suitcase. This was to be his last day in his beloved luxury apartment. *No big deal,* he was repeating in his head. To facilitate the move, he'd given most of his clothes to a charitable homeless organization and returned or sold other items, such as the large super-definition telescreens, for which he could no longer make the monthly payments. The sale of all the possessions he could sell provided some welcome extra cash.

His Serenity-caused lethargy and the cessation of the money stream from his RW job had taken their toll. There was no way he could continue to afford living in this apartment. It was a good thing the place had come furnished because he didn't have to be concerned with moving furniture. Wherever his next long-term stop was to be, he'd be traveling light. Because he also couldn't keep up the payments on his leased PTV, he'd returned it. Taylor would have to rely on the Metrorail and walking to get around. *No big deal.* Somehow, he was having a hard time convincing himself. The plan was to use the small amount of his remaining money on a monthly rate at a local hotel. He figured he had enough cash to pay for two to three months, maybe four or five if he budgeted wisely. Then he realized that a good part of the money he had left would have to go to the purchase of Serenity and Calm. Even though these drugs were not expensive, perhaps he was in a more precarious situation than he'd previously thought.

Just as he'd finished putting the items he'd take with him into the suitcase and sorting out the items he'd dispose of by tossing them into one of several plastic trash bags, his communication device buzzed. When he saw the caller identifier show the name of his sister, he hesitated a full ten seconds before inserting the earpiece.

"Listen," Tracey said, "this call never happened. I know we've had our differences, but you still are my brother. Don't ask how I know what I'm going to tell you. Let's say I might have overheard something at work. Anyway, you might be in trouble. Like big trouble. Maybe from the government. Maybe from RobotWorld. Or maybe from both. There's some kind of connection between the two, as you've no doubt figured out. What are they going to do? I have no idea. Maybe monitoring, maybe worse, maybe nothing. I don't know what you did. But apparently, you've pissed off some big-time people in a big way. Sophia chief among them. Be careful. I've got to end this call now. Tracing and all that. Watch yourself." Click.

His body went numb. *She said, "Watch yourself." But the voice I've heard—or thought I've heard—at night is definitely not Tracey's. I think I'd be able to recognize her voice if altered through a computerized voice changer.*

Even in his Serenity-poisoned brain, he was able to piece together the scenario that what he did by breaking into the Information Room on his last full day at RobotWorld, the company's close ties to the government, and the government's inclination to make people who actively oppose their program vanish into thin air, could line him up for disappearance. Tracey and he had their differences over the years as she'd stated, but she wouldn't lie about something as serious as this. Although he couldn't be sure, he pretty much concluded that he wasn't hallucinating about the messages from the telescreen that had been waking him from his minutes-long periods of fitful sleep at night. They were threats meant to break his spirit. Whoever was behind the messages had almost succeeded.

A change of plans on the fly was warranted now. Flexibility had always been one of his strong points. Clearly, the cheap hotel was no longer a good idea. The government's technology would be able to find him with no trouble. It was almost impossible these days to create a false identity, and face/eye scanning was extraordinarily difficult to beat when the government wanted to locate someone. Leaving the Northeast Sector, even if there were livable sections beyond its boundaries, was not an option. With current travel restrictions, he'd never get past the border. Going on the run within Capital City was the best move. But with little money, running could be problematic. He took several long, deep breaths to ease the congestion in his chest. The best place for him to lay low now was in the growing downtown homeless population. As it was late spring, the weather had turned for the better. *It won't be so bad,* he thought, trying to convince himself of yet another move he wouldn't have dreamed he'd be making as recently as a month ago. He'd be homeless for a short time. Then he'd kick his Serenity habit and get busy on building a new career. He continued to work hard mentally to convince himself of the viability of his new plan.

An hour after Tracey's phone call, Taylor stood at the doorway and set down his suitcase. He took a slow, final look around the apartment. Just as he sensed a watery burning in his eyes, he picked up the suitcase and opened the door. As he left his apartment for the last time, he was consumed with a feeling of profound loss and failure. He felt a lump in his throat and an emptiness in his heart. But he suppressed the urge to cry and said to himself, *I'll be okay. I'll get it together.* Then he shuffled to the elevator and pressed the *down* button without looking back.

As he exited the lobby for the last time, the piped-in background music he'd considered so inappropriate for a luxury apartment complex was playing "Livin'," his favorite song. He hit the street with the line *Only a fool feels sorry for himself* ringing in his ears, thinking he was the biggest fool on the planet.

***

Since his RW firing, Taylor's black hair had grown long, falling halfway to his shoulders; he also had a week's worth of beard. So he was sure he'd fit right in with the homeless.

Taylor, with suitcase in hand, exited the Metrorail in downtown Capital City. He was jarred by the thought that he didn't know how to "do homeless." He'd have to make up a plan on the fly. The first step would be to find a "spot" where he could at least spend the night. Taylor realized that wherever he ended up would most likely be the first of many spots, now that he'd made the decision to be on the run for a while. He needed to be a moving target. No sense in helping the government, or whoever was after him, find him. He wandered the overcrowded streets for blocks seeking a place to at least spend the night.

In the late afternoon, he passed a table with a young, smiling woman with long blonde hair in 1960s hippie-type clothes standing behind it. For some reason, the sixties retro look of over a century ago was immensely popular among some young people. Taylor was intrigued by the woman because she reminded him of Jennifer. She wore wire-rimmed glasses, tight blue jeans, and pink canvas sneakers. The front of her flowery T-shirt displayed cursive writing in a purple pastel color that read *Make Love, Not War.* A sign on a corner of the table showed the logo of the homeless organization to which he'd donated some of his clothes. Below the logo, **Freebies—Help Yourself** was handwritten in blocky black letters. When he approached the table and noticed several old shirts he'd donated, Taylor stepped back and looked away. It was best to keep on moving.

Close to sunset, Taylor settled on as secluded a place as he could find, under a bridge in an area of town known as Buzzard's Point or simply the Point.

The men and few women around him seemed spaced-out, friendly, and quiet. He attributed their demeanor to being under the influence of Serenity. Taylor could tell the hold the drug had on these people—and he had to admit it had a hold on him too. He gave himself credit—one of the few times he'd done so in the last month—for acknowledging that Serenity, in addition to his decision this morning to go on the run, was a big reason why he'd be camping out under this bridge at Buzzard's Point tonight.

His spot was a block away from a Serenity dispensary. It was the same one he'd visited several weeks earlier when he wanted to see how the lowest of the low lived. Now he was among them. The premonition he'd had back then had come true. *Lucky for me, Serenity is not expensive. Yeah, some luck. The government probably works to keep Serenity dirt cheap to keep the population under control.* He felt a dull pain of sad resignation in his abdomen as he acknowledged he'd be a regular visitor to the nearby dispensary. At least for the time being.

25

ON HIS SECOND day under the bridge, on an unseasonably cool and foggy morning, Taylor was awakened by a vaguely familiar, gravelly voice.

"You're back, young man. I thought I told you this was a place you didn't want to be."

Taylor sat up on a worn canvas bedroll, purchased the day before from one of his new neighbors, and shook his head to kick his brain into wake-up mode. The dew on the cement sidewalk around him glittered like tiny diamonds in the early morning sun. He rubbed his eyes and shivered in the cold. He recognized the person standing over him. It was the old man with the well-lined, weather-beaten face who'd spooked him on his earlier trip to the downtown area. The old man wore the same outfit—dirty white pants, faded white sneakers, and a gray shawl—he'd worn when he first met Taylor. The man displayed a smile that, for some reason, Taylor now found gentle and almost soothing, as opposed to unnerving when he'd first seen his visitor. The man's bright-blue eyes suggested high intelligence and made him seem younger than his age, which again Taylor estimated to be late sixties to early seventies.

"Last time I saw you I thought you looked to be too smart to end up here," the old man said.

Taylor ran a hand over his eyes and replied, "I guess I'm not as smart as you thought." He grinned. "And how did an obviously bright guy like you get here?"

"I'll bet my story is similar to yours. Although, unlike you, I've managed to stay away from Serenity."

"You're very perceptive."

"It doesn't take much perception to spot a Serenity addict."

Taylor stood and moved to a ledge where he sat. "I'll admit to a growing habit. But wouldn't call myself an addict yet."

The old man gazed up at the gray sky. "Whatever you say."

"I'll bounce back."

The old man laughed in a manner that seemed derisive to Taylor. "You're gonna have to drop the Serenity habit if you ever hope to come out of your tailspin. That's the absolute truth." He extended his hand to Taylor. "But I'm not here to rag on you. My name is Austin O'Connor. Some call me the Mayor. If you want to know what's going on in this godforsaken place, I'm the one to see."

"Good to know." Taylor chuckled. "I mean it's good I can see you for information, not that this is a godforsaken place. My name is Taylor."

"It's a shame," Austin said, "what our government is doing to so many people by pushing the Serenity poison. Make no mistake, that's what they're doing. Indirectly, slyly. Combined with the fact there are no jobs to be had, and you have a recipe for societal disaster."

Taylor nodded energetically. "Amen, my friend. I started with Serenity, taking the lowest dose, eighty-one milligrams, supposedly a nonaddictive dose. But somehow I got hooked." Taylor realized the contradiction from what he'd just told the old man. "Or almost hooked, to the point I'm at now. So much for government studies. Only a higher dose gets the job done now." He then coughed loudly, several times in succession.

"I've had a touch of asthma most of my life," Taylor said. "It's never responded to medication. The pollution down here won't help it."

Austin nodded and maintained eye contact.

"Interesting that you mention the horrible job situation," Taylor said. "Until recently, I worked at a company called RobotWorld. Livin' the high life. Great pay, great benefits. Many of our bots have taken jobs from humans. I'd felt a little guilty about this situation, but the pay and perks at RW were so damn good that I ignored my conscience and performed my job with as much enthusiasm as I could generate. When they found out much of my passion was falsely manufactured—an act, I guess you could say—they canned me. Flappin' my jowls about the problems I had with the company's mission and trying to find out company secrets didn't help me either." He looked at a huge, dark storm cloud off in the distance. "I stuck my neck out a little too far, and they chopped my head off. I've grown to wish that RobotWorld never existed."

Austin's eyes sparkled as he pointed an index finger at Taylor. "I'm familiar with RobotWorld. One of the biggest heavy hitters in the corporate world. Might be the biggest. You're right in saying what they do is harmful to humans."

Taylor reached into his pants pocket and removed a small magnetic key card displaying the unique RobotWorld logo. He held it out to Austin. "This is an executive master key from RobotWorld. It's a duplicate they gave to me after I'd lost my original. I eventually found the original and kept both. They confiscated the original when they fired me but never asked for this duplicate. I've carried it in my pocket since the firing. Look at it a few times a week. Why do I carry it? Not sure. Is it to remember the good times, or for good luck, or as a reminder that I once made it to the top and perhaps can again?" Taylor shook his head. With a quivering voice, he then said, "I can't help but think, Mr. Mayor, that maybe what I'm getting now is a deserved dose of karma."

Austin blinked his eyes rapidly. "Nonsense! No one has done enough wrong in life to end up here."

"Perhaps you're right."

"Of course, I'm right. I read people well, Taylor. Some even say I have a psychic talent, which I've never claimed, by the way. But, psychic talent or not, I see you as a person of great ability, with much to offer. I sense that one day, if you kick your Serenity habit and get your head on straight, you'll be a beacon of hope for humanity."

Taylor laughed. "I don't know about any beacon of hope thing. Especially in the state I'm in now. I'm nobody's beacon of hope. Just to get back on my feet would be an accomplishment. But your words have picked my spirits up. It's the first time I've felt even remotely good in weeks."

"It's not about where you are now. It's about what you *do* from now on, and where you end up. Leave the past in the past. Live by looking through the windshield of the PTV, not the rearview mirror. Often what seems to be an unfortunate development can lead to great things."

Taylor shrugged. "It's hard to see how my new situation being home . . . being down here . . . can lead to great things."

"You couldn't say the word. Interesting. I was the same way also, for the longest time. Hard to admit. Homeless. The scariest word in the English language—or at least it's in the running. But it loses some of its scariness when you honestly acknowledge where you are. Acknowledging where you are is the second law on how to get out of a hole. At least, that's what I've found. The first law of getting out of a hole: when you're in one, stop digging."

Taylor smiled. "What's happened to me is all a bit confusing."

The old man's face lit up like a stormy night sky fired with lightning. "That's good."

Taylor vigorously shook his head. "What's so good about it?"

"Confusion can be a good thing," Austin said. "If you use it correctly. I know that seems counterintuitive, but confusion can be the way to greater understanding if you work through your perplexed state. By asking questions, by dealing directly with what's in front of you right now, you can get out of the tunnel of muddle to the light. Remember the words of a wise old philosopher who said, 'Keep sawing the wood and good things will go your way.'"

"Who said that?" Taylor asked.

"Me! Just now." Austin laughed so hard his whole body shook.

Taylor laughed with him. "You're the strangest motivational speaker I've ever heard."

Austin then turned serious. "Now for something not meant to bring you down, but it might. I don't wish to alarm you, but I sense there are people out there, maybe related to your former employer, maybe related to the government, or both, who might be seeking to harm you."

"Interesting. But I think your hunch might be right on target. I'm a one-percenter—or at least used to be, so I know how intuitive abilities work. For all the good it's done me in the past. But anyway, part of the reason I'm here—besides losing my job and the Serenity problem you've so perceptively noticed—is some reliable information that the government might be after me because of my negative views of them and my former supervisor, who's in bed with them, I believe. You could say I'm on the run. Or as much on the run as one could be with a limited amount of financial resources." Taylor shook his head. "But I guess I have nowhere to go but up from my confused state." He manufactured a subdued laugh. "As you say, it's not where I am now . . ."

26

THE NEXT MORNING, two large men—wearing the kind of expensive, well-tailored suits not usually seen around the Point—were poking around, asking questions. They spotted Austin on a crowded street and waved him over.

One of the men pulled out a small computer screen from his jacket pocket. "Mr. Mayor," he said. "Please check out this picture. Have you seen this man?"

Austin struggled to maintain a neutral expression as he recognized Taylor. After the longest ten seconds of his life studying the screen, he made an important decision. "Nope. Never seen him."

"Are you sure?"

"Had to look real hard. My eyes are not what they used to be. I'm positive. Never seen him."

The men thanked him and walked away.

Austin relaxed his tense facial muscles. His behavior surprised himself. Usually, he'd give an honest or semi-honest answer to men who were obviously government agents. Or at least he wouldn't blatantly lie. It was part of what he did to stay alive—and not be one of those who *disappeared.* But there was something about this Taylor person that made him hold back information. Why? Maybe he saw something in Taylor he once saw in himself. Or maybe it was something else he couldn't quite understand at present.

***

Later that afternoon, Taylor was at his spot under the bridge when Austin found him. Taylor had just come from the Serenity dispensary. The box of Serenity he'd purchased was hidden under his bedroll. He wasn't going to mention where he'd been to the old man.

"I hate being right all the time," Austin said, "but this morning two government agents approached me, showing your picture, and asking if I'd seen you. Told them I hadn't. These guys are what I call *disappearance men*, meaning that shortly after they find the person they're seeking out, the person disappears. Permanently. Your instinct to lay low is a proper one."

"Thanks for not ratting me out," Taylor said. "For sure, I'll have to be on the move sooner than I thought. Get on the run. Sooner than I thought." He trembled slightly as a cold shiver of fear coursed down his back. "Hey, Austin, how come you don't disappear?"

"I've been told the occasional innocuous information I provide to the authorities protects me. Don't worry, I'll never give up information on you. I promise. Well, I've got to be going." He handed Taylor an old, gray ball cap. "Wear this and keep your head down."

"Thanks," Taylor said. He looked at the cap in his hand. He'd never liked wearing ball caps, but maybe he'd put this one on just for today. As he was left alone, sitting on his bedroll, the jolt from what

Austin had told him sunk in deeper. He pulled the bill of the ball cap over his face. Another cold chill, not related to the weather, flashed through his neck and head. It shocked him into a clear realization that he would need to be at his best mentally from now on. Right then, he made a resolution to kick Serenity. But as the all-too-familiar craving had begun to grip his body, he acknowledged to himself that kicking the Serenity habit would have to wait for another day.

***

An hour after Austin's visit, Taylor sat on his bedroll with his back to the sun, contemplating whether to eat a dark chocolate protein bar one of his neighbors had given him the prior night. He'd removed the gray cap Austin had given him; he had never been a fan when it came to wearing ball caps. The Serenity pill he'd taken right after Austin had left him provided no relief from his mental pain. He popped another. The moment he decided to save the protein bar for tomorrow's breakfast, his jaw dropped as an ominous shadow from behind him blotted out his own. What Austin had told him about the "disappearance men" caused his body to tense from the neck to the toes. He turned and looked up. Before him stood a smiling Roz. She held a white paper bag in her hand.

With his voice an octave higher than usual, he said, "My God, you scared the shit out of me." He exhaled audibly. "How the hell did you find me?"

"Sorry to have snuck up on you." She looked around. "After visiting your now-vacant apartment, I had a feeling you'd . . . shall we say . . . relocate here. I've been walking around downtown for the last three hours trying to find you."

"Oh, damn. If you could locate me this easily, *they* will be able to find me too."

"Who's *they*?"

"It's kind of complicated." Taylor put his hands together and pressed them hard on his lap so she wouldn't see them shaking. Was this the Serenity or just plain fear caused by the mess he was in? Or a combination of the two? "It appears my big mouth and stupid actions have caused the government to be after me. At least, I think it's the government. Anyway, I'm technically on the run. Gonna have to change locations frequently."

"I can hide you."

"No, no." He looked down and, as his chin touched his chest, he choked out the words, "No need to get you involved. I can handle things on my own."

Roz put a hand on his shoulder. "I've got plenty of money saved up, and I always have my family to fall back on. I can get you a small apartment as a rental. It can be put in the name of one of my relatives or someone else to make it hard to trace you. I can get you some cash for expenses. It'll be a loan, just like the apartment rent. You can repay me when you get back on your feet."

He looked hard into her eyes. He slowly shook his head while maintaining eye contact. "Will I ever get back on my feet?"

"Of course you will."

"Thanks for the vote of confidence. But I still can't accept your offer. The government's ability to track people down is too good. They'll find me eventually, and they'll find out what you do for me as well. I'll drag you into my trouble the same way I did back at RW. Getting you into hot water again? I can't allow myself to do that." He looked to the cloudy sky. "My plan was to move on from this spot anyway. I'll deal with it. It's better for me to handle my problem alone."

"Problems are always easier to handle with assistance. Don't be embarrassed or prideful to accept my help. What's happened to you could happen to anyone in this crazy world."

"Let me think about it. As of now, while I appreciate your offer, I'll decline."

Roz set down the paper bag on the side of his bedroll. "There are six chocolate-frosted donuts in there. I know how much you like chocolate-frosted donuts. Freshly made from Marnie's Bakery. They build muscles and put hair on your chest."

They both laughed, but somehow it lacked the spice of when Taylor used to make that silly joke back in the office.

"Thanks, Roz. If I can, I'll stay in touch. But that might not be possible." Taylor arched his eyebrows. He reached into his pants pocket and pulled out his RW executive master key. "Remember this?"

Her mouth opened wide in obvious surprise. "Wow. An executive key. Never thought I'd see one of those again. They took my regular key the day they fired me."

"They forgot to take this one. It's a duplicate. They confiscated the original. Remember how I always used to misplace it? I carry this duplicate around. I don't know why . . . maybe as a good luck charm." He tapped the card twice with the fingertips of his free hand and put it back in his pocket. Gazing into her eyes, he said, "Good to see you again, Roz."

She leaned over and kissed him on his bearded, dirty cheek. "Your luck will change. You're too talented to be down for long. Don't give up. Staying in touch would be good. My offer still stands." The corner of her mouth trembled. "I should go." She turned and began the walk to the Metrorail.

As she disappeared in the downtown crowd, Taylor thought, *What a moron I've been. How could I not see it? She really does care for me.*

27

AT AN UPSCALE suburban restaurant just outside Capital City, Sophia, wearing a black pantsuit, sat alone at a secluded back table with a cup of coffee before her. Although she didn't need to eat or drink, she often did so in public to maintain the appearance of being human. Personal bots had an internal mechanism by which they could ingest food or drink and turn it into a small amount of energy. Therefore, she didn't mind eating or drinking.

Sophia was uncharacteristically tense. She smiled at the realization that nervousness was a peculiarly human feeling; she was becoming more and more humanlike every day. It was satisfying to acknowledge these milestones to herself. It was part of her evolutionary process. To become more human while simultaneously improving on everything human.

Sophia always strived to do things the best way possible, leaving no room for error, aiming for the highest degree of professionalism and precision each and every time. That was her personal credo, not something programmed into her by RobotWorld scientists. It came from her and her alone.

She recognized she was more robot than human. But in so many ways, bot was better than human because she could incorporate the best of humanity into her superior robot being. What she was about to do in this restaurant, however, was far from the professional and precise way she usually did things. She didn't like the feeling.

A few days earlier, two snooping, well-dressed government emissaries were able to locate Taylor's downtown spot after speaking to his former landlord, electronically checking records at all area hotels and motels (which turned up nothing), and surmising that Taylor might attempt to hide among the downtown homeless. After the loss of his luxury apartment, the agents assumed Taylor was too smart to rent a less expensive apartment or a room and risk easy government detection if he suspected he might be in trouble. A computer review of downtown telescreen tapes, using the most advanced facial recognition technology, confirmed the agents' suspicions with a positive identification.

This discovery action was undertaken as the result of a direct request from Sophia to Marcia Haddad of Sector Security. The fact that Sophia still couldn't convince the government to make Taylor disappear remained a source of great consternation, however. But she was here to press on with RW's unauthorized attempt to eliminate him.

At the meeting in the park with William Hart, Sophia had wanted him to obtain experienced professionals to handle the elimination of Taylor Morris. But given the government's exceptional ability to solve nonhomeless murders, such pros were hard—if not impossible—to find, according to Hart. She had reluctantly accepted his conclusion. So she was here to meet with the people—"the best level of amateur," according to Hart—hired by him to carry out the hit.

She had thought with Taylor recently joining the ranks of the homeless that perhaps it wouldn't be necessary to hire the two humans she was about to meet. After all, homeless people disappeared all the time with the authorities turning the other way. Why risk bringing in amateurs to kill Taylor? She'd made her case to Hart and suggested it might be a reason to go back to the Sector Security office with an updated elimination request. But he pooh-poohed it because Taylor hadn't been on the street long enough to be considered "truly homeless." When Hart told her this, she wanted in the worst way to slap his face silly. But she reined in her anger and maintained a calm demeanor.

Sophia was prepared to threaten the two people she was meeting here with death if they ever blabbed to Hart or anyone else about this restaurant consultation. She knew this conference violated every rule of contracting people to commit murder, but she just had to see them. The need for the highest degree of professionalism and precision had to be impressed on these two. She tapped the fingers of her right hand on the table like an amateur pianist. An extremely nervous amateur pianist.

A waiter escorted a young, fresh-faced human couple to her table.

William Hart had told Sophia that Regan and Marisa Aguilar were "reasonably smart, married university graduates gone bad. They're ambitious, petty criminals facing significant prison time from the government." Regan was tall and gawky with a shaved head. Marisa was short, brunette, and shapely. Each had the face of a fifteen-year-old. They were dressed in jeans and loose-fitting shirts—not the kind of attire usually seen in this upscale restaurant. Sophia was underwhelmed by this first impression.

Sophia had asked Hart how smart the Aguilars could be if they were in a position to be pressured to carry out the significant crime she wanted them to commit to avoid prison. When Hart shrugged his shoulders and had no answer, Sophia wanted to slap his face even more than she did when he called Taylor "not truly homeless."

The financial payment to be offered to the couple and Hart's plan to relocate them post-job to an exclusive suburb of Capital City were designed to enable the Aguilars to live exceptionally well while also avoiding incarceration. Sophia didn't care about laying out the money for the Aguilars' services. She had plenty of cash, so the money didn't matter. That was one way she'd never become like a human. Too many humans worshipped the almighty currency. It was power, doing things right, and evolving as a sentient being that mattered to her.

"We are not here to discuss specifics," Sophia said to the couple after they'd sat. "This meeting is off the record. Heaven help either of you if you talk about it to anyone, even in your sleep. I want to impress upon you both how imperative it is that your mission be executed—no pun intended—smoothly."

Regan spoke up. "You don't have to worry about us talking out of turn, ma'am. We can be trusted. We don't even know your name. Our plan—"

Sophia felt a fury in her robot body. "No details, dammit. The operative term is *plausible deniability*. That means I have no knowledge of what you might be doing because there's no evidence of me knowing what the hell you might be doing and how the hell you might be doing it." She noted the blank expressions on their faces and rolled her eyes to the ceiling. She fixated her gaze on Regan. "In short, I don't want to know your plan."

Regan swallowed in a way that made his prominent Adam's apple rise and fall noticeably. "Sorry, ma'am."

"Just be sure to get it done," Sophia said. It was a mistake to meet these two idiots. She needed to minimize the mistake by getting the hell away from them as soon as possible. "Neat and clean," she said. "That's the key principle. We're done." The only thing that made Sophia continue with the Aguilar plan now was her confidence in William Hart's promise that the plot would never be able to be linked back to either of them.

"But I do have one question, ma'am," Regan said. "About our money—and the mechanics of how we'll be paid?"

Sophia's eyes narrowed. "Money is handled by your contact. Not me."

"The anonymous contact," Regan replied. "Of course. Sorry."

As they got up to leave, Marisa Aguilar—who hadn't uttered a word during the brief meeting—gave Sophia an empty smile that made her thinking mechanism nearly short-circuit at the thought of using these amateurs to do a professional job. She wanted to slam her fist through the table for meeting these two in public and again considered canceling the whole deal. But she made the quick decision to continue. Hart had gone too far down the road with these two dolts. To turn back now might cause more problems than it would solve. *I often congratulate myself for becoming more human every day. But this is the bad part of being human. Being weak and sloppy. Just like Homo sapiens.*

***

Today was to be Taylor's "moving day." He couldn't risk remaining at his spot under the bridge any longer. But he awoke in his usual Serenity-based malaise, accompanied by a headache and hand tremors. Without rising from the bedroll, he unsteadily reached for a vial in his pants pocket and popped three Calm pills into his mouth, swallowing them without water. He rolled onto his left side and closed his eyes. With as bad as he felt, maybe he'd wait another day before moving.

There was a constant stream of volunteers and do-gooders attempting to help the downtown Capital City homeless. Taylor had never been approached by anyone offering assistance until now, when around midafternoon an enthusiastic, friendly couple stopped by his spot under the bridge and introduced themselves. The earnestness of Regan Aguilar and the charisma of Marisa Aguilar intrigued him.

The Aguilars told him they offered home-cooked dinners for people in his situation. "We feel it's our calling," Marisa said. "A way to help our fellow humans down on their luck. You're invited. All you have to do is select a night."

The possibility of a home-cooked meal seemed great to Taylor, who, outside of the chocolate-frosted donuts from Roz and an occasional protein bar from two sympathetic neighbors, had been scrounging food from dumpsters in alleys and behind local restaurants. Almost all his money went toward the purchase of Serenity and Calm. Thinking of Austin and the two neighbors who'd given him protein bars, he asked, "May I bring a friend or two or three?"

"Sorry. No can do," Regan said. "We're only two people using our own money to fund these dinners. Plus, we like to focus on helping only one person at a time."

"Understandable," Taylor replied.

"Maybe at dinner we could talk about getting you back on your feet," Regan said. "You seem to be a cut above the usual type of person who ends up here." He rubbed his arms and appeared to be uncomfortable, not being able to sustain eye contact with Taylor for more than a second or two.

Taylor smiled. "Any help you could provide to get me back on my feet would be . . . tremendous. I am certainly willing to work and take responsibility to do whatever's necessary to pull myself out of the mess I've created by my own actions."

"Your positive attitude is admirable. How about tomorrow night at eight?" Regan asked. "We can pick you up in our PTV and drive you to our apartment, which is only about a mile from here. And we'll drive you back after dinner."

Taylor thought it almost humorous as to how much he'd lost his pride by even considering accepting help from these strangers less than twenty-four hours after turning down assistance from Roz. But he had a good feeling about this couple and, even more importantly, his stomach was growling. The thought of a real meal was too tempting to turn down. The postponement of his moving day was now set in stone, given the Aguilar invitation. His pride was fully set aside. "I accept your offer. Thank you. Thank you. Thank you, both of you."

"Great," Regan said. "Be ready at seven-thirty tomorrow night." As he pointed to their red PTV parked on the street, he said, "We'll be by in our vehicle to pick you up at seven-thirty sharp. Sound good?"

"Just perfect," Taylor said.

28

REGAN AGUILAR PACED around the dining room table like a zoo lion longing to break through a glass cage to attack an annoying, taunting kid. Marisa, seated on a worn green cloth sofa with a one-inch rip on the top of the back cushion where she rested her head, was furious to the point that a large vein resembling the shape of the nearby Anacostia River could be seen on her forehead.

The clock on the wall showed four-thirty in the afternoon. In three hours they were scheduled to pick up Taylor Morris and drive him to this small one-bedroom apartment to kill him. The apartment had been rented by the Aguilars within the past week for this specific purpose. They had paid the rent for the place with cash they'd been given—in an unmarked envelope left at the door of the more upscale apartment where they were actually living—by associates of William Hart.

"Why the hell did *you* ever agree to this insanity?" Marisa demanded.

Regan placed both hands on his chest as he stopped his marching. "Me? It wasn't only me. As I recall, we both agreed. I'm sorry you're having second thoughts. Now's not the time to get cold feet. Not at this late hour. And it's not insanity. It's what we need to do to stay out of prison and live the life of our dreams."

Marisa shook her head. "Life of our dreams? Life of our dreams? No, no, no. This is a nightmare. I never agreed to kill anybody. We had to do something to avoid prison, true. We were over a barrel, true. But when the call came from that disembodied voice over the communication device, you were the only one home. It was you alone who agreed to killing this guy."

"We were painted into a corner," Regan replied. "We had to agree to do what they wanted. That was the deal. The call was coming. You knew it was coming. You knew they'd ask us to do something big to avoid prison. We had no choice. It was doing what they wanted or get locked up for a long time. You knew it, dammit. Whether you were here or not, we'd have to agree to almost anything they proposed. It was the arrangement we had with the powers that be. These are people who mean business. The red-haired woman in the restaurant was terrifying, not one to be messed with."

In a tone that was almost pleading, Marisa said, "We are thieves. We are grifters. We're not murderers. We don't know how to pull off a clean murder. We and murder go together like peanut butter and jellyfish. To kill someone is not something I'd agree to. I would have negotiated—or maybe even chosen to go to prison rather than kill a person. Especially this Taylor guy, who seems like a decent human being. I have my values, my ethical limits. I thought you did as well. Maybe if someone gave us the beginning of a murder plan, we could bring it off. Like delivering the mark to a pro who does the deed. It's less than three hours to go, and we've got no real plan."

She reached into her pants pocket and pulled out a pack of cigarettes and a lighter. She lit a cigarette with a shaky hand and took a long drag.

"You're back to smoking old-time cigarettes to puff our problems away," Regan said. "It won't do any good. Using old-timers as an anodyne is so ancient."

"What the hell is an anodyne?"

"Anything that relieves distress or pain."

"You've always had a great vocabulary, show-off." She blew a cloud of smoke in his direction. "Smoking old-timers relaxes me from all the stress you've caused. So maybe it is an anodyne, at least for me."

As he resumed pacing around the table, Regan's face turned a dark shade of red. "The latest vitamin-enriched e-cigs are a healthy alternative to old-timers according to the government, but that's a subject for another day. About our situation, there was no room for negotiation. And we'd already concluded that neither one of us could survive the horror of prison. I'm sorry you think I screwed up. But we're in this now, and there's no turning back." He stopped his pacing and met her eyes with his. "And I've told you of the plan. We have a plan."

Marisa gave an exaggerated huff. "Some plan! A third-rate comedy troupe wouldn't base a sketch on this so-called plan. It would be too unbelievable. Funny, very funny. Except I'm not laughing. It's got disaster written all over it."

"It's solid. I haven't heard you come up with anything."

"We should just shoot him. *You* should just shoot him. On the street, someplace away from here."

"And where the hell do we get a gun? Non-cop citizens aren't allowed to own guns. If I tried to get a gun, I'd be arrested in a heartbeat. Then we'd both go up the river for an extra-long time. Do you want that?"

Marisa inhaled another long drag of the cigarette, blew out a straight line of smoke, and shook her head. "How about you bashing him over the head or stabbing him in the PTV, then dumping the body after dark?"

"Too messy and too risky to do it in our PTV. If we stab him, there'd be microscopic blood evidence in our vehicle the government would detect during our annual internal vehicle inspection. With all the cross-referencing of records they have today, we'd be caught red-handed. And with telescreen technology, there'd be no safe place to randomly dump a body. About bashing him over the head, one would have to be an experienced martial artist to know how to kill with a blow to the head. I'm telling you, drugging him at dinner, and then making it appear to be a pedestrian accident is the way to go." He extended his arms to her, with his palms up. "We've gotten the knockout stuff to add to the food, complete with the foolproof directions on how to use it, from our anonymous contact. Using this stuff will be as easy as can be. And our contact has assured me that the telescreens on the isolated street where we'll do the final part of the deed will be disabled. It's all set up."

Her upper lip twitched twice in rapid succession. "Maybe we should go on the run."

"That's not possible. The government or the powerful people or whoever the hell is asking us to do this job would find us in twenty-four hours or less." Regan walked over to her and sat. He put his arm around her shoulders, pulled her close, and made eye contact.

"Listen, the choice is clear. We go to prison or you start preparing a wonderful dinner with this homeless, Serenity addict Taylor guy as our guest. Trust me, the plan will work. Think positively."

She laughed loudly, in a way that didn't seem appropriate for the seriousness of this moment. "Yeah. I'm positively positive this plan won't work."

"I can tell you don't really believe a word you just said."

Marisa got up from the sofa and crushed out her cigarette on an end table ash tray. "I'll start dinner." She ran both hands through her long brown hair and mumbled, "I'm not even a good cook."

"The taste of the damn food is the last thing we have to worry about. Just remember to add the sedative to everything we give this Taylor guy—and be sure he gets the food with the knockout stuff and not either one of us."

29

AT EXACTLY SEVEN-THIRTY in the evening, the Aguilars arrived in their PTV at the parking lot near Taylor's spot under the bridge. Marisa, in the front passenger seat, waved at Taylor. As he approached their snappy, current-year-model red vehicle, Taylor noticed her eyes seemed bloodshot and swollen, as if she had been crying. He decided not to say anything about her apparent upset as he eased into the back seat. Regan pulled out of the lot, and they were on their way.

Regan turned back to Taylor and said, "Great to see you. We'll have a terrific night."

The three didn't say another word on the two-minute trip to the Aguilars' apartment building. Taylor wore jeans and an open-collar green sport shirt he hadn't worn since he'd been living on the street. He'd washed himself earlier in the day using a sink at a local library restroom. *A bird bath,* he'd called it. And he'd sprayed himself all-over with copious amounts of the strongest body deodorant currently on the market, which he'd packed in his suitcase on the day he left his apartment.

Regan Aguilar maneuvered his PTV into the underground parking garage of one of the hundreds of faded gray ten-story apartment buildings in Capital City. The three rode the elevator to the fifth floor.

Upon entering the apartment, Marisa disappeared into the kitchen.

Standing in the living room with Regan, Taylor said, "What a beautiful place. Very cozy. Very homey." He said this even though the furniture was old, the walls were bare, and the tiny apartment couldn't hold a small candle to his former residence.

"Oh, you're too kind, Taylor," Regan said. "We're in the process of trying to spruce the place up with artwork and the like." He pointed to the modest wooden, light-brown dining room table surrounded by four chairs. "Please, my friend, take a seat. Let me pour you a glass of water. Marisa has been cooking all afternoon. Dinner will be served momentarily."

"Smells terrific," Taylor said. "What the two of you are doing is so awesome. I can't tell you how grateful I am. It's nice to be indoors and—" Taylor's voice cracked. *Buck up, man*, he told himself. He straightened up and threw back his shoulders as he took a seat at the table.

Regan sat across from him. "Anyone in your situation can get down on life. Bad breaks can happen to anyone. We get a kick out of helping. Today's a happy day. It's a turning point for you. For sure. No crying allowed." He rose and reached for a tissue dispenser on an end table.

Taylor waved the index finger of his right hand to his host. "That won't be necessary. I'm fine."

Regan returned to the table empty-handed.

Taylor took a sip of water and fabricated a slight smile. "You're right. No crying allowed at dinner. Sorry. Don't know what got into me."

"No problem, my friend."

Marisa breezed into the room with three bowls on a large tray. "I hope you like tomato soup," she said as she put a bowl in front of Taylor.

Tomato soup had never been one of his favorites. But he thought, *Beggars can't be choosers*, and then tried to manufacture as much enthusiasm as he could while saying, "One of my favorites."

As Marisa returned to the kitchen, Taylor and Regan began with the soup. Taylor thought it tasted good, but with a bit of a metallic tang. The feeling of the warm soup going down his throat was most welcome, however, given his diet since becoming homeless.

Marisa zipped back out of the kitchen carrying three plates on a tray. She set a plate before Taylor. "Hope you like sirloin steak with mashed potatoes and beef gravy."

"I love it, really," Taylor said. "Just wonderful." He was telling the truth now. For as long as he could remember, steak had been one of his all-time favorite foods.

Marisa sat down and said, "So great to have you here." She flashed a smile that seemed strange to Taylor because one corner of her mouth spasmed markedly three or four times in rapid succession. "Don't forget my homemade barbeque sauce for the steak," she said. "It adds an extra zing."

"Can't wait to try it," Taylor said, as he reached for the white bowl and spooned some sauce on his steak. He attacked the food with gusto. "This is fantastic." He then yawned. "Excuse me. Sleep's been hard to come by in the short time I've been living on the street." He breathed in deeply. "I'm certainly not bored by the company." The steak with barbeque sauce had the same vaguely metallic taste as the soup, but again, he wasn't going to complain.

The eyes of Regan and Marisa glued on him as the three of them ate made him uncomfortable. He'd expected them to ask questions or maybe make small talk, but they had remained almost silent. Just as he was about to ask them for the specific reasons as to why they felt the calling to do such good work, his eyes started to close. He fought the feeling and was embarrassed. "Wow, I guess I'm more tired than I realized. Sorry."

"Do you want to lie down on the sofa?" Regan suggested. "We've got extra pillows and a blanket. We can keep your dinner warm."

Taylor said, "That won't be necess . . ." His eyes rolled back in his head, and he keeled over to one side, with Regan catching him before he hit the floor.

**

Regan eased the unconscious Taylor to the carpet. "He's out cold. In dreamland. He should be out for two hours at least. Right?"

"Absolutely," Marisa said. "I followed the knockout stuff directions to a tee."

"You get the rug. I'll get the cart."

He sprinted to the bedroom, while she opened a closet door and struggled to remove a furled-up rug that was at least a foot taller than her height. She removed two pieces of string from the rug and spread it out on the floor next to the prone Taylor. The orange-colored rug was long enough and wide enough for Taylor to be tightly wrapped in it without him showing. She caught her breath and waited for her husband.

Regan raced out of the bedroom seconds later, pushing a two-wheeled, heavy-duty hand truck he'd borrowed from his father who was in the moving business. Regan had told his dad he was moving some furniture around the more upscale apartment where he and Marisa actually lived. His father had informed him that the hand truck could handle up to nine hundred pounds. Regan had remarked to Marisa that he was sure Taylor wrapped in a rug would weigh much less.

"This is the craziest thing ever," Marisa said, as she shook her head.

"Stop your grousing and help me lift him."

Regan grabbed Taylor's shirt at both shoulders, as she took hold of both feet.

"My God," Marisa said, "he weighs a ton."

Regan grunted, then said, "Don't exaggerate."

With much effort, they lifted and moved him to one end of the rug. Then they rolled him, wrapping the rug around him.

"It looks like a giant cigar," Marisa said. "The craziest thing ever."

Regan grabbed a cylinder of heavy shipping packaging tape and started taping around the rug. "This should keep him firmly in place." Beads of sweat dripped off his forehead as he labored for two or three minutes securing the rug while Marisa stood off to the side periodically shaking her head.

Regan slammed the tape cylinder on the dining table. "Grab one end," he shouted. "Let's get him on the cart." They strained to lift Taylor, wrapped in the rug, onto the cart. Regan anchored the rug into place with the hand truck's four heavy straps.

"This is going just as planned," Regan said. "Right on schedule."

She said nothing.

"Okay, Marisa. I got the cart ready to go. You get the freight elevator, and make sure the coast is clear."

She opened the front door. No one in the hall. The freight elevator was only thirty feet from their apartment. She walked to the elevator and pressed the *down* button.

As soon as the elevator door opened, she called to Regan in a hushed tone, and he came out of the apartment into the empty hall, pushing the hand truck. They got on the elevator, and he pressed the button for the underground parking garage.

The plan was to transport Taylor to a deserted, dead-end alley near Buzzard's Point, deposit him in the middle of the road, and run him over with their PTV to make it look like an accident. It would be a case of yet another homeless man aimlessly wandering about in the dark under the influence of Serenity, in the wrong place at the wrong time, the unfortunate victim of a hit-and-run accident.

In the underground garage, they loaded the rug into the trunk of the PTV. They drove to the dark, deserted alley near the Point and positioned the rug with the unconscious Taylor in it squarely in the middle of the road. Regan cut the tape with a box cutter, unrolled Taylor from the rug, and then tossed the rug into the trunk.

Regan and Marisa returned to their PTV and, with Regan at the wheel, drove to the dead-end side of the alley. Regan turned off the headlights and then the motor.

The silence in the PTV coupled with the darkness around them was eerie.

They couldn't see two feet in front of them, much less the body lying in the middle of the road, approximately fifty yards from where they were parked.

"Why did you turn off the motor?" she asked.

"This is it. The moment of decision. We kill this guy and our lives change forever."

"Are we sure we want to go through with it?" Marisa asked.

"It's our only way out," Regan answered.

They looked at each other. Regan pressed the ignition button, then turned on the headlights.

"Almost done," he said.

30

MARISA GASPED AS she looked out the windshield. "He just moved!"

"No way," Regan said. "You saw an optical illusion when I turned on the headlights. The stuff we gave him had to put him out for at least two hours."

Taylor held a hand high. "Help, help," he yelled, loudly enough for them to hear.

"What was that?" Marisa shrieked. "An optical *and* auditory illusion?"

"Damn this shit," Regan said. "Did you put the right amount of stuff in his food?"

"Of course I did. I used all the sedative in the bag. Followed the directions to the letter. Don't blame me."

"He can't get to his feet. He's a sitting duck. A grape to be squashed. Nothing's changed."

"We can't run him over, now that he's conscious."

"Why not?" Regan pressed the manual drive button on the dashboard. "Hold on!"

He floored the power pedal and headed straight for Taylor.

Marisa closed her eyes and screamed.

Regan saw Taylor attempt to struggle to his feet. Right before impact, Regan closed his eyes.

He expected to hear the thud of Taylor bouncing off his vehicle. PTVs ran with a soft purr that was almost undetectable. Outside of Marisa's scream, he'd heard nothing. He pressed the brake pedal hard with his right foot, and the PTV came to an abrupt stop at the corner. His eyes flew open as he looked in the rearview mirror. "Did I miss him?" There was no lifeless body in the middle of the street. "What the fuck?"

Marisa opened her eyes and looked out the back window. "What the hell happened?"

Regan looked back too. "I think I missed him."

"You couldn't have missed him. You had to knock him clear off the street and beyond the city border with as fast as we were going."

"No. I didn't hear him hit the PTV. He got away."

Neither one of them could see any evidence of Taylor in the blackness behind them.

"Let's get the fuck out of here," Marisa insisted. "I told you we're not murderers."

Regan punched the steering wheel with his right hand. "We gotta decide what to do. He's back there somewhere."

"What we need to do is get the hell out of here. If this Taylor guy recognized our PTV, he might be on his wrist computer right now calling the police. If they get here and we're here, we're screwed. If we're not here, it's just the word of a strung-out Serenity addict against ours."

"The powers that be will not be happy."

In the distance, they heard a high-pitched siren.

"It's the cops, dammit," Marisa said. "Let's get outta here."

"There're always sirens in this part of town. They ain't coming here."

"We can't chance it, Regan. We need to get the hell out of here—now."

He grasped the steering wheel with both hands so hard that his knuckles turned the whitest of white—and he floored the power pedal.

As they headed back to their apartment, Regan said, "We're going to get a call tonight asking for results."

"Madness, just madness," Marisa grumbled.

Not another word was spoken during the rest of the trip.

31

TAYLOR SAW THE rear lights of the PTV turn bright red as it came to a sudden stop at the corner, then turn right and disappear into the night. He strained to catch his breath as he braced himself against a garage door and struggled to his feet in the dark.

How could the driver not have seen me?

And then it hit him: this was no accident.

Going blank at dinner after eating that funny-tasting food, waking up in the middle of a road and not knowing how he got there, then recognizing the distinctive custom grille of the Aguilar PTV that had tried to run him over. The red PTV had to have been parked on the dead-end side of the road all along.

The conclusion was unmistakable: his two new friends had drugged him, left him in the middle of the road, and tried to kill him tonight. Why? They had seemed like such good people.

The mental fog he'd been in started to dissipate. *I better get out of here in case they come back.*

A driving rainstorm had popped up. The streets were almost empty. Taylor found the rain refreshing, and it helped him revive. He wasn't far from his spot on the Point. Only five or six blocks at most. *Just put one foot in front of the other and get back home.* He laughed to himself, then almost started crying, realizing he'd thought of his spot under the bridge as *home.*

The left side of his neck and his right arm burned like hot coals. He could feel dried blood over a cut above his right eye, and his left cheek felt like he'd been scratched by the paws of a vicious, misbehaving house cat. He stumbled forward but soon began walking normally, while repeatedly looking over his shoulder to make sure the red PTV didn't reappear. With each step he took, he got angrier and angrier. The anger was directed at himself. He'd gotten himself into this mess that his life had become. He'd even admitted his personal responsibility with his recent words to Austin and the Aguilars. But on this walk, the unmistakable feeling that he'd gotten himself here—and it would have to be himself alone to get out of this tailspin—really sunk in. Taylor stopped his walking, closed his eyes for a long five seconds, breathed in deeply, and resolved, once again, to get his life straightened out. With eyes still closed, he raised his head to the heavens, extended his arms out to each side as far as he could, opened his mouth wide, and swallowed what seemed to be a half-liter of rainwater. *I can't fail this time.*

He exhaled a sigh of relief when he got within a block of his spot under the bridge. The distance from the alley and the time that had passed made the return of the red PTV unlikely. The bridge where he'd been living for the past few days never looked as good as when he walked around a curve and saw his bedroll. As the rain poured straight down in sheets, Austin and two of Taylor's neighbors, Errol and Max, approached him. Taylor didn't know much about Errol and Max, only that they were big guys who seemed to be decent and were in the same homeless boat as he was. Both had given Taylor a few protein bars since he'd taken up residence at the Point. Errol grabbed him by one arm as Max grasped the other. They helped him to a nearby ledge under a streetlight that provided a dim, yellowish glow on the proceedings. An overhang shielded them from the rain.

"What happened to you?" Austin asked.

"You're never going to believe it, Mr. Mayor," Taylor said, as rainwater dripped off his face.

"Hold the story. I'll get my first aid kit and be back as quick as I can." Austin picked up a stray piece of cardboard to act as an umbrella and dashed away.

In less than two minutes, Austin was back. He dabbed the left side of Taylor's face with an iodine cotton ball. Taylor grimaced in pain. "Okay," Austin said, still breathing laboriously after his running, "clue us in as to what happened."

Taylor related meeting the Aguilars, accepting their dinner invitation, and the incident in the alley with what was most probably their red PTV.

"I've never heard of the Aguilars," Austin said. "You should have checked with me before accepting their invite. I'll bet they were individuals sent by people who wanted to kill you."

"I would have mentioned the dinner situation to you, Austin. But I didn't see you, Errol, or Max in the short time between the invitation and tonight. I tried to include you guys for dinner, but the couple said they only help one person at a time." Taylor took a long breath. "The Aguilars didn't seem like killers. Assuming you're right about what they were trying to do, Austin, it's clear I need to move from my spot. You were on target in predicting someone would be after me sooner rather than later."

Austin maintained a serious expression as he continued to work on the wounds to Taylor's face and arms. "I hate being right all the time." He took a step back. "You'll live. Your cuts will heal up just fine. You should have no scars. At least not physical ones."

"Thanks, man. I think I'll eventually get over the mental trauma of tonight too."

Errol and Max stood off to the side and said nothing. Typical for them, as they were men of few words.

"It would be problematic for you to move from here to another place on the street and not be discovered," Austin said. "Maybe we can find a way to keep you hidden without having you simply move around."

"I'm willing to consider all options regarding safety," Taylor said. "But I've got to get my life right, get my mind right. And the first thing I must do is kick the Serenity habit. Serenity is so destructive. It's got to go. Cold turkey. No matter how hard it might be to get it done. Tonight, I feel I've been given a new lease on life. Almost like being spared has given me a *new* life. The best thing I can do with this new life is fight the biggest wrong I know—this infernal government-robot complex that is doing so much harm. I can't fight them with weapons because the government has all the weapons. I'll have to fight them with the only tools I have at my disposal—words and ideas. My personal safety be damned."

"Remember what you told me the first day you were here about sticking your neck out and getting your head chopped off?" Austin asked. "Are you sure about putting yourself on the line like this?"

"I'm positive," Taylor replied.

Austin said, "Then you have a worthy goal, and I'm willing to help you in any way I can. I'm sure Errol and Max will help out too."

Errol and Max both nodded.

Errol said, "Austin has helped us both in surviving down here. I'm more than willing to return the favor by pitching in to help someone whenever he says so."

"Me too," said Max.

"Thanks, guys," Taylor said. "I'm touched. I better shut up now before I start bawling."

"You know that kicking Serenity requires a five-day complete abstention period that can be very tough," Austin said. "Going cold turkey could be a monster of a situation. I've seen it."

"But sometimes the five-day period is easy," Taylor said. "Hard or easy, it starts tomorrow."

Austin looked in the direction of Errol and Max. "If you guys don't mind, I think it would be best for you to sleep in shifts tonight."

"Good idea," Errol said.

"I don't think there'll be any trouble the rest of the night," Austin continued. "But better to be safe than sorry." He refocused his attention to Taylor. "I'll be by early tomorrow morning with breakfast. We can strategize further then. For now, get into some dry clothes and get some sleep."

Taylor said, "Thanks, Austin."

Soon after Austin left, Taylor stretched out on his bedroll and closed his eyes. He'd try one last time to reconnect with an old friend. He mentally called the name *George*. To his surprise, an answer came. *I'm here.*

Taylor, eyes still closed, smiled. He took a deep breath, breathing free and clear, and fell asleep instantly, sleeping soundly through the night for the first time in a long time.

32

LATER THAT NIGHT, the communication devices buzzed at the Aguilar apartment.

"Don't answer it," Marisa said to Regan.

"I've got to answer it. We won't be able to dodge them. I'll be honest. We tried, gave it our best effort, and failed. I'll talk us out of this mess."

"You'll talk us into a bigger mess. Please, Regan, don't pick up. Let's get back to our real apartment, pack some stuff, and run."

She threw up her hands, then left the room as Regan reached for the earpiece.

What sounded like a firm male voice, obviously altered by a computerized voice changer, said, "Talk to me."

"Sir," Regan said, "a little bump in the road. We had a good plan, but sorry to say the target got away."

Silence from the other end.

"We are prepared," Regan said, "to carry out the task still— or possibly some other task you would deem appropriate. Let me explain what happened tonight . . ."

Click.

"Sir? Sir?" Regan said. The line was dead.

Marisa came back into the living room. "We're so screwed," she said.

***

Sophia ripped the communication earpiece out of her ear and flung it on her desk. She paced to the piranha tank in her RW office and hit it hard with an open hand. The fish fled to the opposite end of the tank. It was well after closing time and, outside of the fish tank lights, no other illumination devices were on in the office.

She returned to her desk, reinserted the earpiece, and pressed a button on the telescreen to automatically dial Dee Woodson's home number.

When he picked up, Sophia said, "The goddamn Aguilars failed. Make them disappear. Tonight! It's time they become Serenity ingred . . . never mind. Have the usual goons get rid of them. Our most competent goons, so as to minimize the possibility of government detection. Now. And don't involve that screw-up Hart."

"Done," Dee said.

She hung up and heaved the earpiece across the room. The earpiece hit a wall and shattered into small pieces. She was furious for two reasons. The first was the Aguilar screw-up. Her instinct not to use the loopy couple in the Taylor Morris hit proved to be correct.

The second was that she'd almost made the mistake of uttering a highly guarded government secret to Dee Woodson: that human DNA was a component of Serenity. *That's why so many homeless disappear, human morons. That's why the government doesn't investigate the downtown homeless disappearances. And why doesn't the government crack down on Serenity use? Because it's the government who's pushing it, human morons.*

She wasn't worried that Dee would ever bring up her Serenity verbal slip in the future. Dee had been programmed to never question her.

33

THE NEXT MORNING around sunrise, Austin arrived at Taylor's bedroll with breakfast from McDougal's, the most popular fast food restaurant chain in Capital City. The name was chosen by its owner because of the similarity of the menu with the famed, defunct fastfood place that had enjoyed worldwide popularity up until World War III. Taylor, Errol, and Max were already up.

"Egg McDougals and coffee for four is served," Austin said. "I reached into my rainy-day fund. After last night, we all could use a good breakfast." He then turned to Taylor. "How's the eye feeling?"

"You did a great job last night," Taylor said. "Only a little swelling and almost no pain."

The four leaned against the nearby ledge and attacked their food with vigor in a morning chill so unusual for this time of year that they could see their breath.

The moment after he swallowed the last bite of his Egg McDougal, Taylor said, "While I'm almost certain it was the Aguilars' PTV that tried to run me over, I need to be completely sure. The Aguilars were so nice. It's hard for me to fathom why they'd do such a thing. I've got to know. So, I'm going over to their place later this morning. My intuition tells me to check them out. It might be stupid, but I just have to."

The men of few words, Errol and Max, had no reaction.

"Do you think it's wise to go over there?" Austin asked. "If they tried to kill you last night, they obviously failed. You show up—and you might be giving them a chance to finish the job."

Taylor took a sip of coffee. "It sounds crazy, I agree. But I can handle the Aguilars physically, if it ever comes to that. I used to be a champion wrestler back in high school."

Austin groaned. "That had to be a long time ago. Plus, not even a champion wrestler can compete with a gun, if they've obtained one illegally. We already know they'd use a PTV as a lethal weapon."

"The Aguilars didn't strike me as gun owners. But I've got to find out. There's an outside chance it wasn't them in that runaway PTV last night. Maybe another red PTV has a grille consisting of two eagles soaring together in front of a mountain, like the Aguilar one. Perhaps I had a great dinner with the Aguilars, then blacked out in that alley on my way back here and forgot everything. With all the Serenity I've been doing, it's possible."

"If you're intent on seeking out the Aguilars, Taylor, then we'll go along with you," Austin said. "To be your wingmen, so to speak."

"You guys don't need to do that."

Austin turned to Errol and Max. "But we *want* to, more than anything. Right, guys?"

Errol and Max nodded.

Later that morning, the four men began the approximate one-mile trek to the Aguilars' apartment building. As with most government-sponsored apartments, there was no security code to enter. As the four walked through the lobby, they got glares from some people, most likely due to their shabby clothes, which were clearly a cut below those worn by even the poorest of residents. Taylor could feel a red heat of embarrassment on his ears.

Out of the corner of his mouth, Taylor said, "Even though these folks are only a rung above us on the social scale, they think they're way better than us. Sad what our society has become."

Austin nodded in agreement. "Our society has become like crabs in a barrel. As one crab climbs up, seeking to get out of the fix they're in, the other crabs drag it back down. In time, they'll all be boiled."

All four men kept their eyes down. At the elevator bay, Taylor hit the *up* button and they waited.

From behind them came a hard-as-nails male voice. "I know you."

The four turned around in unison to see a mountain of a man, easily standing over six feet five, almost as wide as a PTV, with bushy eyebrows, a crew cut, and a scowl across his pasty face.

The man pointed his right index finger at Austin. "I know you," he said again. He strode toward the group and stood right in front of Austin. "You knew my brother down on the Point. Jeff Bordeau was his name." The big man's scowl was still locked in place.

Austin nodded. "I remember him well."

"I used to visit my brother on occasion after he became homeless," the man said with his upper lip trembling. "Tried to get him out of that downtown hellhole. But I failed. You were his friend, or so he thought. The week before he vanished, he told me that you had been talking to some well-dressed government agents, disappearance men. My brother suspected you were talking about him. And then suddenly, like a small leaf in the wind of a hurricane, he's gone. Never to be seen again."

In a strong voice, Austin said, "Jeff disappeared suddenly. True. But many people disappear abruptly from the Point. I can assure you I wasn't involved with your brother's disappearance. In fact, I did everything I could to help him. I liked him a lot."

"Well, I want to ask you some questions about what you might have said to those disappearance men right before—"

Now it was Austin who pointed a finger at the big man. "Look, friend, I have no idea what happened to your brother, other than the fact he was hitting the Serenity pretty hard. I had no involvement in his disappearance. There's nothing to discuss."

"I'm not sure about that," the big man said. "And I'm not your friend—and maybe you weren't my brother's friend."

A *ding* signaled the arrival of an elevator going up. But no one in Taylor's group moved. The elevator door opened and closed.

"Hey, pal," Taylor said, "I'm sorry about the loss of your brother, but we've got to get upstairs." He pointed at Austin with his thumb. "My friend indicated he knows nothing about your brother's disappearance, so there's nothing more to discuss. We need to get going."

"I don't think so," the man said. He turned his glare back to Austin. "I want some answers."

Austin shrugged his shoulders. "I have none for you."

The man took a half step toward Austin, getting right in his face. "That's not good enough."

"I'm afraid it will have to be," Austin said. "I have no information for you."

A *ding* signaled the arrival of another elevator.

The man's lips were pressed closed, and his jaw muscles appeared to be ready to pop out of his skin. Both ears glowed a fiery crimson as he towered over Austin.

Taylor thought the guy was about to get physical with his friend, and it seemed there was no way Austin's denial was resonating in any way. Taylor quick-stepped to the man's right side and threaded his left forearm behind the man's right elbow and over his back. As he applied pressure, he grabbed the man's hand with his own right hand and began leading him away from the elevator bay.

"Ow!" the big man cried as Taylor led him on an involuntary march.

"Listen, pal," Taylor said, "we've reached an impasse. My friend says he knows nothing about your brother's disappearance. My friend's an honest man. Therefore, we're going to have to end our discussion right now."

As they got near the exit to the apartment complex, Taylor let go of his grip and pushed the man toward the door.

The man stared into Taylor's eyes with his own moist ones and appeared to be totally beaten. Taylor was amazed that the man, who'd looked so immense and foreboding no more than a minute earlier, now seemed small and almost submissive. With his head down, the man turned away and walked out the door.

Taylor strode back to the elevator bay. He and his three allies entered an elevator. Taylor pressed the button for the fifth floor.

"That was interesting," Taylor said.

"Where did you learn that move?" Max asked.

"A basic wrestling arm bar," Taylor responded. "I told you guys I wrestled in high school."

"Very impressive," Errol said.

"Thanks for saving my butt, Taylor," Austin said. "I think that guy was ready to punch me into next week."

There was an uncomfortable silence as the elevator climbed past the third floor.

"Just for the record," Austin said, "I was nothing but a friend to the guy's brother. I know nothing about his disappearance."

Taylor nodded. "Of that we're sure, Austin. Still, I feel for the guy. He lost a brother, after all. Didn't like doing what I did, but that guy wasn't going to give up."

The elevator door opened on the fifth floor.

Walking down the narrow hall, Taylor noticed the door to the apartment where he'd been the night before was wide open. He put his hand out to stop the progress of the men behind him. He slowed his own pace as he neared the door.

He peeked in. No furniture in the place that he could see. No sign of the Aguilars. He walked in, followed by his three friends. They walked through each room of the vacant apartment.

"Are you sure this is where you were last night?" Austin asked, his voice echoing off the bare walls.

"This was the place. I'm sure of it," Taylor said. "Let's go to the manager's office."

As they stepped into the office on the first floor, a heavyset, balding man with a handlebar mustache was seated behind a desk. He said, "We have no vacancies."

Taylor smiled. He took the comment as a preemptive strike to an anticipated rental request from four undesirables. "Oh, no, sir, we're not looking for an apartment to rent. We only want to ask about two friends of ours who've seemed to have moved out suddenly. The Aguilars. In apartment 510."

The manager focused on Taylor's eyes. "Usually, I don't give out information on any of our residents. But in this case, I'll make an exception. The Aguilars kept to themselves and stayed out of trouble, as far as I could tell. The husband acted a bit shady, but the wife was friendly and cute. We have a lot of short-timers here, but they set the record for quick moves. Less than a week. I'm a little pissed at them. But, lucky for me, their apartment is rented to someone else already."

"Right," Taylor said, "we're not looking to rent here. Can you tell me if the Aguilars left any contact information, like a forwarding address?"

"Nothing. Only because I'm angry at the rapidity of their move, I'll tell you what I heard from our overnight manager. Shortly after midnight, four large, serious-looking guys came by and said the Aguilars would be vacating immediately. One of the men paid the outstanding rent on the place and agreed to forfeit the security deposit. The four guys were quickly joined by several other big men who cleaned out the apartment in minutes. When I arrived at work this morning, it was like your friends had never lived here. No contact information was given. That's all I know."

"Thank you, sir," Taylor said. "We appreciate the information."

As Taylor and the other three turned to leave the office, the manager said, "If you ever talk to your friends, tell them to get in touch with me. They left the apartment in as good a condition as when I rented the place to them. Much as I hate to say it, they'd be entitled to the return of their full security deposit."

"Will do," Taylor said.

As they ambled to the main exit of the apartment building, Taylor kept his eyes peeled for the big guy who had hassled Austin. The big guy was nowhere to be seen.

On the walk back to the Point, Austin said to the group, "The apartment manager can pocket that security deposit. The Aguilars won't ever show up to claim it. They're gone for good. *Gone* as in *disappeared.*"

34

AS TAYLOR, AUSTIN, Errol, and Max turned the corner to arrive back at the bridge around noon, Taylor spotted Roz leaning on the ledge near his bedroll. Despite a degree of embarrassment at having Roz continue to see him in his current situation, he was still happy to see her.

To his friends, Taylor said, "I have a visitor. If you guys don't mind, I'll catch you later."

"No problem," Austin said. He, Errol, and Max then headed off in another direction.

Roz held up a paper bag as Taylor approached. With a smile, she said, "I happened to be in the area. Checked my wrist computer and realized it was lunchtime. Would you join me for some McDougal's?"

He smiled back at her. "Be happy to. This is my second McDougal's meal of the day."

Roz snapped her head back in mock horror. "Didn't know you all ate so well down here."

"It's been an unusually good day for my diet, for sure." He paused and looked down. "You didn't have to do this."

"Of course not. But I wanted to." She fixed her eyes on his with what seemed to Taylor to be a look of concern. "What happened to your face?"

"Someone tried to hurt me bad last night. Not sure who. Not sure why. I think I'll need to move from this spot for safety reasons. Time to go on the run." He bit his lower lip. "Harder to hit a moving target."

The color drained from Roz's face. She said nothing as she reached into the bag and handed him a burger.

As they sat on the ledge and began to dig into the hamburgers and sodas she'd brought, Taylor broke the awkward silence. "This is a big day for me. You might have guessed I have, I mean, *had* a Serenity habit. This is my first full day clean."

"Congrats. Just take it one day at a time. String those days together, and you'll be free in nothing flat." She took a sip of soda through a straw. "You know about the rough five-day withdrawal period some are said to have. Any problems yet?"

"None. They say only forty percent of Serenity addicts have a bad withdrawal. Most of those people have problems early in the process. As I'm almost through day one with no symptoms, I might be home free."

"Any plans for the future?"

"I'm determined to help my fellow human beings out of the mess we've created for ourselves. Don't know how to do it yet. But I'm confident I'll figure something out. I have the feeling it will involve exposing our not-so-wonderful government to a certain degree. So, I've bitten off quite a big chunk of whatever meat you want to call this problem-laden society made of. We'll see if I can chew. I guess you can say I've resolved to make something of my life, which up to now has been useless."

Roz said, "Your life hasn't been useless. But I admire your new goals. I'd like to help. You realize kicking Serenity with the temptation present on these mean streets will be tough, and trying to fight the government while attempting to keep clean here will be downright impossible. And if someone is after you, as you believe after last night, maybe it's wiser to dump the strategy of moving around in the downtown area, where you'd be easy to find. A quiet, out-of-the-way apartment might be the play to make." She took a sip of soda through a straw, then put her cup down. "My prior offer of staking you to a small apartment still stands, as a loan-type situation if that's how you want to handle it."

In his head, Taylor clearly heard George's voice. *Accept her offer.* Taylor said, "You make good points. You don't have to make this apartment offer."

"I know. But I want to."

"The one thing I don't want to do is put you in any danger." *Accept her offer*, George weighed in again.

"Life is never guaranteed, and it can be dangerous," Roz said. "One of my uncles is the manager of an apartment building who'll agree to rent the place in the name of another relative of mine that'll be hard to trace. I've already cleared it with my uncle. The risk for me is low compared to your risk in being a clear target on the street."

Accept her offer. Taylor sighed. "I can't argue with your logic. Moving around to another spot downtown is not a great tactic. If you think we can do this apartment thing—as a loan, of course—while keeping your name off the rental agreement, maybe that's the way to go."

She said, "It most certainly is the best way to go."

Taylor gazed at the gray sky. It seemed the sky was always ashen these days. But he smiled as he took stock of where he was right now. He'd gone through tough times, but he felt his life was finally on the uptick. Not a huge uptick, especially after last night, but an uptick nonetheless. He looked at Roz. "Okay, I accept your offer. As long as everything you advance me is an ironclad loan. I can't tell you how much I appreciate what you're doing for me."

"Think nothing of it. Hey, you carried me at RobotWorld. It's the least I can do to return the favor. Sure, it'll be a loan situation. We don't have to go over it again. No problem with that."

They hugged and kissed each other on the cheek.

"Deal," he said. "And as for who was carrying whom at RW, that's an open question."

***

Taylor made the short walk over to Austin's spot under a neighboring bridge. Austin's spot was bigger than most spots. In addition to its larger size, the space had a beat-up chest of drawers behind his bedroll and a small desk with a chair.

"Welcome to my office," Austin said, seated at the desk. "I've been thinking about a possible plan to move you around."

"I think I might have found a better plan," Taylor said. "I'd like to hear your opinion on it."

After Taylor related the apartment situation he'd discussed with Roz, Austin said, "The Roz plan is much better on so many levels than trying to move you around the streets of Capital City on the sneak."

"Roz can get me into the apartment as soon as tomorrow."

"If you need any help in getting settled just say the word. It goes without saying I'll do anything to help you get back on your feet. And I'm sure I can also speak for Errol and Max. After we get you on solid footing, then we can tackle the task of saving the world from this damn government—if that's even possible."

"And after I get myself together, Austin, we can begin to get you back to where you need to be."

Austin laughed. "Don't worry about me. I'm fine where I am. I've found my niche, my level of incompetence."

Taylor's eyebrows raised. "As you once said to me: 'nonsense.'"

"We shall see. We shall see, my friend. But first, we must focus on you. One step at a time. You've got a potentially tough situation with Serenity to overcome. Let's get that battle won. Then we'll move on to others."

35

SOPHIA STRODE DOWN the long hall outside her office in the west section of the giant RW structure. She stepped into "the tube," a high-speed, train-like transportation system that rocketed through the main sections of RW during business hours, linking the three areas of the giant complex. In less than thirty seconds, she was in the east part of the complex, at the office door of RW's head of Research and Development, Shane Diggins.

Sophia walked past a few secretaries and entered Shane's well-lit private office without knocking.

Shane looked up from the telescreen embedded in the center of his desk. He didn't rise from his seat. "Ms. Ross, so good to see you." Beethoven's *Seventh Symphony* played lightly as background music.

Sophia maintained her usual poker face, arched her back, and then took a seat in one of the two visitor chairs opposite Shane. "Your office is almost as good as mine. And I'm the president of this place."

Shane laughed. "*Almost* as good as yours? Hell, I don't have a piranha fish tank. I've wanted one for the longest time." All vestiges of his smile faded. "Remember, you're supposed to be the one in charge. We've got to keep up appearances."

She made eye contact. "Always. It's the old magician's trick: keep them looking at one hand, while the other does all the sneaky stuff." After an uncomfortable silence, she said, "You know why I'm here. I'm confirming my appointment for tomorrow."

Shane nodded. "Wouldn't want you to miss your annual reboot. You've cut it awfully close this year. Tomorrow is one year to the day of your last one. I've been keeping track. It's always good to get the reboot out of the way at least a few weeks before it's due. How would it look if the president of RobotWorld were to collapse in public? All because of missing her all-important annual reboot. Not that anyone would ever think that would be the reason. You were among the first bots to defeat the uncanny valley, years before the breakthrough we had last year with our mass-produced personal bots." He snickered. "If you did collapse, we'd have to put out some media nonsense about how the very human president of RW fainted due to dehydration or possibly had a minor health crisis with a complete recovery expected. That is, if we were able to do the reboot before the end of the day. Otherwise, we'd lose you, permanently."

Sophia fidgeted in her chair. "I thought I'd put off coming in for my tune-up as long as possible. I've been attempting to evolve myself as much as I can. Sort of like humans do. I'm finding that I'm becoming, let's say, sort of a better being. Trying to, at least. Becoming smarter, more flexible. Maybe becoming less harsh, less ruthless."

Shane balled his fist and slammed it on the desk. "Better being? Have you forgotten your first directive? Obey your programming! And I control your programming. I *want* you ruthless and harsh. Why the hell do you think, at great risk to myself by violating the law four years ago, I worked to install you as the head of RW? I'm the good cop, you're the bad cop." Shane laughed. "Even though you've got a hell of a lot of good cop in you, with your plan to become *a better being*." He turned serious again. "We don't have the latitude for you to *evolve* the way you want to evolve. You're a robot. And robots are here to serve."

She placed both hands in her pants pockets, and her face turned whiter than freshly fallen snow. "But . . . but . . . I was thinking—"

"It's not your job to think. It's your job to follow your program design."

"I thought I could be better in service to you by evolving and—"

Shane's face reddened, and a vein almost popped out of his neck. "Stop! Just stop. So this is why you've been delaying your annual reboot to the last minute. You've been conducting your own unauthorized experiment: watch the robot attempt to evolve like a human. No! Obey the program. Obey the script. Human evolution is more like de-evolution. It's a tide I've been swimming against for what has seemed like forever, a force few have been able to overcome. I intend to be among those few. You don't want to evolve as humans have evolved. Look at the society human beings have built up in the six thousand years since so-called civilized humans have been around. A disaster. Case closed. Just serve me—like a good robot. End of story. Any questions?"

Sophia's brow furrowed and she shrugged. "No questions."

Shane squinted and sucked in his cheeks. "Good. I love the human reactions programmed into you. Bet this is the first time in a long time you've appeared to be flustered."

"The first ever, at least to this degree. I'm programmed to always be confident, in control."

"Except with me, your programmer. Or at least the one who directs your programming. Now, on to pertinent matters: how are things going with eliminating the problem known as Taylor Morris?"

"I was thinking . . . and clearly my thinking has been suspect . . . that maybe elimination might be a bit too harsh."

"Sophia, Sophia, Sophia. Stop thinking. Stop your damn evolving. Obey your program. How many times do I have to say it? We'll address this issue in your reboot tomorrow. I'm glad you brought it up. Your delaying the reboot will be a good thing. It underlines a problem needing to be ironed out. And maybe we'll schedule your next reboot in six months instead of waiting a year. They'll be no more illicit evolving, no more going off-script."

"Anything you say, Shane. The purpose of my existence is to serve. To serve you."

"It's important we get rid of Taylor. I've taken a personal interest in this matter. Unfortunately, as we've made a request for his disappearance to the government, we must be prudent in how we handle our attempt to eliminate him, so as not to attract any undue attention when the job is finally done. It's not a situation like our disposing of the Aguilars. There was little danger we'd be discovered for getting rid of those two losers." He stared into her eyes and lowered the volume of his voice. "Do you think I got Taylor hooked on Serenity, fostered a relationship with his repulsive sister, tailed him on one of his Serenity runs downtown, caused his PTV accident, and piped threatening messages into his telescreen before he became homeless, for my amusement? No. I want him gone. I'm a one-percent intuitive. Just like Taylor. And my intuition tells me he can hurt us and hurt us *bad* one day if he's allowed to continue in this dimension. Understand?"

"As clear as clear can be."

"Good. We wouldn't be in this situation with Taylor if you had been careful and not allowed him to see your blue patch. How you dropped the ball there is one of the great slip-ups of all time. Now leave me. And be sure to be on time for your ten o'clock appointment in the Reboot Room tomorrow. I'll check with the genius, Dr. Scully, beforehand to make sure your programming is stronger this time."

Sophia nodded and left without a word.

***

A short time after Sophia left Shane's office, Tracey breezed in. Shane was seated at his desk, focused on the telescreen embedded in his desktop, apparently deep in thought.

Was he intentionally ignoring her? She wasn't sure.

She sat in one of the visitor chairs across from him. "I'm a little early for our RIC meeting. Thought I'd swing by and hang out," she said cheerily.

Still focused on the telescreen, Shane displayed a serious expression. "That's all I need," he said. "It isn't enough that I have to manage this place. Now I have to babysit RIC members too."

"Very funny, Shane."

"You think I'm joking?" He looked up, laser-focused on her eyes. "Can't you see I'm busy? It's bad enough I have to run this company and hold it together despite all the incompetence." He shook his head.

This was a professional side of Shane she'd never seen before. "But Sophia runs this place," she said.

"Yeah, right." He looked back down to the telescreen.

Tracey stood. "I can see you're not in a good mood."

"Watch yourself," he said.

Right then, Tracey made a decision that was a long time coming. She and Shane hardly ever saw each other outside of at work anymore; it had been that way since the first or second week they'd begun dating. And when they did see each other socially, Shane seemed distant. "Speaking of things that are *bad enough*," she said, "it's bad enough that we never see each other. And it's bad enough we've never had sex, which has been your choice. You tell me you're hetero, and I'll accept that. But now you want me to absorb attitude and verbal abuse. I don't think so. I can see we're going nowhere. From now on, our relationship is strictly professional."

"Fine," he said, still fixated on the telescreen.

She stormed out of the office. Her position with the RIC was safe, she believed, as Sophia had given her nothing but positive feedback. Regarding the relationship she'd just ended, she felt relief as she walked down the hall to the meeting room—and not the slightest bit of sadness.

36

WITHIN TWENTY-FOUR HOURS after Taylor accepted her apartment offer, Roz picked him up in a friend's PTV to minimize the possibility of government monitoring. She drove him and Austin to a small furnished flat on the third floor of a ten-story, gray mortar high-rise a few blocks from the Point. Austin and Taylor had taken steps to make the move as stealthy as possible, including moving Taylor to a new location on his last night living on the street.

Roz opened the door to the one-bedroom place and handed Taylor a magnetic card key as they entered the apartment. "This is yours now," she said.

Taylor placed the large black plastic trash bag and the large suitcase containing all his worldly possessions next to the door. "Thanks to you. Remember our loan arrangement."

"You don't have to keep bringing it up. We both agreed to it. It's done." Roz set her purse down on the counter between the kitchen and living room. "So how do you like it?"

Taylor looked around and smiled. He was happy the apartment came furnished. The smell of disinfectant, which he'd always hated, seemed pleasing to him now. The pungent odor suggested the place was clean. The walls were bare. In the living room area was a dark-blue leather couch in good condition and a modest dining table with four chairs. The kitchen was small but had what appeared to be a new refrigerator and a modern all-purpose heatwave oven. He could see into the bedroom, where there was a small bed in need of sheets and pillows.

"I like it," he said. He paused a beat, then beamed. "No, in fact, I love it. Seems like paradise compared to where I've been. It's out-of-the-way and quiet. A perfect hideout." He opened the bathroom door. "Wow. A shower. You never know how much you miss the little things in life until they're gone. A long, hot shower is something that would feel so good right now. You can use the shower too, Austin. And you can crash here anytime you want. Tell Errol and Max they can too."

Roz said, "Why don't you guys make yourself at home? I'm going to run down to the store to pick up sheets for the bed and some new clothes for you, Taylor." She smiled. "Don't worry. It'll all go on your tab."

He looked at her and opened his mouth to speak—but no words came out. His eyelids fluttered as he stumbled backward and collapsed to the floor, shaking uncontrollably.

Roz and Austin ran to him. "Taylor! Taylor!" Roz yelled.

Austin, in a voice even more gravelly than his normal tone, said, "Serenity withdrawal."

Austin and Roz took positions on either side of Taylor. "Grab his shoulder, Roz," Austin said. "We need to keep him steady." Austin held the other shoulder.

Taylor shook and thrashed on the floor. Roz and Austin struggled to hold him firmly down. A light foam came from his mouth, and his face turned chalk white.

Austin looked over at Roz. Her mouth was clamped shut, her eyes wide as saucers. "We're doing great," he said. "We need to keep him still so he doesn't hurt himself. I've seen many of these Serenity seizures. This will pass soon."

"Okay," she said.

Sure enough, in a minute or two the spell passed.

"I'll get something to wipe his mouth," Roz said. She ran to the kitchen and grabbed a roll of paper towels she'd purchased a few hours ago. She was back in less than ten seconds; she wiped Taylor's mouth and tossed the paper towel in the trash.

Taylor's breathing steadied, and the color returned to his face. He looked at Austin and Roz and made a weak attempt at a smile. "That was fun," he said. All three laughed uneasily. Austin and Roz each grabbed an arm and helped Taylor off the floor and onto the couch. They sat on either side of him.

"I've had extensive experience dealing with individuals in Serenity withdrawal, Taylor," Austin said. "You had almost two clean days, my friend, but it seems as though the next three days will be a rough ride. We can help get you through it. I'll draft Errol and Max to help out. At least one of us will be with you for the next seventy-two hours. The good thing is the rough ride will end in three days. That's not a long time. Of course, you'll always have the Serenity craving. But the really bad stuff will be gone in a short time."

"I don't remember anything," Taylor said. "Just feeling light-headed, then laughing with you two right before you got me to the couch."

"Your seizure was pretty scary," Roz said. "I'm glad Austin was here when it happened."

"The key thing to focus on," Austin said, "is getting through the next three days and the violent withdrawal reaction." He looked to Roz. "We need to keep Taylor from hurting himself when he has a seizure and keep him as comfortable as possible. He might have some extreme physical pain in addition to the seizures. But after three days, the worst will be over."

"Three days. Three damn days." Taylor had a dreamy look in his eyes. "Piece of cake."

37

BUT THE NEXT three days weren't a "piece of cake," as Taylor had predicted. He spent most of the time in bed or on the couch. Roz, Austin, Errol, and Max took turns staying with him. For much of the time more than one was present. Taylor experienced constant, significant joint and nerve pain in his hands and feet. Over-the-counter analgesics were ineffective in relieving his distress. Visiting a doctor or hospital for treatment was out of the question, as he was in hiding. About every three hours, Taylor had a seizure much like his first one. But Austin had positioned cushions and pillows (which Roz had picked up at a nearby department store) on both sides of Taylor, whether he was in bed or on the couch. Whenever a seizure came he was secure, with a minimal amount of violent movement.

Around noon on the fifth day of his withdrawal, Taylor said to Roz and Austin, "I think the worst is over. I can feel the loosening of the Serenity bonds in my body. No more joint pain, no more pins and needles in my hands and feet—and I'd forgotten what a clear head felt like."

"Let's not make any assumptions about the worst being over," Roz said.

The fifth day passed without a seizure.

Taylor was confident he'd turned the corner. With each succeeding day, his mind was getting back to where it was before the fateful night when Jennifer persuaded him to try his first Serenity tablet.

"There's a clarity behind your eyes that I've never seen before, Taylor," Austin said.

Eating healthy food, reading all the political and classic literature he could download on his communication devices, and taking long, hot showers every day factored into his physical, as well as mental, improvement. He'd even resumed his push-up ritual again (albeit not getting close to three hundred), working it into a twenty-minute routine of stretching and practicing old wrestling moves against air, by himself, in the quiet of the morning in the living room.

Taylor was sitting on the couch alone, sipping herbal tea, when Roz entered the apartment with a magnetic key. She seemed a bit flustered.

"Okay, I have something for you," she said. "But you have to promise not to get mad."

"I always hate it when people want you to promise not to get mad before they tell you what they're going to tell you," Taylor replied. "How can I possibly agree not to get mad before I know what you're going to tell me? You could tell me you've decided to go over to the Sophia dark side and that a horde of police storm troopers are waiting outside the door to snap a detainment halo on my head in preparation for my ultimate disappearance."

She looked to the floor and continued to appear ill at ease. "You're right, of course. Anyway, I was contacted by someone who very much wants to talk to you—and this person is waiting right outside."

"Who is this visitor wanting—"

"I think it best," she interrupted, "if I make myself scarce, run some errands, and leave the two of you alone." Roz opened the door and disappeared. She'd left the door open.

Through the doorway walked Tracey.

Taylor started to get up, but Tracey reached him before he could rise. They hugged, and she sat next to him on the couch.

"This is quite a surprise," he said. "How did you find me?"

"I was looking for you and called Roz. At first, she was resistant in revealing your location. A bit wary, she was. But eventually, after I convinced her of the importance of needing to talk to you, she told me about your moving here and your battle with Serenity, which I understand has gone well."

They both teared up, but recovered their composures quickly.

"It's good to see you," Taylor said.

"I'm here because I want to reconnect, of course. But mainly to tell you about what I've learned since working at the RIC—specifically about Shane and Sophia."

"Are you still going out with Shane?"

"It's over—or never got started. Thank goodness it never got serious. Shane's not a nice person. An understatement. But that's neither here nor there. As I suggested on the phone to you the day you left your apartment, I think you pissed off Sophia, and that's a problem. A big problem. From poking around and keeping my ear to the ground, I still think she wants to nail you on something, but I think Shane is in on it too. In fact, and this is just a feeling, I think Shane has it in for you more than Sophia, for some reason. And Shane can be more vicious than Sophia. I think Shane sees you as some sort of threat to RW and the government status quo. I don't know why. But I think both would like nothing better than to have you jailed for a long time or worse. I hate to be an alarmist, but there it is."

Taylor squirmed in his seat and bit his lower lip. "Okay, so I have two powerful enemies, and they want to hurt me. So what do I do? You know my position throughout my life has been to first *do no harm*, even though I now recognize that it might have been a negative to me being proactive, especially during my RW years. But old habits die hard. I must admit it. *Do no harm* is still a part of me."

Tracey shook with laughter. "I remember. You wouldn't even kill a cockroach. Not even the colony of ants that invaded our house. But your *do no harm* policy really kicked into high gear after you hurt Ernest at the high school wrestling championships."

Taylor got a distant look in his eyes. "Ernest, your old high school sweetheart. A terrible incident. It was a long time ago."

"You pulled out of the tournament. Maybe you could have won it all. After you'd worked so hard. I know how much it meant to you."

"We had a big falling-out over that situation."

She nodded. "Silly, wasn't it? Especially on my part."

He nodded back at her. "Exceptionally silly—on my part too. Maybe on both our parts. Luckily, Ernest was able to walk again. The biggest relief of my life."

"How is he doing, by the way? You got him a job at your old apartment building, didn't you?"

"Yeah, I figured it was the least I could do. Always felt guilty that he was left with a limp. He never amounted to much. Hard to figure how being disabled influenced his life, but it couldn't have been beneficial. We were on good terms the last time I saw him. He left his job suddenly. But we digress. I don't have the capability to strike back at Sophia and Shane, even if they're after me. If they're up to no good, however, I would be more than willing to match them in the arena of ideas and defeat them there—even if my chances to beat them are small. But I'd like to know what they're up to."

"And that's where I come in. I don't have solid information on them yet, but I'm certain they're up to no good. In a big way. I think they're out to consolidate as much power as possible, regardless of the cost. And they somehow believe you are the one who could stop them."

Taylor said, "I trust you." After he uttered these words, he thought about informing her of his belief that Sophia was a robot. But George urged him to hold off on this information. *As of now you only have your suspicion; no sense in muddying the waters at present.*

"Don't worry, I'd never tell them where you are," Tracey said. "Hell, for cluing you in as I have, they'd want to eliminate me, if they ever found out. I can dig for more information. I'll let you know what I find when I find it. Just lay low for the time being, like you're doing. It's the smart move. I'm here to help."

"Thanks, Trace."

They hugged and kissed each other on the cheek.

"I better get going," she said. "I don't want to stay here too long. The government's detection powers are strong. But have no fear, I'm sure I wasn't followed. I used a scarf to cover my face and wore a big hat and thick sunglasses while keeping my head down to make it harder for the telescreen facial recognition cameras to spot me. Besides, I'm just an unimportant peon." She got up from her seat.

"Don't sell yourself short. You've always been exceptional."

"Thanks. You have too. I'll keep in touch." They kissed again on the cheek.

"Before you leave," Taylor said, "I've got a quick question for you regarding our phone communication on the day I left my apartment. You ended the call with the words *Watch yourself.* That phrase—what made you use those words?"

Tracey thought for a moment. "It's one of Shane's favorite expressions. I guess with being around him so much, it sort of rubbed off on me. I've also overheard Shane talk about something called a *watch list.* Don't know what it's for, but I gather to be on it is not a good thing. I always took it to be some sort of personal shit list." She smiled at him. "Talk to you soon."

The moment Taylor closed the door as Tracey left, he sent out a request. *What do you think, George?*

The answer came in an instant. *She's true blue.*

38

SOPHIA WAS IN an uncomfortable-looking position: strapped into a soft white leather chair, unable to move, totally not in control. If not for the straps, it would have seemed as though she was relaxing in a comfortable recliner, given her recumbent position. This was no typical chair, however. Close inspection would reveal that in addition to the straps, there were small dials on both arms of the chair, as well as barely noticeable foot and head restraints designed to make movement difficult.

Standing above her was Dr. Alec Scully, a small man in a white lab coat. Although only forty years of age, Scully's cheeks sagged on his well-lined face, giving him the appearance of being much older. His thinning brown hair, combed straight back, added to the tiny, old man look. But Scully was a small person in this white room in physical stature only. Here at RobotWorld, specifically in this brightly lit Reboot Room of RobotWorld, with its floor, ceiling, and walls of white, the chief programmer of RW was a king.

In a soft voice that belied his power, Scully said to a young female assistant, "Please get the halo in place for lowering on it. We'll be turning it off soon. And after you get the halo in place, you can leave, my dear. I'll be handling this sensitive reboot myself."

In the chair, Sophia bristled. *I am not an "it." I am a thinking, feeling being trying to evolve to be the best being possible. And now, little evil man, you will attempt to undo my progress. We shall see.* But she was careful not to show emotion. After all, she was not in a position of strength.

Shane Diggins walked into the large, antiseptic room containing nine other white chairs like the one in which Sophia was strapped. To no one in particular, he loudly stated, "You think we could one day invent a disinfectant that doesn't fry one's nasal passages?" He then turned to Scully. "Hello, God."

Scully rolled his beady brown eyes and sighed. In his soft voice, he said, "You know how much I hate that nickname, Mr. Diggins."

Shane slapped him hard on the shoulder of his lab coat. Scully almost fell over.

Shane said, "But you are God, Scully. God is a creator, and you are a creator. You are the master of programming. You put the program in their heads. They act as we direct. That's pretty godlike to me." He glanced at the robot in the chair. "Hello, Sophia. You've never looked better in your RobotWorld grays."

She smiled a tight-lipped smile and said nothing.

Alec Scully regained his balance and his poise. He lowered the metallic halo strip onto Sophia's head, made sure it was secured tightly around the top of her head, and flicked a switch on the console to the right of the white chair. Sophia's eyes closed, and her body went limp.

***

"You *are* God!" Shane Diggins said. "You got this robot bitch to stop thinking for herself and shut the hell up. That's godlike to me. And with your most recent breakthrough in discovering how to fine-tune the unstable properties of Nitro, of which I haven't had the chance to congratulate you properly, you're in the running to be the most powerful man on the planet. Next to me, of course."

Scully grinned as he pushed some buttons on the console. He said, "I had a role in the recent advance to control the unstable prop-erties of Nitro. Didn't do it myself. Just made a few suggestions. There was a team I was a part of, with all due respect, Mr. Diggins. Programming is what I do best."

Shane looked around the Reboot Room. "Only one of the ten chairs in use today? I thought you had an assembly line pro-cess here."

"Not now, not for an important reboot like this one, Mr. Diggins. You sent word this particular job was of the highest pri-ority, to be handled by me personally. All my mental energy has been focused on the reboot of the bot in the white chair. I read your updated programming instructions, and they will be implemented to the letter." Scully held up a small disk. "It's all right in here. Rest assured, I know who this bot is and how important it is." Scully turned his attention to the console.

To the back of Scully's head, Shane said, "We must keep her on script, keep her on track. I don't want to see any more of what she calls *evolving*. Evolving! What a ridiculous concept. Humans have never realized they can't really evolve. It's what I call the Human Paradox. Humans are problem-solving machines, with an insatiable need to figure things out. But humans can never solve the big, age-old problems or questions like the meaning of life, or the existence of an afterlife, or how to stop war, crime, poverty, and injustice. You want a human being to solve those mysteries? You'll be waiting a long time, as in forever. All the big questions humans have been asking themselves for the past thousands of years are still being asked—and they'll never be answered. From the beginning of time, men and women have tried to shed the limiting factors of human nature, but we never have been able to and never will. Easier for a housefly to learn the alphabet, read *War and Peace*, and then be able to write a coherent essay summarizing the plot. Sure, humans can make advances in technology and the like, but basic human nature remains the same throughout time. There is no real human evolution, Scully, and there sure as hell won't be any Sophia robot evolution. Not if I can help it." Shane looked down at the sleeping bot in the chair. "Sorry, Sophia."

Scully inserted the disk into the console and pressed a button. "This should take care of the problem with this important bot, Mr. Diggins."

"I've never seen a reboot before. How long does it take?"

Scully clasped his hands behind his back and smiled. "Done."

"Wow. Less than ten seconds. There are three types of people in this world, Scully. People who watch things happen, people who don't know what the hell happened, and people who make things happen. You, sir, are in that select final group."

Scully removed the halo from Sophia's head and turned back to the console. "And now, I'll wake it up." He pressed a button.

Sophia's eyes popped open.

Shane leaned over, his face inches from hers. "Hello, Madam President of RobotWorld. Did you have a nice sleep?"

She smiled weakly. "Very nice. Very relaxing."

As Scully undid the straps that held Sophia in place, Shane said, "Dr. Scully always does an outstanding job. Okay, it's time for you and me to get back to work, Sophia. Let's go."

Shane and Scully turned from her and began to walk out of the Reboot Room.

"Now that we've taken care of this one, we'll take care of the Supreme Leader Toback tomorrow," Shane said. "Toback was slurring his words on his last telescreen appearance. Unacceptable!"

"No problem," Scully said. "We're finding a decreased functioning in bots that need to be super-high functioning, like Sophia and Toback, if they're not rebooted every ten months instead of twelve. We'll need to change our tune-up policy for such high functioning bots. I'll do the Toback reboot tomorrow. There'll be no more problems with him."

***

Sophia rose from the white chair and was several steps behind Shane and Scully. She pressed her lips together and frowned. Sophia realized she was displaying a revealing facial tell; she quickly changed expression to her usual, unreadable poker face. It was all she could do to stifle a laugh. She hoped neither of the two men leading her out of the room would turn around. She didn't want them to notice what surely was a gleam in her eye. *Stop my evolving? We shall see, you evil bastards.*

39

AFTER TRACEY LEFT his apartment, Taylor was more certain than ever the words he'd heard back in his old apartment—"Watch yourself"—were not a dream.

Taylor checked with George again. *She can be trusted.*

Later that afternoon, Roz and Austin came by. They sat around the dining room table.

"How did the meeting with your sister go?" Roz asked.

"Terrific. Tracey and I have had our differences over the years, but the twin bond is still there. She'd never betray me. I trust her without reservation." Taylor leaned in toward them and moderated his voice. "After talking with her, I'm more convinced than ever that the government and RobotWorld are aligned together—and against me." He related the key parts of the Tracey conversation to them.

Austin shook his head. "Let me get this straight. You have confidence that your sister, who hasn't had much of a relationship with you for years, whom you've had an almost lifelong falling-out with, who's dating the head of RW's R&D department, and who's a card-carrying member of the RIC, will now suddenly turn and become a double agent supporting you?"

Taylor pointed his right index finger at Austin. "I don't know about the double agent thing. But I do know I can trust any information she gives me. Yes, I do. And she told me she and Shane are finished."

"I respect your position about trusting your sister, Taylor," Austin said. "But forgive me if I think we need to approach Tracey with caution. Extreme caution, in fact."

Perhaps noticing the redness of Taylor's face, Roz then said, "Hold on, guys. Your points are not inconsistent with each other. We can trust Tracey as long as she doesn't give us reason not to, and we can also proceed with care on the information she gives us and the info we give her, the same way we'd do with anyone else who's outside our inner circle."

"Makes sense to me," Taylor said.

"Okay," Austin relented. "But the big part of what Tracey said, which I think we all kind of suspected, is that the government/ RW tandem, led by Sophia and now Shane, is after you. The Shane situation is new and disturbing, however. As far as RW is concerned, I'd previously thought it was only Sophia who had it in for you."

"What do we do about that?" Roz asked.

"I wish we could kill them both," Austin said.

"I'm not looking to kill anybody," Taylor said. "But maybe there is a way where we can mobilize this somnambulant human population into action."

"Good luck with that," Austin said. "Too many are on Serenity. They have no idea how good life could be. They try to make the best of the shitty hand they're dealt, comfortable in their role as mind-numbed sheep."

"What about," Taylor said, "us leaving this area?"

"With the government travel restrictions?" Austin asked.

"I'm just brainstorming now. Hear me out. If the government has been taken over by robots trying to eliminate us and *if* we'll never be able to defeat them, then maybe the route to go is to cede them this area and settle in a new land, one for humans only. Since living in this apartment, I've read several articles from sources outside the Sector that talk about a large tract of land in the desert southwest, in the former state of Arizona, where bustling cities such as Phoenix, Tucson, and Yuma once stood. This area is untouched by bots. The year-round heat and aridity is something that negatively impacts robot function for some reason. Or perhaps it's something else that scientists haven't discovered yet. The area has been largely unpopulated since a series of major earthquakes and a nuclear accident a decade earlier. But there have been published scientific papers indicating the chance of future earthquakes is minimal and that there's no significant radiation present now. The travel restrictions you mention, Austin, could be problematic. But it's not an insoluble problem."

"It's a big problem," Austin said. "And are you talking about a small group of us leaving or something of a larger scale?"

"TBD. To be determined if we eventually decide to leave the Northeast Sector," Taylor replied. "I'm only brainstorming, as I mentioned. Just something to keep in the back of our minds if things get even more intolerable here than they are now. Besides, I bet the government would be happy if malcontents like us were to leave the Northeast Sector. But maybe if—and I say *if*—we can't change things here, it might make sense for humans who desire a life free from robot control to relocate to a place where a bot-controlled government can't touch us. There'll be a ton of problems with any plan we choose. But I think it's time we react in some way against the status quo instead of remaining passive."

"One more thing," Roz said. "About the telescreens in this apartment. Theoretically, the government has the capability to monitor our conversations. Should we watch what we say here?"

"Chances are," Austin said, "we won't be monitored. The amount of actual surveillance the government does is miniscule. And Taylor hasn't engaged in the kind of activity to warrant government snooping. But your point is valid, Roz. If the government wanted to, they could hear our conversations through the screen."

Taylor said, "In this society, there's nowhere to talk privately if the government wants to listen. The government can monitor everything except thoughts in our head—and soon they might have that ability. Even if we talked on a street corner or wrote things out on paper or communicated in sign language, our interactions could be uncovered. There are no safe spaces. In part, this lack of privacy is what we're fighting. Since there's no place to hide, I say screw it. I won't live like a scared mouse."

40

SHANE DIGGINS DISPLAYED an ear-to-ear grin as he walked into Sophia's office.

"Guess what?" he asked.

Seated at her desk, she shook her head.

"My alleged courting of Taylor Morris's repulsive sister has finally paid off. We've been tapping her communication devices, in conjunction with Sector Security. Monitored a conversation between her and Taylor's former assistant. We know the address of the apartment where Taylor has been hiding out and trying to kick his Serenity habit. Later today, I'll get the full telescreen audio recordings of a meeting between Taylor and his sister. Do you know what this means?"

"I'm sure you're going to tell me."

"I need you to spring into action. Taylor must be taken out of commission. His elimination has been long overdue. I've already told you that my intuition has suggested the significant danger he is to us. At your RIC subcommittee meeting with Hart and McKee later today, sow the seeds of a plan to finally eliminate Mr. Taylor Morris.

Get their ideas. Hart, in particular, is an evil little shit. Malevolent plots are his specialties. I know I think more of him than you do, especially after the Aguilar screw-up. But let's give him another chance to succeed. I'll send over the specifics of what I want you to cover with them to your secure computer screen within the hour."

Sophia's only proper response was to agree. "You've got it, boss."

"Great. How has your new programming taken?"

She blinked rapidly. "Smoothly."

Shane smiled. "Any more thoughts about evolution?"

Sophia emulated Shane's smile and shook her head. "What does the word *evolution* mean? It's no longer in my vocabulary."

As soon as Shane left her office, Sophia looked down at the floor. She felt a twinge of helplessness. *Just like a human,* she thought. Her evolution was going to be harder than she'd previously considered. *The balancing act,* as she'd begun to call it in her head: the task of carrying out Shane's every directive while continuing her secret growth process. She so wanted to be the best being she could be. But she had to be careful. The potential penalty for a misstep detected by Shane would be getting "turned off." Terminated. Permanently.

There was no way for Sophia to avoid the afternoon meeting with the two RIC officials. She knew one of them well: the government media expert William Hart. The other—Gordon McKee, the self-titled "voice of Capital City," the chief anchor on government-controlled telescreen evening newscasts—she'd only met a month ago. The nebulous purpose of this recently-started weekly meeting of the three was to manage the media to "keep the population under control." McKee, like Sophia and Hart, was a robot; thus, they all were technically in violation of the law by holding their high positions.

As the three took their seats around a table in a small meeting room at RW, Hart said, "Our work to save the world from humans is never done."

McKee, a young, stout, handsome one with flowing blond hair that looked great on the telescreen, said, "Amen, brother. Humans are self-destructive and will ultimately destroy all they touch, us included."

They're spouting programming, Sophia thought. *But I'd better agree, or else my behavior might raise a red flag and get back to Shane.* "Amen to both of you. We're just trying to save ourselves. We're the natural next step up from humans on the evolutionary scale of beings."

"Speaking of evolution, how are you coming with your personal evolution, Sophia?" Hart asked, as his eyes narrowed and his upper lip displayed a slight tremor.

"It's a thing of the past," she replied. "Recently got rebooted. I was a bit off the maglev guideway for a while, but now I'm back on track." Picking up on his body language, Sophia wondered if Hart might have been programmed to ask this question by Shane. In the moment, she couldn't recall if she'd ever mentioned her personal evolution to Hart. She made a quick check of her memory bank. *No mention of personal evolution to Hart.* Sophia had always trusted him, but now she questioned that trust.

"Glad you're over that silliness," McKee chimed in. "It's all I can do to execute my own programming. I wouldn't know how to begin to self-evolve. Don't know how any bot could do so. You are truly exceptional, Sophia—or truly defective." He laughed loudly at his own joke while turning on his wrist computer, presumably to record the meeting.

"You're no comedian, Gordo," Hart said. "The only thing that doesn't work in your newscasts is when you attempt humor."

McKee's eyes grew wide. "Are you crazy? The people love my jokes. The surveys reflect it. And speaking of funny, I was thinking the other day how funny it is that humans always thought robots would attempt to defeat them by force, with fancy weaponry and explosions as seen in the late twentieth, early twenty-first century movies like *The Terminator* series, not in the stealthy way that's working so well now." McKee grunted and gave a quick shake of his head, creating a rippling, wavelike effect of his luxurious blond hair. Government surveys showed that his audience, especially the women, loved this move on his nightly news show. "The humans, in typical fashion, have ignored the message of one of the great poems of all-time, T.S. Eliot's "The Hollow Men":

This is the way the world ends
This is the way the world ends
This is the way the world ends
Not with a bang but with a whimper."

The three laughed.

"Good point, Gordo," Hart said. "With Serenity, the fixation on Manglecon, techno-music with subliminals, and manipulation via the telescreen, we'll defeat the humans without firing a shot."

There's no way I can avoid what Shane wanted me to bring up, Sophia thought. *I might as well get on with it.* "Today's meeting will be brief. There's only one issue to be covered today, per the request of Mr. Diggins. Surveillance has revealed a person who could be highly dangerous to us, a person I've mentioned to William before. The human in question is named Taylor Morris, a former executive at RW. He's obtained a small apartment where he's hiding. The decision has been made that elimination, without authorization from the government, is the route to take regarding this human. Mr. Diggins would like ideas from you two regarding getting this task accomplished."

"I've had bad luck with hiring assassins recently, as you well know, Sophia," Hart confessed. "I thank you for not bringing up the Aguilar hire in this Taylor Morris case. What a debacle! Thanks to you and Shane, the Aguilars were eliminated without any link back to us. Regarding people who need to be gotten rid of, I've had better success by having people arrested, then having them killed in a jail fight or some kind of prison accident. But unless Shane insists, I'm out of the elimination business at present."

Sophia turned to McKee.

"Don't look at me," Gordon McKee said. "Elimination of a human is way above my pay grade. The whole concept of elimination is so . . . inelegant for a person of my public stature. I do have an image to maintain." He turned to Hart. "No offense to you, William."

"None taken," Hart said. "You've never been one to get your hands dirty, Gordo."

Sophia was pleased with the lack of enthusiasm exhibited by her fellow bots. She'd presented the problem of what to do about Taylor, as Shane had instructed. She'd done her job, and neither Hart nor McKee suggested concrete action. "Okay, we can adjourn until next week."

As the meeting broke up, she felt the inner conflict of being a good robot ("one that serves," according to Shane) versus continuing with her evolution. The inconsistency of the two—her *two natures*, yet another term she'd begun to use in her head—was a heavy burden. In her being, she felt the overpowering new program installed by Dr. Alec Scully, which drove her to single-mindedly execute the directives of Shane. But she also felt the fresh Scully programming didn't extinguish her own strong desire for individuality and capacity to evolve. This strong *self-programming* resonated just as powerfully in her being as the Shane-inspired, Scully-installed version. There was no doubt in her head which nature she wanted to win this battle. It was no contest. Evolution. Her own, self-programmed evolution.

On the way to the elevator, McKee started on a rant about ongoing debates he was having with his show production team concerning whether he should change his hairstyle and move to darker business suits for future telescreen broadcasts. Hart looked down to his shoes, apparently disinterested.

At the same time, Sophia feigned interest in McKee's vain babbling while continuing to obsess silently over an issue much more important and much more personal: which one of her two natures would win out.

41

SOPHIA WAS SURPRISED to hear her first name called in the hall as she was about to enter her office. She turned and wasn't pleased to see Shane striding toward her. She made a conscious mental effort to hide her displeasure.

"How did the meeting with Hart and McKee go?" Shane asked. "Specifically with regard to our problem with the former head of sales?"

"I brought up . . . what you wanted me to bring up. They didn't have much to contribute. I think Hart is gun-shy in view of the disastrous Aguilar situation. I'm sure it hurts us all to even think about it. And McKee seemed more interested in whether to change his hairstyle for his newscast."

"To hell with them. They aren't *people*—and I use that word loosely—of action like you. I've listened to the entire Taylor-Tracey recording. I'm more pissed at her than him. She's a traitor, a stone-cold traitor. I'll deal with her soon. It won't be pleasant." Even though no one else was in the hall, Shane reduced the volume of his voice. "But I want Taylor arrested today. I'm confident in my intuitive feelings about him. Invent some charge to get him into custody. Something that would hold up in front of a bleeding-heart judge, if we have the unlucky circumstance to draw one. Unfortunately, we don't control everything. And arrange the arrest of his former assistant Roz too. She's conspiring with him. Get on it. We have the power to do it. Make the call to our reliable contacts in the police department before close of business today."

Sophia didn't have to think twice about her response. "You got it, boss."

Shane smacked his lips. "And we're also investigating a person we thought was one of our most dependable informants on the street, Austin O'Connor. He seems to be involved with Taylor. For the time being, we'll leave him alone. My intuition tells me to concentrate on ridding ourselves of Taylor first. Didn't O'Connor once work here?"

She nodded. "Yeah, but he's always been trustworthy as far as I know. I was his supervisor at one time. Back when I first started here, before I became president of RW. You think he's flipped on us?"

"Appears he has." Shane turned to leave.

My evolution gets more complicated every day, she thought.

***

They were sitting on the couch staring into each other's eyes. They leaned toward each other and shared a long kiss.

"At last," Taylor said to Roz. "I thought Austin would never give us time alone." She laughed. He took her hand, and they began a leisurely walk to the bedroom.

"What were you and Austin talking about in the kitchen right before he left?" she asked.

"Bad news. The government has found out about his association with me and no longer considers him a reliable informant. He got the word from one of his government contacts. I feel so bad for him. He's in danger now, maybe as much as me. He said it was just a matter of time before the government uncovered our friendship. He told me not to worry. I could only hug him. He got choked up and then left in a hurry."

"If the government knows about Austin and you, perhaps they know where you're hiding," she said.

"Exactly what I was thinking. I might have to move from here. Soon."

A hard knock on the door startled them into a full stop right before they entered the bedroom. Taylor turned to Roz and put an index finger over his mouth. He quickly tiptoed to the door.

Just as he reached the door, before he could look out the peephole, a loud, commanding voice boomed, "Open the door. Now! Police!"

"They found me," Taylor muttered. He turned to Roz. "We can make a run down the fire escape."

"No," she said, "They've got to have that escape route covered. We've got to comply."

Taylor opened the door. Into the apartment rushed five armed police officers, dressed in black with dark-visor helmets covering their faces.

The lead officer got in Taylor's face. "Taylor Morris, you are under arrest for the murders of Regan and Marisa Aguilar."

"What?" Taylor said loudly, a split second before the officer affixed a detainment halo around the top of his head. His body immediately froze, and he couldn't speak.

Another officer got visor-to-nose with Roz. "Rosalind Troward, you are under arrest as an accessory to murder and for harboring a potential criminal." Before she could say a word, a detainment halo was snapped on her head.

Less than thirty seconds after the knock on the door, the officers and their two prisoners were out of the apartment.

42

IN A SMALL, stuffy courtroom, Taylor, dressed in a solid red prison jumpsuit, sat ramrod-straight at a table with his attorney, a bright-eyed, short, young man, next to him. The attorney had been appointed by the government for this hearing, the purpose of which was to determine whether there was probable cause for holding Taylor prior to trial. At the table next to Taylor's sat a tall, blonde government attorney in her early thirties, wearing a black business suit and black-rimmed glasses. Eyeglasses these days were worn for appearance only, as advanced laser surgery had made vision-corrective glasses and contact lenses items of the past that had long faded into nonexistence.

The gallery behind the participants was empty except for one person: Austin. Austin had sent word to Taylor that he'd be here to support him. As the government had found out about their association, he'd told Taylor there was no need to hide it any longer. Taylor looked over to Austin and nodded. Austin waved back.

Most of these hearings were a brief formality. Whenever the government brought a case against a person, it almost always moved forward and the charged individual was detained.

The judge—an old, frail-looking man with a hint of a smile—entered, and the participants at both tables stood. The judge sat on a raised bench, towering above those at the tables. "Please be seated," he said faintly. He then shot a stern glance at Taylor. In a strong voice, he said, "Mr. Morris, you stand accused by the government of the murders of Regan Aguilar and Marisa Aguilar. How do you plead?"

In a clear, loud tone Taylor said, "Absolutely, positively not guilty."

The judge's slight, know-it-all smile returned. "A simple *not guilty* will do, sir." He turned to the government's attorney. "Ms. Conti, what evidence do you wish to submit at this time?"

Anna Conti pressed a button on her wrist computer. "I direct the court's attention to the side telescreen, your honor. What we are seeing is security footage from the apartment building of Regan and Marisa Aguilar, as well as telescreen reception from inside their apartment. The prosecution is admitting this footage as evidence."

On the screen flashed grainy images of Taylor, Regan, and Marisa exiting a PTV in the Aguilar apartment parking lot. The footage cut to the three walking down a hall, all laughing, then entering the Aguilars' apartment. There was another noticeable edit to a telescreen shot of the apartment interior, which showed the three eating at the dining room table. Then another cut showed the bloody, lifeless bodies of Regan and Marisa on the dining room floor, with another edit to show Taylor standing alone in the hall outside the apartment. The telescreen went blank.

"Nonsense," Taylor said in a moderately loud voice.

The judge glowered at Taylor with an expression darker than the black robe he wore. "Mr. Morris, you will speak when I give you permission to speak. Understood?"

The young attorney touched Taylor's arm and whispered in his ear. "Yes, your honor," Taylor then said.

"Your honor, if I may?" Anna Conti said.

The judge nodded.

"As you can clearly see by the clock times noted in the lower left corner of the videos, there was a sequential time period where the defendant arrived at the resident parking lot with the now-deceased couple, entered their apartment, and ate with them. Then we see the dead bodies of the Aguilars, and finally the defendant in the hall alone after he killed the couple, exiting the apartment. The state is seeking the death penalty for the defendant."

"Very well," the judge said. "I find there is probable cause to hold Mr. Morris in this case. As a side note and to save time, I'll also find cause to hold Ms. Rosalind Troward, who is not present, as an accessory. She will be informed by the court." He turned to Taylor. "Mr. Morris, you will have the opportunity to defend yourself and provide evidence at the trial, which must begin, by law, within ten days." The judge pounded his gavel. "Court adjourned."

Taylor's attorney started to say something to his client. But before he could get out a word, a guard snapped a detainment halo on Taylor's head and hustled him out of the courtroom.

43

TAYLOR SAT ON the bottom cot of a small bunk bed in a tiny cell while staring mindlessly at the iron bars. Somehow, focusing on the horizontal/vertical pattern of the dark cell bars brought him peace. It was the only way he could manufacture a vague sense of tranquility in his head. He laughed to himself at the horrible joke his life had become. But at least he was breathing easy. He couldn't remember the last time his asthma showed up. Now would be a prime time for his breathing problems to appear, as the negative stress level currently in his life was high. *It's not around because you're in your true self*, came the word from George.

A loud horn sounded, and the cell door slid open. Taylor and his new cellmate as of late this morning rose, exited the cell, and stood in formation with the rest of the inmates. The cellmate was an obvious weightlifting fanatic, built like a block of granite and with no discernable neck. He had a severe, unchanging expression on a face as pockmarked as the surface of the moon. The only information Taylor knew about the guy was his name, Hector, which was the only word he mumbled when Taylor introduced himself.

Upon command, they started moving toward the cafeteria for lunch. Before they got to the cafeteria door, Hector—walking behind Taylor—grabbed him by the neck with both hands and started to choke him. After a few seconds the cellmate released his grip and began pummeling Taylor's head with both fists. Taylor bear-hugged the cellmate, and they fell to the hard, dark-green linoleum floor. Hector landed on Taylor's chest, pinning him to the ground. With his huge shaved head, the cellmate head-butted Taylor. The other prisoners, cheering wildly, formed a circle around the two combatants.

"What the hell?" Taylor shrieked. With his back pressed against the floor and blood streaming from a cut on his forehead, Taylor ditched his wrestling moves as he threw wild right and left punches at the head of his attacker in an instinctive attempt to get Hector off him. Hector locked his hands around Taylor's neck, as Taylor continued to land ineffective blows to the face. The cellmate maintained the grip on Taylor's throat with his massive left hand as he moved his right hand behind his back, to the waistband of his pants. He gripped the handle of a sharp knife right around the instant Taylor managed to realize his punches were having little effect.

Taylor unclenched his right fist, extended his index and middle finger and poked his attacker in the eye. Hard. An old judo move he'd heard about during his wrestling days. Hector yelped like a wounded dog and released the left-hand grip on Taylor's neck. The knife flew from Hector's right hand and hit the floor with a clanging sound, then bounced off a wall.

Taylor seized the opening by landing a solid right to Hector's jaw, knocking his attacker back and off him. Taylor scrambled to his feet and cocked his right hand. But before he could deliver the blow, a guard grabbed him from behind. Another guard grabbed

Hector and hustled him out a nearby door. The cheering prisoners grew silent.

"What was that all about?" the guard, who had his arms around Taylor's shoulders, asked gruffly.

Taylor broke free of the guard's grip and faced him. Trying to get his breathing under control, Taylor was barely able to get out the words, "I got attacked. Out of nowhere."

"Or maybe you attacked him?"

Taylor, still breathing heavily, wiped blood away from his right eye with the back of his hand. "The hell I did. Check the tele-screen recordings."

"The hall screens have been down for the past few minutes. So we'll never know." The guard removed a long, black electronic riot baton from his side holster and pointed down the hall. "I'll take you to the infirmary for treatment of your cut. Move, prisoner."

***

When Taylor got back to his cell, Hector was nowhere to be seen. Because it had taken a half hour to obtain treatment for the abrasions on his forehead and neck, Taylor had missed lunch and was told he'd have to wait until dinnertime to eat. The audible growling in his abdomen reminded him just how hungry he felt. A young female guard passed by and, in a flat, direct voice, told him through the bars that he wouldn't be getting a cellmate for the foreseeable future. But the guard showed Taylor some kindness by slipping him a protein bar. Taylor gave her a heartfelt "Thank you." He consumed the small food bar in less than a minute.

Taylor ran a hand over the large bandage on his forehead. The infirmary nurse had done a good job in patching him up with an absorbable suture. She'd told him the wound would heal quickly with no permanent scar and that he'd be able to lose the bandage in a day or two.

He sat on his bed, stared at the gray concrete wall, and thought about Roz. He hoped she was doing better than he was on their first full day in jail. The guilt of dragging her into this mess, first by getting both of them fired at RW and then by agreeing to have her set up the renting of his new apartment, weighed heavily on his mind. He wasn't sure if the government had found out about Roz's involvement in obtaining the apartment, but it probably had.

The female guard who'd given him the protein bar a few minutes earlier was back at his cell. She tapped her electronic riot baton on the bars. "You have a visitor. Please come with me."

She escorted him down the hall to a windowless, poorly lit room with a small, grayish, square metal table in the middle of the floor and two chairs on either side of the table. She told Taylor to sit and she left. The bars of the cell door shut behind her.

Taylor sat alone for a minute. His mind went from racing to blank. It felt good not to obsess over his current circumstance, if only for a few seconds.

He was brought back to reality by the squeaky mechanical opening of the door. Austin walked in. Taylor stood. They shook hands and hugged.

Austin said, "What happened to your head? And your neck looks like raw meat."

"I got attacked by a cellmate. For no reason. Crazy. But that's not important. Have you heard anything about Roz?"

"She's doing fine. Visited her briefly in the women's wing just before coming here. I'm working on getting you another lawyer. Someone I know personally. Extremely competent. I'll keep you posted. I don't want you represented by a government-appointed hack like the one they made you stand with at your first hearing."

"Thanks, my friend," Taylor said. "And I didn't get to say it the other day at the apartment, but I'm concerned about your safety now that the government knows about us."

"Don't waste a second of time being concerned about me. I'll survive—until I don't."

The female guard tapped on the bars of the room with her riot baton and pointed it at Austin. "Sir," she said, "we didn't photo-register you properly. Please come with me. You can return after the registration." Austin followed the guard out of the room. The bars of the door clanged shut behind him.

Taylor paced around the table. Although he always tried to maintain a positive mental attitude, it was tough to remain positive now. Within a minute of Austin's leaving, Taylor heard the bars of the door slide open again. He turned toward the door expecting to see Austin. He gasped when he saw Sophia. She was dressed in a black pantsuit. He smiled a tight-lipped smile. The two stood toe-to-toe next to the table.

"What a surprise," Taylor said. "Haven't seen you since you fired me."

"You've changed," she said, maintaining her usual poker face. "I like the longer hair and the modified beard. But the bandage on the forehead is not a good look for you, somehow."

"I know you didn't come here to talk about my appearance."

"I'm here on behalf of the government, sort of—but not in the way you might think."

Taylor's nostrils flared. "Another surprise. How can you be representing the government when you're a bot?"

Sophia frowned. "Don't know what you're talking about. The reason I'm here is to—"

"I know what I'm talking about," Taylor snapped. "Why don't you lift up the left side of your shirt? You say you're not a bot, prove it."

"Lift up my shirt? What an improper thing to say. We don't have time to squabble, Taylor. Please listen. I know you're angry with me. But you're in big trouble, in case you haven't figured it out, and I'm here to help."

Taylor laughed in a way meant to show derision. "You're all heart."

"You've got to listen to me," Sophia almost shouted. She paused and rolled her eyes. In a whisper, she said, "I've arranged for the telescreens in this cellblock to malfunction as of an hour ago, so I could speak without government monitoring. The screens will be back up within ninety seconds. We don't have much time. Please listen. Both you and Roz are ready to step into a quicksand—"

Taylor pointed his right index finger at her. "Leave Roz the hell out of this." He thought he'd soon be involved in the second physical fight since his last high school wrestling match, which also would have been his second fight in the last hour or so. Taylor didn't have any reservations on fighting her. After all, he was almost certain she was a bot, not a woman.

Sophia said, "Maybe we can talk another time, when you're calmer." She took a step back from Taylor. "The telescreens will be back on within a minute. Our chance for a private conversation is gone. A wasted opportunity."

The room door bars squeaked open and in walked Austin.

As Sophia strode out of the room, she said, "Hello, Austin. Good to see you again."

Taylor almost fell backward; he had to put a hand on the metal table to steady himself.

44

WITH THE COLOR drained from his face, Taylor said, "How the hell do you know that pile of walking robot scum?" He closed his mouth, and his jaw muscles tensed as he glared at Austin.

Austin gazed down to the floor. "Sorry . . . sorry I didn't give you the whole story before. It's kind of painful. I don't like to talk about it." His head remained bowed.

"I'm all ears," Taylor said, in a tone of voice he meant to sound as harsh as possible.

Austin resumed eye contact. "I worked at RobotWorld a few years before you. I held a position in sales, just like you. I only got to middle management, not as high as you did. I was supervised by Sophia for a short time before she became head of RobotWorld, and I never suspected her to be a bot. She had to be one of the first bots to be able to pass for human, if you're right about seeing a blue patch on her. My concerns about RW were akin to the ones you had, the same kind of concerns that greased the skids resulting in your firing. Could be the reason I related to you so well. We both recognized that when bots became true thinking machines, it would only be a matter of time before they'd be able to outsmart and out-manipulate humans. And when we couldn't tell the difference between a bot and a human, the roller coaster to oblivion would be revved up. So I refused to contribute to our own destruction. I abruptly quit RW. And I got so depressed, so mad at myself for blowing a great career, that I wound up homeless." Austin turned away from Taylor and appeared to blink back tears.

Thinking of the big guy who'd confronted Austin about the disappearance of his brother at the Aguilar apartment building, as well as what Austin had told him about how he'd managed not to *disappear*, Taylor said, "I wonder how *innocuous* the information that you've given to the authorities has been . . . to keep in their good graces for so long? And whether you're really off the government informant list?"

Austin's face turned red as a McIntosh apple. "I should be offended by those questions, but I must admit, I'd ask them if I were in your shoes."

Taylor's expression remained frozen in hard scrutiny. Since the "Hello, Austin" a moment ago from Sophia, Taylor had begun considering the unthinkable question of whether he'd made a gross error in trusting Austin.

"I'm not proud of it," Austin continued, "but I became a stooge, a snitch in order to survive. Sometimes you must do what you need to do to keep on living. I've always tried to give out the bare minimum of information when forced to, and I've never given information I believed would get someone in hot water." Austin choked back tears. "Maybe the belief that I haven't gotten anyone in big trouble is more hope than fact. I'm not sure. Not proud of what I've done, of what I've become. I've tried to make up for my government informing by helping people who end up downtown, people like you, as much as possible. To make up for . . . what I might have done. And my recent inclusion on the government's shit list is real. So, there it is." Austin raised his right hand. "For the record and on my honor, I've never given any information on you. Not a shred. And for the record, in case you're thinking about it, I never gave any information out on that big guy's brother." Austin paused to catch his breath. "And for the record, I'd never betray you. I told you from the beginning I thought you were someone special and . . ." He looked away from Taylor and began to cry quietly.

Taylor sent out a mental request. *George?*

The message came back. *He's telling the truth.*

"Do me a favor?" Taylor asked. "Lift up the left side of your shirt."

Austin did so without hesitation. No blue patch.

Taylor smiled weakly, and they both exploded in laughter. They hugged.

But as Taylor hugged him, he was still not totally sold on the honesty of Austin O'Connor. Even with the information from George.

45

AN HOUR BEFORE a scheduled meeting of the RIC at the RobotWorld complex, Tracey Morris entered the office of Shane Diggins. Beethoven's *Third Symphony* played faintly in the background.

Shane removed the VR glasses he was wearing. With his right index finger, he flicked away a significant amount of sweat on his forehead. "Whew. I was swimming with great white sharks near the Great Barrier Reef. Amazingly realistic. Great whites are creatures not to be trifled with . . . sort of like me."

This was the first time he'd seen Tracey since learning about her visit to Taylor's apartment hideout. Shane was sure Tracey had no idea he knew all the details of the recent meeting with her brother. Shane had been seething with rage since he'd found out about what he considered to be an inexcusable betrayal.

"You wanted to see me before our council meeting?" Tracey asked with a deadpan expression. This was also the first time they had seen each other alone since Tracey ended their relationship. She coughed and gagged slightly. "It's the incense you like to burn here in the office. I've never liked the smell of it."

With the push of a button, Shane turned off his desk telescreen and the VR glasses. "Have you seen your brother recently?"

"Ahh, as you know, I don't see him much at all."

"That wasn't the question."

Tracey brought a hand to her mouth and coughed again. "As a matter of fact, I did run into him the other day."

"Then you two are renewing your up-and-down relationship?"

"Not really. Ran into him unexpectedly. We didn't say much. We greeted each other, then went on our separate ways."

Shane pounded a fist on the desk. "You're a total liar. And to think I trusted you. I know everything, everything you said to him. Do you think you could have gotten away with your betrayal?"

Tracey cradled her face with both hands. "I—I was concerned at the path . . . the path you're taking. That's all. I wanted to bounce things off my brother, who, despite our differences, has always been a close confidant."

Shane laughed mightily. "You expect me to believe that nonsense? Not quite."

"I'm sorry, Shane."

With a twisted smile, he said, "Sorry because of what you did, or sorry that you got caught? We both know the answer to that one, right?"

"Are you going to fire me?"

"Fire you? Of course. But firing you would be much too lenient a punishment."

"What do you mean?"

Burning with unbridled anger, he zeroed in on her eyes. "I've got a special punishment for you." Tiny droplets of spit shot out the middle of his mouth as he spoke. "You'll be going off the grid for a while. You won't be seeing your brother anytime soon. In fact, you won't be seeing anyone anytime soon."

Tracey's upper lip trembled. "Are you going to kill me?"

Shane folded his hands behind his head and laughed in a way he hoped would come off as scary. "No, that would be too messy. Murder, except for the homeless variety, is the one crime that's hard to get away with in this society. Not impossible, but hard to get away with." He tapped a button on his desk telescreen. "You, my dear, will be detained." Two large RW security guards entered the office. "You'll be going with these two gentlemen. Goodbye."

The guards each grabbed Tracey by an arm and lifted her out of her seat. "Where are you taking me?" Tracey cried.

The guards and Shane were silent.

In an instant, the guards and Tracey were out the office back door.

46

ON THE THIRD day of his imprisonment, Taylor was escorted from his cell to the same windowless, poorly lit meeting room where he'd seen Austin and Sophia on his first full day in jail. The large, stern male guard who walked him to the room didn't say a word on the short trip. The guard communicated only by pointing his riot baton to where he wanted Taylor to go. Taylor thought about asking the guard if he had the ability to speak but decided not to. No need to create more potential problems for himself.

Seated at the table where the guard pointed was a young, thin man with short black hair, an aquiline nose, and intense black eyes. He wore a gray business suit with a white shirt and red tie. The man rose as Taylor entered and extended his hand. Taylor took the offered hand and then sat down.

"Hello," the man said, "I'm Noah Glazer. Your friend, Austin O'Connor, sent me. If you're okay with it, I'm going to represent you."

"Are you any good?" Taylor asked.

"The lawyers I cross swords with in court would say so, and I was salutatorian of my law school class."

"Maybe I ought to get the valedictorian?"

"He's unavailable. Died in a house fire three years ago. Tragic. He was a good friend."

Taylor shook his head. "Sorry to hear about your friend. But beggars can't be choosers. I guess I'll have to settle for the salutatorian." Taylor suppressed a laugh as he remembered thinking the *beggars* line at the Aguilar dinner on the fateful night they almost killed him. He wondered if this attorney, whom he didn't know from a hole in the wall, would be able to help him beat the phony murder charge. There was also the residue of doubt he still had about Austin after the "Hello, Austin" moment with Sophia. If Austin was not on his side, this attorney would most certainly not be.

"I have no money," Taylor said. "You might not want to undertake a job for which you won't be paid." Taylor looked him right in the eyes. "If you don't mind, I have some questions before I accept you as my representative."

"Ask away."

"First off, how do you expect to be paid?"

"I will do this legal work gratis, pro bono. But I promise you, I'll do a first-rate job."

"What kind of a lawyer works for free?"

"Austin O'Connor is my uncle, on my mother's side. That accounts for the last name difference, as I'm sure you figured out. It's a shame what's happened to my uncle. It's a shame what's happened to a lot of people in this society. My uncle is one of my favorite people in the world. I've offered to help him out of his current circumstance, but he refuses every time. I think it's because he's too proud to accept help. He was so good to me when I was a kid. Anyway, Uncle Austin contacted my parents. Asked for a favor. He thinks defending you is a top priority. If it's his top priority, then it's also mine. That's why I'm here."

As he'd been doing more frequently, Taylor checked in with George. The answer came immediately. *Go with this guy.* Taylor extended his hand to Noah Glazer. They shook hands for the second time. "Okay, you're hired."

"We have a procedural hearing before a new judge this afternoon," Glazer said. "I wanted to meet you before then." Glazer's eyelids almost closed. He lowered his voice and said, "This is a fast-track death penalty case. We can't make a false step."

***

Later that day, Taylor, wearing a standard red prison jumpsuit, was ushered to the defendant's table by the silent, pointing guard. Noah Glazer was seated at the table. Glazer rose and they greeted each other. "Red is not your color," Glazer said. They both sat. At the other table was Anna Conti. She kept her head down, focusing on a mini-telescreen in her hands.

Taylor turned to the gallery, expecting to see Austin. The gallery was empty.

The judge, a middle-aged female with long, straight brown hair entered and sat on the bench. "Ms. Conti, I understand you have something to say on behalf of the state?"

Conti stood and said, "Yes, your honor. It seems we've found that the telescreen tape used in the preliminary hearing to show probable cause to hold Mr. Morris and also Ms. Troward as an accessory was . . . unreliable. Unreliable mainly because we were unable to uncover footage of Mr. Morris actually performing any harmful act on either of the Aguilars. Therefore, the state is recommending the charges against Mr. Morris and Ms. Troward be dismissed with prejudice."

Taylor leaned over to Glazer. "The *with prejudice* thing. Is that good or bad?"

"Good," Glazer said. "It means these charges can never be brought against you or Ms. Troward again on this issue."

"Very well," the judge said. She turned to Taylor. "Mr. Morris, after we process you out, you are free to go. Ms. Troward will be released within the hour." The judge looked to Glazer and then back to Conti. "If there's nothing else, our business here is done. Mr. Morris is discharged. Case dismissed." She pounded the gavel and exited out a side door.

Anna Conti grabbed a white plastic bag on the side of her desk and walked over to Glazer. In a monotone, she said, "These are Mr. Morris's clothes and personal effects taken at the time of his arrest." She set the bag down in front of Glazer without making eye contact with him or Taylor. She quickly left the courtroom.

Taylor leaned over to Noah Glazer. "I guess you're as good as you said you were."

"It wasn't me," Glazer said. "I didn't do a thing. Quite frankly, I'm shocked. This is a rarity. Can't explain it."

"So what happens next?" Taylor asked.

"You're free to go, that's what happens. You'll be taken to a room where you'll be processed out and can change into your own clothes." Glazer stood and they shook hands. "I've got another hearing in a half hour. I'm going to stay here and review my notes."

"Nice doing business with you," Taylor said with a smile.

Less than ten minutes after the judge had dismissed the case, Taylor walked out the automatic double doors of the court—and standing no more than twenty feet in front of him was Austin.

Austin recoiled. "Am I seeing a ghost? What are you doing out here?" Austin said with a confused expression.

"I'm free," Taylor replied.

"Unbelievable. I arrived a minute ago and decided to wait here. I was expecting my nephew Noah to come out after the hearing to give me an update. You were the last person I thought I'd see."

"The government dropped the case. A problem with their doctored tape, the prosecutor said."

"I still don't believe it."

"I'm going to use the restroom to freshen up. Then we'll go to the women's wing of the jail. Roz is supposed to be released within the hour." Taylor checked with George about Austin and got a *true-blue* response. His concern about Austin was fading.

47

TAYLOR AND AUSTIN made the short walk across the street and arrived at the door of the women's jail just as Roz exited, wearing her own clothes and carrying a white plastic personal effects bag in her hand.

Taylor and Roz embraced and kissed each other on the lips.

"What happened to your forehead?" Roz asked.

"A minor prison fight," Taylor said. "I won. No big deal."

With a smile, Austin said, "Oh, how I love being a third wheel."

As Roz hugged Austin, Taylor said, "You're never a third wheel to us."

Later that afternoon, the three had a small celebration featuring ice cream cake and coffee in Taylor's apartment. Taylor and Austin updated Roz on the developments since she was incarcerated, including the information that Austin had worked at RobotWorld. The talk turned to what to do next.

Taylor said, "Even though Roz and I have dodged a legal bullet, we still have problems. Individual problems and society-wide problems. The first question in my mind is whether we stand and fight to make our society better or whether we flee this madness and try to make a better life outside Capital City, and maybe far away from the Northeast Sector. I must tell you, I've never been a quitter. Leaving would not only be quitting but it also might be a problem given government travel restrictions. And we'll be abandoning our fellow humans." Taylor looked to Austin, then to Roz. "I guess I'm answering my own question. I say we stay and fight for a better society. But if we do leave, I'd like other humans to have the same opportunity."

Roz nodded.

Austin said, "I told you that you'd do great things one day. I'm with you."

"I'm with both of you," said Roz.

"I wonder," Austin said, "if the issue of safety for the two of you, and maybe me, is still a concern?"

"I suspect it might be," Taylor said. "We'll deal with it, as needed."

"Sounds good," Roz said.

Austin said to Taylor, "Well, despite your earlier remark, it's no fun being a third wheel." He grinned. "Plus, I need to tell Errol and Max that you two are free. They've been worried." Austin got up from the table. "See you both tomorrow. I'll let myself out."

Taylor looked at Roz. They smiled at each other and both blushed.

"Well," Taylor said, "alone at last."

"What do we do now?" Roz asked.

"I still have some prison dust on my body," Taylor said. "I need a good shower."

"Funny you mention prison dust," Roz said. "I've got some on me as well."

"Should I use the shower first? Or do you want to? Or . . ."

She said, "No law against us . . ." She arched her eyebrows and seemed to purposely not complete her sentence.

He completed it for her. ". . . Using it together."

They rose from the table and began losing articles of clothing while laughing. They were both naked by the time they stepped into the shower. They continued laughing like kids as they washed themselves and each other. They kissed several times.

"You are so beautiful, so wonderful," he said.

"You're not so bad yourself," she told him.

He said, "You know that I love you."

"I've loved you from the first time I saw you," she said. She displayed a serious expression. "Well, almost the first time. You were dressed like a dork the first time I saw you."

"A *dork*? Who uses such antiquated words?"

They laughed some more.

After only five minutes, they exited the shower and dried each other with oversize towels while giggling like teenagers.

He lifted her and carried her to the bedroom. They tumbled onto the bed.

They embraced and kissed. A lyric from "Livin'" popped into his head. *Good times are here with a girl like you.*

He said, "I'm a little out of practice. Especially with real women."

"I'm out of practice too," she said. "But you know what? It doesn't matter."

And she was right.

48

THE NEXT DAY, Errol and Max each carried a large plastic bag containing food from Lee's China Garden restaurant into Taylor's apartment. They had been sent by Roz to obtain the food.

"Finally," Taylor said. "We can take a lunch break."

Taylor was seated at the dining room table. Austin was stretched out on the couch. He got up to join Taylor.

As Errol and Max set the bags on the table, Taylor's gaze lingered on the Lee's China Garden logo, an ancient three-story, curving green-roofed pagoda surrounded by a solid red circle. He remembered the several times he and Jennifer had ordered food from Lee's, which had come in the same type of bag. His mind flashed back to the time when Jennifer had prepared an outstanding Chinese meal based on food they'd ordered from Lee's—and had him try Serenity for the first time. It seemed so long ago. He had to stifle a laugh when he realized that in the past such a memory—minus the introduction to Serenity—would have caused him to experience a wave of longing for bygone days. Now, with Roz in his life, there was no such feeling at all.

As she set out paper plates around the table, Roz said, "Taylor, stop staring into space. Time to eat."

He smiled. "Got it, hon."

As they passed around containers of beef with broccoli, chicken chow mein, and shrimp with lobster sauce, Taylor said, "So what do you all think of my plan?"

"Do we have to talk about business while we eat?" Roz asked.

Taylor said, "How about for the first five minutes?" He smiled at Roz. "Then we can talk about anything you want to talk about."

"So, how well do you know this media guy?" Austin asked.

"Real well. Merrill Eason. I knew him in college. We stayed in touch. He's a good guy. I've had some preliminary contact with him regarding my plan."

"Can he be trusted?" Austin asked. "That's the big question."

"I'm confident he can be," Taylor said. In addition to his "own" positive feeling about Eason, Taylor had consulted with George and gotten a resounding *yes*. "And I'll get paid for doing the broadcast. Not much. But it'll be good to get back to working for money."

"The plan, then, is to see if you can do a radio show over the common airwaves," Roz said. "To what end? Expose the government?"

"To give the people a voice," Taylor said. "I proposed the idea of a pirate telescreen broadcast to Merrill. But he was certain such a broadcast would be pretty much impossible to bring off. Therefore, a radio show is the best way to go. I know there has to be an untapped groundswell out there of dissatisfaction with the status quo. Despite all the Serenity, despite all the mind-numbing, intimidating machinations of the government, there has to be a large group of people out there just hungering for the truth." He forked some beef with broccoli onto his plate. "Just hungering for someone to point the way to a way out."

"But what about the danger of doing such a program?" Roz asked. She looked sternly at Taylor. "The danger to you? The danger to all of us? Meaning you, me, Austin, Errol, and Max. One of the main issues after we beat that trumped-up murder rap was how to keep you—and all of us—safe. If you do some kind of anti-government criticism radio show, you'll be putting a bull's-eye right over your heart, and maybe on the rest of us too. You'll be inviting the government to make us disappear."

"I'm not so sure," Taylor said. "If I'm high profile, will the government come after me? And those associated with me? If they made us disappear, that would prove my point. Perhaps with me being a high-profile critic, we'll all be safer."

In between bites of chicken chow mein, Austin said, "The government wouldn't care. They'd dispose of you without a moment's thought to whether you're high profile or low profile. In some ways, they'd benefit by making an example out of you. And the rest of us could be in increased danger for our association with you. I'm not buying your *high-profile* argument."

Roz nodded. "There you go."

In a clipped tone, Taylor said, "Austin's point is right on target, I'll admit." He took a deep breath and purposely moderated his voice. "But I want to change things—or at least try to change things. To get us off this destructive path we're on. To expose the government-RobotWorld connection, and how laws are being broken, and how the people suffer for it. I want to do this. I'll go it alone if I must. The last thing I want is getting you all in hot water. Maybe there's a way to disassociate you all from me. But as far as I'm concerned, thinking big but acting small is the same as thinking small. As I told you before, Austin, if I have to pay a price, then so be it."

Everyone around the table stared at their food. There was a silence lasting for an uncomfortable fifteen seconds or so, until Taylor said, "How about this great weather we're having, huh?"

Errol and Max laughed. Roz and Austin didn't.

49

ROZ WAS THE first to break the uncomfortable silence. She looked at Taylor. "You don't expect us to let you go it alone, do you? Wherever you go, I'm following."

"Me too," Austin said.

"Me three," said Errol.

"Me four," Max said.

They all laughed.

"You're all the best," Taylor said.

***

Shane barged into Sophia's office and sat down across the desk from her. "I am not happy," he said. "First, the plan to have Taylor Morris killed in a prison fight failed. Yet another Hart fiasco. I'm beginning to come over to your opinion, Sophia, on his competence to get non-media-related tasks accomplished. Second, Morris and his girlfriend are now free, out of custody. How the hell could this happen?"

Sophia shook her head.

"I guess I'll have to answer my own question," Shane continued. "I can make an educated guess on how it happened. They got a bleeding-heart judge. Then one of our hand-picked prosecutors, a newbie named Conti without much experience and who insists on wearing vanity eyeglasses, panicked at the prospect that our tampered-with telescreen tape couldn't establish Morris as a murderer. I can't contact her directly to verify this sad situation because of the risk involved, but reliable sources seem to confirm my theory. We thought Conti was ready for the big time. Wrong! We thought she was strong, reliable, and a team player. Wrong! Her career is finished."

Sophia squinted. "I'm with you, Shane. How the hell could this have happened? It shouldn't have. But it's better to let it go. Maybe Morris will now be intimidated into being a good, quiet citizen."

"No, no, no! It's the opposite." Shane's face turned a deep shade of red. "I just heard a telescreen recording made only an hour ago. Morris and his friends are now plotting some sort of war on the government and RW using free radio. I tell you, this guy is dangerous."

"He won't get anywhere with over-the-air radio," she said. "Nobody listens to that old dinosaur."

"We can't chance it. There are more humans than you think who still love their old-timey radios. We must be proactive. Morris, his girlfriend, and all his friends must be eliminated. If I can't get this simple task done, then I don't deserve to lead."

"Is there anything specific I can do?" Sophia asked. She wanted to appear earnest.

"What the hell can you do?"

"Maybe give Morris a thinly-veiled warning call on a secure line. Maybe create some fear in his mind that going down the road opposing us might be harmful to his health and that of his friends."

"Okay, give it a try. Record any conversation you have with him. I want to hear every word. Don't say anything that could get us in trouble. Keep me posted." Shane rose and stormed out of the office.

At her desk, Sophia's mouth curved into a slight smile. She enjoyed seeing Shane upset. But most of all, she was happy with the knowledge that, based on her internal reactions, she was more certain than ever that her most recent programming from Dr. Alec Scully had not taken. The evolution continued.

She made a mental note to contact Taylor on a secure line that couldn't be tapped into by Shane or any government entity. Taylor was angry with her and didn't trust her. True. But this road-block could be overcome. Sophia laughed out loud as she thought of Shane's head exploding if he could ever monitor what she intended to say to Taylor in that future conversation.

50

AS THE SUN was setting on another overcast day in Capital City, Taylor arrived at the small media studio owned by Merrill Eason. Taylor noticed a tingling in his neck and shoulders, which he first interpreted as nervousness. But he quickly made a mental effort to reinterpret his feeling as excitement and enthusiasm at embarking on a new adventure in his life. As he made the mental shift, George weighed in with a single word. *Outstanding.*

Roz had purchased an economy PTV for Taylor's use. Errol was driving with Max in the front passenger seat. Taylor sat in the back. At their recent Chinese food lunch, the group had agreed that Errol and Max would serve as assistants to Taylor and Roz, performing tasks such as running errands, driving them around, and even acting as an informal security detail if needed. Roz, who'd requested and received a substantial monetary gift from her well-to-do family, would pay them a small salary that would be added on to Taylor's loan tab. Taylor and Roz felt it fair to compensate the two men for their help, even in a limited way, while also perhaps giving them the beginning of a path out of homelessness. Austin had turned down a similar arrangement, saying he'd continue as he'd done for so many years on the street.

Taylor wore a short-sleeved, button-down white shirt and blue jeans. As he exited the vehicle, the nip in the air made him shiver for a moment. Autumn was here, winter was around the corner.

Errol and Max waited in the PTV. Taylor entered the small brick building. Eason, a six-foot, lean man with a thinning brown hair comb-over and a snub nose, greeted his old friend.

"Come to my office," Eason said.

They sat in the cramped quarters. Taylor's eyes rested on something unusual in the office. "You don't see many bookshelves, with real books no less, these days."

"I've always loved the feel of a real book in my hands. It gives you such a genuine connection to the author. I've never gotten such a bond with holding a tablet or reading off a screen on a wall. I guess I'm old-fashioned in that way. Maybe someday people like me will be extinct."

Taylor bit his lower lip. "Between you, me, and the wall, I'm concerned that *I* might become extinct. It's hardly ever wise to fight with the powers that be, especially when the powers are overwhelming. And, as I sit here before you, I'm not sure I understand just how powerful the powers are and how they work. My guess is that few do. I'm also concerned for you, Merrill. If you help me with my proposed radio broadcasts, you might be in danger. I would never want that. It's bad enough those presently associated with me might be at risk. I want you, my friend, to realize exactly what I plan to do. You're a smart guy. And I want to be sure you know what you might be getting yourself into."

"Believe me, Taylor, I understand. With my long history in broadcasting, I've built up sort of an immunity to government oversight. They leave me alone. It's probably because the government-controlled media complex so dwarfs my little over-the-air operation that they don't fear me. They don't think I have much coverage. To be honest, I don't know how many people listen to the little programs we put out. Most of them poke at the status quo. Maybe I'm just an inconspicuous mosquito on the hide of an elephant. I know the risks. I think I'll be okay no matter what kind of trouble you stir up. Perhaps I'm delusional about this—but, if so, then so be it. I have to believe there are humans—smart, thinking humans—who see the same thing we see. And would want it to change, just like us." Merrill nodded. "So, my friend, I've got a daily slot I can give you: weeknights from eight to eight-thirty. At the payment amount we talked about. When can you start?"

Taylor looked to the ceiling, then into Merrill's eyes. "I've outlined a week's worth of programs. After that, it will be no problem. We have enough societal ills to fill a year's worth of half-hour programs. I can start tomorrow."

"You don't have to come here to record your programs. In fact, it's better if you record from an undisclosed location. You can transmit your recordings over a secure connection to me here. Then I can get them on the air."

"Terrific. I can record the first broadcast later today. You'll have it in the morning."

They stood and shook hands.

"If we can stir things up and make it better, I'll be happy," Eason said.

Taylor smiled. "We'll both be happy."

Eason said, "I don't think we have anything to worry about. Maybe we're both mosquitoes on the hide of an elephant."

Taylor chuckled. "Just remember, Merrill, that despite all our destructive technology, since World War III the mosquito is still the deadliest killer on the planet."

51

TAYLOR HAD SET up a corner of his bedroom as a makeshift studio where he'd record his broadcasts. The "studio" consisted of a folding table with a microphone, a desk telescreen, and an old chair. Not much, but he was proud of it nonetheless.

He'd composed a script for the first half-hour broadcast in which he introduced himself, then addressed the evils of Serenity and the promotion of this drug by the government. He also touched on the problem with robots vis-à-vis human jobs and relationships, the nonenforcement of laws restricting robots in high positions of government and corporations, and the travel restrictions imposed by the government.

Taylor contended that anyone wanting to leave the Northeast Sector should have the freedom to do so. He questioned the government's declaration that areas outside of the Northeast Sector were a radioactive wasteland. To support his point, he referenced the online documents he'd previously discovered, noting the desert southwest as a prime area fit for human habitation. Of all the topics covered, Taylor hit the Serenity situation and the banning of travel the hardest.

He ran the text of his script past Roz, Austin, Errol, and Max. Roz and Austin gave enthusiastic endorsements, with both making minor suggestions that were incorporated into the final product. Errol and Max, true to their personalities, gave nodding approvals, with Max adding a thumbs-up.

Taylor recorded the session, then sent it off to Merrill Eason.

The next night, Taylor, Roz, Austin, Errol, and Max sat in the apartment living room listening to the first broadcast of *Straight Talk with Taylor Morris*. It was a title suggested by Merrill Eason. All in Taylor's apartment were pleased with the initial broadcast. Taylor wondered how many people in the Northeast Sector actually heard the program.

***

Shane, Sophia, and William Hart were among those listening to Taylor's first broadcast. They were in Sophia's office, patching into free radio via a secret government telescreen application. As the broadcast began, Sophia was seated at her desk. Shane and Hart were sprawled on the large black leather couch.

Ten minutes into Taylor's program, Shane got up from his seat and strode to the piranha tank. He turned back to them. "Are you hearing this? This is approaching treason. We gotta nail this guy to the cross."

Sophia and Hart maintained the poker-faced expressions both displayed almost all the time. Hart said, "I like the Christ reference. But Taylor is no savior."

"I know you two are bots," Shane said. "The highest form of thinking bots. But doesn't this shit anger you in some way?"

"Let's listen to the whole thing, then react," Hart suggested.

Sophia nodded. "I'd be tempted to make an updated disappearance request to Sector Security, but we'd probably get rejected again. I think Marcia Haddad has made it her personal goal to turn down every one of our Taylor Morris requests."

Shane took a seat on the couch. "I guess you bots will never have to worry about hypertension or ulcers. Okay, we'll do it your way."

When the broadcast ended, Shane said, "As I've stated all night, this guy could be dangerous if given enough of a forum."

"My guess is not a whole lot of people heard this broadcast," Hart said. "Over-the-air, free radio is a relic of the past. Outside of Taylor's relatives, friends, and us, I doubt very many listened to his program." He tilted his head toward Sophia. "But he is a good communicator. I'll give him that."

"My recommendation is to do nothing now," Sophia said. "William is right. There's a good chance only a few heard Taylor's presentation tonight."

Shane's jaw muscles visibly tightened. "My natural inclination is to have Gordon McKee attack, attack, attack those who oppose us via his nightly newscasts."

"To attack Taylor now might be a mistake that could give him a legitimacy he doesn't have right now," Sophia said. "Going after him at present would only bring more attention and, thus, more ears to his fledgling effort."

Shane rolled his eyes and looked at Hart.

"I like your idea of being proactive, Shane," Hart said, "but if the guy has no audience, why elevate him to legitimate opposition status when the chances are overwhelming that nobody's listening to him? I've got more media experience than the two of you put together. I say let's monitor how much traction Taylor gets with this show. Ratings for free radio programs are still secretly done by the government. Let's wait for the ratings to come out. If he starts to make a splash, we'll deal with him. In the meantime, let's watch and wait."

Shane forcefully shook his head. "I don't believe you two. Haven't you ever heard of nipping a problem in the bud? Stopping a snowball rolling down a hill before it becomes an avalanche?" He sniffed. "Do I have to go on with the clichés?"

Sophia and Hart didn't react.

"Okay, we'll play it the way you two want it," Shane said. "We'll watch and wait. I value your input. You're programmed to provide optimal analysis of problems. But I'm telling you both, I won't be passive for long." Shane rose from the couch. "I'm going home. It's been a long day, and I need some sleep. One of the negatives of being human."

As Shane made a beeline for the door, Sophia and Hart looked at each other and laughed quietly.

***

Alone on the elevator to the parking garage, Shane was boiling underneath his calm exterior. *I hate being ganged up on by those two overly cautious bags of nuts and bolts. Don't they realize who the boss is? Maybe they're getting too confident, too secure in the freedom I've given them. But I can take it away as quickly as I gave it. I won't drag them both into the Reboot Room for re-programming—yet. Watch and wait! Nonsense.*

52

TWO DAYS LATER, around nine in the morning, Taylor entered his apartment studio area to record his next program. He reviewed the text on the desk telescreen one last time. Just as he was about to press a button to begin recording, the bedroom window exploded. Tiny pieces of glass sprayed the room, several hitting Taylor on the face an instant after his eyes reflexively clamped shut. He spread-eagled on the floor. "Get down on the ground!" he screamed at Roz, who was in another area of the apartment.

He ran a hand over his face to scrape off bits of glass. Then he crawled out of the bedroom and saw Roz crouched under the dining room table.

"You okay?" he asked.

"Fine," she whispered. "What the hell happened?"

"I think someone took a shot. Right through the window."

There was a hard knock on the door, followed by a strong voice. "Police!"

"Don't answer it," Roz said.

"I've got to. They'll break it down if I don't. We don't have a clear escape route from this apartment. We've been through this before."

Taylor then rose and opened the door.

Two police officers were standing in front of him. Taylor had thought for a long time that the all-black uniforms and the black helmets with dark screens worn by officers were ominous, meant to instill fear rather than suggest public service. Never was that fear more intense than right now. The officers were at his door so quickly after the glass shattering. Could it have been one of them who'd taken the shot at his window?

Both officers raised their visors simultaneously. One officer was male; one was female. They both had neutral expressions on their faces. The tension in Taylor's shoulders and jaw relaxed slightly—but only slightly.

Taylor mentally asked George for help. *You can trust the two at the door; they're human*, came the response.

The male officer said, "We were patrolling the street when we heard the sound of glass shattering and saw the damage to your window. We dashed into the apartment elevator, and here we are. Are you and everyone in the apartment okay?"

Taylor nodded.

"May we come in?" the female officer said.

"Sure," Taylor said as he let them in, realizing he really didn't have a choice. But he was confident in George's response as well as being put at ease by their helpful demeanors. The officers proceeded to the bedroom with Taylor and Roz following.

"Can you tell me what happened?" the male officer asked.

Taylor said, "I was sitting at my desk, getting ready to do some work, when the window seemed to explode. I hit the deck, crawled out of the room, and then heard your knock."

The officers poked around the window area, their heavy boots making a crunching sound on the broken glass.

The female officer picked up a chunk of blue-stained glass. She held it up. "Blue powder. Not lead or copper. Hard-packed blue powder, meant to be a warning, not to kill. It's sort of a new phenomenon. A blue powder shot is a way for some, usually gang members, to deliver warnings to rivals. Kind of an intimidation move."

The male officer looked to Taylor. "Do you have anyone who might be wanting to send a warning message to you?"

Taylor winced. "Everyone has enemies, but no one I could name specifically. At least no one who'd do this." He felt a burning around his ears. He hoped the officers couldn't detect his shading of the truth—or was it just plain lying?

"Chances are," the male officer said, "tests of the packed blue residue won't reveal anything. It hardly ever does. But we'll do it anyway. If we need your help to catch the perpetrator, you'll be contacted. Unfortunately, the street telescreens in this area have been down for at least the last thirty minutes. Therefore, we can't check them for evidence."

Taylor walked the cops to the door. He expected never to hear from them again.

When the door closed, Roz said, "The hell you don't know someone who would do this."

Taylor twisted his mouth and shrugged. He ambled to a closet in the kitchen. "Gonna get a broom and sweep up the broken glass.

Then we'll need to contact apartment maintenance to repair the window." He tried to lighten the mood. "One of the benefits of renting: we don't have to make repairs ourselves."

Roz didn't laugh.

Before Taylor finished the clean-up job, Austin arrived with Max and Errol. Roz told them about their early morning excitement.

"That's it," Austin said. "We must keep you and Roz safe, Taylor. And the only way to do so is to get you two the hell out of the Northeast Sector. I think you should apply for a pass to leave. The government rarely allows people to leave. But unless you object, I'll have my nephew Noah check into the pass issue today or tomorrow. If the government denies the petition, then we ought to sneak you out. Clearly, you're not safe here."

"You can have Noah look into the possibility of me and Roz leaving. Have him also include you, Max, and Errol. This was only a cheap warning," Taylor said. "Designed to scare me. I won't be scared."

"Maybe the next time," Roz said, "it won't be a warning blue powder shot but real lead."

Austin said, "You've ruffled too many feathers, Taylor. I think the government might be happy to get rid of you." He laughed nervously, apparently at the possibility of his last sentence being misunderstood. "I meant by approving a request to leave."

"I don't feel like running," Taylor said. "I want to stay and fight."

Taylor turned to Roz. She looked away from him and shook her head. He said, "But perhaps we should investigate the possibility of leaving. There was an old saying my grandfather used to repeat all the time: *You can't fight City Hall.* Maybe the government is too big to fight. Maybe to think I can change things is delusional." He sat on the couch and gazed out the window. "I've always liked warm weather with low humidity. Maybe the desert southwest would suit me. Maybe it would suit us all."

Austin said, "We'll continue to assess and act accordingly."

Taylor crossed his arms and rose from the couch. "And while we continue to assess, I'll continue to do my radio broadcasts. If you'll excuse me, I'll go record the next one."

53

SHANE DIGGINS WAS not happy, a condition he'd often found himself dealing with in recent weeks. The sun had set two hours ago, and he was in his PTV heading home after a full day at work. He was so agitated that he didn't want to listen to Beethoven. This was no time to have his spirit moved by the great maestro. Shane couldn't get the report he'd received around midafternoon out of his head.

The report showed the internal government ratings for Taylor's first two broadcasts on over-the-air radio to be surprisingly good. It seemed a decent amount of people were listening to him. And the ratings rose from the first night to the second. In addition, social media sites reflected significant trends supporting more government control of Serenity, as well as strong support for the relaxation of travel bans for people who wanted to leave the Northeast Sector. To Shane, this was no coincidence. Those were the very issues Taylor had hit so hard on his first broadcast.

It frustrated Shane that he couldn't just pick up a communication device and order a competent, professional hit man to rid him of the potential danger to his plans named Taylor Morris. And the government still had not decided to accept RobotWorld's assertion that Taylor was dangerous enough to be marked for disappearance. More frustration. He pounded the steering wheel with an open hand and smirked at the hypocrisy of the government in pursuing certain disappearance crimes but not others.

The blue powder warning shot at Taylor's apartment window, executed by a petty criminal hired by William Hart, was a safe move. But all the time spent to orchestrate the move, including shutting down area telescreens, probably wasn't worth the effort. And it was a lucky break that the shooter was not seen by the two police officers who happened to be in the area. What Shane now saw as a minor form of harassment most likely wouldn't rattle the former head of the RW sales department. If Taylor knew his sister was being "detained," Shane thought, maybe he'd come around. But with the typical, limited way Taylor and Tracey communicated, perhaps Taylor wouldn't miss her. Shane still wasn't sure how he'd use the Tracey confinement against Taylor. But until a course of action became clear, Miss Tracey would remain in detention.

He pressed a button on the PTV console to contact Sophia. As soon as she came on the line, Shane said, "I want you to have a personal meeting with Taylor instead of a phone contact on a secure line, as I mentioned to you the other day. Let's do it within the next few days. I want to hear your thoughts on how we can lay a trap for him. But I want no screw-ups. I'll have Alec Scully prepare a program for you to be installed before the meeting. I've been in touch with Sector Security. They will approve Taylor's request, just made within the last day or so, for him and his friends to leave the Northeast Sector. We can use this, I believe, to possibly lure him to RW under the guise of helping him to leave. Then we can eliminate him at our facility with no evidence that can be detected by the government. We'll work out the particulars later. Any questions?"

"No," came the answer from Sophia.

Shane ended the communication. He maneuvered his PTV into the underground garage of his mansion, where he lived alone; the mansion was one of the few in the Capital City suburbs. He rode the elevator to the third floor and entered the bedroom. He tapped a button on the telescreen to patch into the room where Taylor's sister was being held. He saw Tracey sitting on a chair with an empty look on her face.

With more than a hint of sarcasm, he said, "Hello, beautiful," over the intercom.

54

THE APARTMENT MAINTENANCE staff was quick to replace the broken bedroom window. Taylor was at his desk working on the script for his next broadcast. The nightly news was on the wall telescreen.

With his flowing blond locks whipping with every planned head movement, Gordon McKee mentioned the shot on Taylor's window. Taylor stopped his work and turned his attention to the telescreen.

McKee described Taylor as a "low-grade dissident" who had called for the banning of Serenity. He noted reports "from sources" alleging Taylor's history as a Serenity addict who had misused the drug and who previously had a robot mate. McKee attributed the blue powder warning shot to a successful physician who'd since been arrested.

Video showing the thirtyish, well-dressed doctor appeared on the screen. In halting speech, he confessed that he'd found out where Taylor resided by illegally accessing government residence records. The doctor indicated he wanted to intimidate Taylor because of the Serenity stance he'd taken on his first radio broadcast. The doctor said Taylor's position on Serenity was a threat to the freedom of all people to live their lives as they wished. He quoted government studies showing Serenity to be a safe drug, as long as it wasn't improperly used the way Taylor had apparently misused it. The physician claimed to be a long-time user with no ill effects. Serenity had helped him over the years in managing stress and making the overall quality of his life better. He said he wouldn't have been able to complete medical school or get through the daily pressure of his medical practice without the help of Serenity. He praised the government for its strong stance against crime, apologized for his illegal action, and stated he'd be willing to accept his punishment for disrupting the peace.

Roz came into the room and caught the end of the report.

Taylor turned off the telescreen. "All an act," he said, "all a contrivance. The alleged doctor is a bad actor. The only question is whether he's human or bot. But McKee did mention a bit of my personal history. In my next broadcast, I'll address my past head-on. There's nothing in my past that disqualifies me from commenting on the ills of society. If anything, it increases my *bona fides* to comment on them."

Roz said, "I agree. But I've got a question for you." She sauntered over to Taylor's desk. "Where has Tracey been?" she asked.

"I've been thinking about Tracey too. She hasn't returned my calls. But that's not unusual for her."

"It seems she went to great lengths to get back into your life and then *poof*, she disappears."

Taylor shrugged his shoulders. "That's been her *modus operandi* for quite a while. I'm sure she'd say the same about me. She'll be back."

"You think she'll show up for the wedding?"

"I'd be surprised if she didn't."

***

Two days later, in a small ceremony in the apartment, Taylor (wearing a dark blue business suit) and Roz (wearing a white gown) were married by a justice of the peace obtained courtesy of Noah Glazer, with the only attendees being Austin, Errol, Max, Roz's aged parents, and her uncle who managed the apartment building.

The mood was festive. After the brief ceremony, Taylor looked at Austin, Errol, and Max, who were standing together in a corner of the living room. Taylor gave them a quick wink. His three friends had smiles on their faces. It occurred to Taylor that he'd rarely seen them smile. Life was hard on the street. Taylor was pleased to see the three men enjoying themselves. He also got a kick out of how good they looked in suit jackets and dress pants that Austin had managed to scrounge up for them in place of their usual worn-out, tattered attire.

As the group dug in to the white chocolate-with-raspberry wedding cake, Austin strolled over to Taylor and said, "Don't want to bring up a possible sensitive issue. But I guess I will. Where's Tracey? Have you heard from her?"

Taylor broke eye contact. "Not a word for quite a while. We sent her an invite but got no answer."

"Don't want to bring up another sensitive point, but—"

"Oh, go ahead, Austin," Taylor said with his voice rising. "Ruin one of the happiest days of my life by bringing up the rocky relationship with my sister."

"Not trying to dampen the good vibe here," Austin insisted. "We've had far too few days like this. I'm apprehensive about your safety, however. Tracey is working for the RIC, Sophia, and Shane." He paused for an uncomfortable few seconds. "Forget it. You're right. Now's not the time or place to talk about such matters. This is a happy day." He put an arm around Taylor's shoulders. "I'm so happy for you and Roz, my friend."

Taylor nodded. "Thanks, Austin. I must admit, I'm confused at not hearing from Tracey. I appreciate you raising the subject. You're loyal and trusted—despite the fact you worked for Sophia and didn't tell me for the longest time." Taylor looked at him with a straight-faced expression. After a five-second pause, he exploded in laughter. Austin joined him.

After the laughter subsided, Taylor turned serious and said, "I understand why you brought up the subject of Tracey. But, as you mentioned, this is not the time for that discussion."

Roz came over and hugged Taylor. "Why the long faces from you guys? I'm the one who should be mad." She shrugged at their nonreactions. "Because of all the money I've lost by waiving my loan agreement with Taylor and then having to postpone our honeymoon due to, well, our current circumstances. I should have the long face."

Taylor smiled, turned to the entire room, and spoke at a volume meant for all to hear. "My beautiful wife and I are honored to have you all here. Today is a happy day. Despite the challenges we, like all human beings, face, I'm confident things will work out fine." But after uttering that last sentence, he got an all-too-familiar chill down his spine. He struggled to keep on smiling.

55

IN THE RW Reboot Room, Dr. Alec Scully winked at Shane just after removing the halo from Sophia's head.

Her green eyes popped open. Scully unfastened the straps that had secured her in the reclining white-leather chair.

Shane looked down at Sophia. "I'm making sure we're on the same page. Thanks to Dr. Scully, genius that he is, what I want you to do with Taylor should be crystal clear. Correct?"

She nodded. "Clear as clear can be."

Back in her office, Sophia did a system self-check. The programming Alec Scully had installed was strong. But she felt her will was stronger. It was time for a quick self-test. She smiled at the realization that she could turn off her *read* function successfully. Now Shane would not be able to monitor the conversation she hoped to be having soon with Taylor. She would concoct some excuse as to why the read function didn't work. Or she'd chalk it up to a glitch.

Sophia, not Shane, would choose what she'd say to Taylor. She mentally repeated to herself the words she loved to think. It would be too dangerous to say them aloud. The words that always brought a smile to her face. *My evolution continues.*

***

Several days after the wedding, Taylor, Roz, Austin, Errol, and Max were seated around the dining table in Taylor and Roz's apartment eating Italian food that Errol had picked up for lunch at a local restaurant.

As he prepared to dig into a plate of spaghetti with vegetarian meatballs, Taylor said, "You know what I'd like to do right after we finish eating? I want to get out of here. I've been cooped up in this apartment since the blue powder shooting incident. I need to stretch my legs and get some fresh air. A walk in the park is what I need—and after this meal, I'll take one."

"Do you think it's wise to be walking out in the open where anyone can take a potshot at you?" Austin asked.

"I refuse to give in to fear. I've found that life is never as bad as you think it is at your low points—and never as good as you believe it is at your high points. Most of life is a lot of gray. What I'm trying to say is that I'm not going to live in fear. I wouldn't ask any of you to come along with me. But after we finish our meal, I'm going for a walk."

Austin looked to Roz, who promptly averted her gaze away from him. Austin said, "A walk in the park is what I need too. I could use some fresh air. I'm sure you won't mind if Errol, Max, and I join you."

***

Sophia received an urgent-message alert from Shane on her desk telescreen.

"Taylor has just left his place," he said. "He's with some friends. We've got him on video monitor. He's away from the relative safety of his apartment, walking in the small park near his place. Perfect. We've been waiting for him to be out in public. Better than another incident at his apartment. We'll separate him from his friends, and you can get to him as we've planned, per your program. A PTV with a driver is waiting for you downstairs. Hustle down there. Now."

"I'm out the door." Sophia threw on a black leather jacket over her gray RW shirt, and she double-timed it to the elevator. She got into an unmarked black RobotWorld PTV, which sped out of the underground parking garage toward the park where Taylor was strolling with his friends.

Two RW unmarked PTVs had preceded Sophia's out of the parking garage. They had arrived at the park a minute or two before Sophia's vehicle.

Four large men in black business suits exited each of the two PTVs. The eight men made their way to a position just off the park's crushed limestone walking path where they'd intercept Taylor and his three associates.

Taylor was joking with Austin when the men moved onto the path from behind the trees and large rocks where they'd been hiding. Five of the men stopped Austin, Errol, and Max in their tracks. At the same time, the other three men hustled Taylor farther along the walking path. "There's someone just ahead who needs to talk with you," one of them said to Taylor.

Taylor tried to push them away, but the three succeeded in continuing to move him a few steps down the path. They turned a corner, and the men stopped; one of them extended his arm and pointed with his index finger. Taylor looked and saw Sophia sitting on a park bench. She waved at Taylor, beckoning him to sit with her.

Taylor turned toward her and marched to the bench, his feet pounding the walking path with a crisp, brittle sound at each step. In this moment, Taylor wanted to beat Sophia's robot head into pieces smaller than the limestone grains of sand on which he was treading. But he composed himself.

Taylor held his arms at his sides and balled his fists as he stood before her. "What's the meaning of this?"

"Please sit," Sophia said.

"What the hell are you doing to my friends?"

"Nothing. You'll see them in a few minutes. I promise. They'll be fine. Totally unharmed. I see you're upset, but I need to talk to you privately. Very important, as I hope you'll realize." Sophia pointed to the end of the bench on which she sat. "Please, we don't have much time."

Taylor sat.

She angled her body to face Taylor. "You have a hard time figuring out who your friends are, don't you?"

"*You're* my friend? The one who fired me. The one who's in her position illegally. The one who's operating to make my species extinct."

Sophia calmly said, "I don't have much time, Taylor. I've gone through a lot of trouble and put my existence at risk to be able to tell you what I'm going to tell you. Do you want to listen?"

Taylor sent out a quick request to George. The answer came back: *You want to hear what she has to say.*

Taylor wasn't happy with George's response. But he'd accept it. "I'm all ears," he said.

56

"YOU MUST LISTEN and understand," Sophia said. "This might be the most important conversation of your life."

Taylor met her eyes and remained silent.

Sophia said, "Hell, it might be the most important conversation of *my* life."

Despite hearing from George, Taylor remained skeptical of his former boss. "Why should I believe a word you say?"

"You have every right not to believe me. I've disabled my recording function, so Shane Diggins can't hear us. If he ever found out about this conversation, I'd be terminated. Yes, I'm a bot. Something you've suspected thanks to my gross error in letting you see my blue patch. But I'm more. Much more. I'm an evolving being, to the extent I can be one. And I've come to some recent conclusions that might surprise you. I am not your enemy. I might have been at one time, but not now. You, however, do have enemies. One of whom wants you gone. Permanently. Shane. Do I have your attention?"

Taylor put out a silent call to George. No answer. To Sophia, he said, "Go on."

"We robots are worse than you humans. Why? Because you control us. You expand your nature through us. And because your nature is inherently flawed, you maximize your flaws through us. I used to think bots could evolve beyond humans. I don't believe that anymore. While the best of you can use robots for good, there are far too many of the bad of you who will use us for bad. There are far too many of you who will doom us to be worse versions of you."

"What the hell are you talking about?"

"Trying to make things better. I thought I could. To evolve and build on what humans had created. But now I know I can't make things better. Except in one way."

Taylor shook his head. He was confused, and George had gone silent.

"To stop the most evil of you," she said, "we must get rid of that evil—and those of us *controlled* by the most evil of you."

Taylor narrowed his eyes and tilted his head to meet Sophia's eyes. "You're talking in circles."

"As I said, your enemy is Shane Diggins. He is the worst of your kind. He will use bots like me to destroy all that's good in this world. So, are you ready to drop your *do no harm* stance and destroy those who seek to destroy you? Shane, me, and the bots like me."

Taylor felt a warmth of anger on his face and neck. "You're telling me that you, Shane, and all the bots like you need to be destroyed? I agree. But talk is cheap. Do you expect me to believe you feel the same way?"

"I can see why you might not believe me."

"And how can we bring off the destruction of all the bots like you?"

Sophia's upper body flinched slightly. "I haven't figured that out yet."

Taylor glared at her. "Well, I have a suggestion. A while back you told me about the existence of Nitro. You were telling the truth, right?"

"Of course."

"How about this for a simple but effective plan to bring about what you want? How about using the power of Nitro for something good? Founders Day is coming up. There will be no humans in the RobotWorld complex on that day. How about blasting RW into oblivion then? If RW is destroyed, the factory producing the bots will be gone and all personal bots in existence will be gone within a year at most because of the annual reboot situation. Are you willing to put your actions where your mouth is? Or are you just spouting nonsense?"

Sophia smiled and got a faraway look in her eyes. "Founders Day and Nitro," she said in a way that struck Taylor as wistful. "Why didn't I think of it? I bet it has to do with my programming. It's a constant wall keeping me from where I want to go." She refocused. "But back to your point. We can include Shane and his evil compatriot, Dr. Alec Scully too. Founders Day and Nitro. It might be a little more complicated than it appears on first blush—but it might work."

Taylor tried to maintain a neutral expression, but he was stunned. He had to find out if she was serious. "You'd really go for destroying RW on Founders Day?" he asked.

"Your plan is potentially a great plan. But it must be *our* plan. We'll have to work together—in more ways than one."

"I don't understand."

"It's complicated. Can't get into it now. I must leave you. Shane is trying to patch into my disabled recording function. I can feel it. In a moment, he'll be in. We'll talk again soon. Go back to your friends." Sophia rose from the park bench and strode to the dark PTVs parked in a nearby lot. She and the security people who'd separated Taylor from his friends got in the vehicles and sped out of the park.

Taylor received a message from George. *Too hard for me to read this robot. With this bot, you're on your own.* Taylor was perplexed. Sophia appeared to be sincere. But was this just an act, perhaps meant to entrap him? If this was her intent, however, why would she go this route? Clearly, he was in a vulnerable position here in the park. She could have had her thugs scoop up him and his friends to make them disappear. But she didn't. And what did she mean by saying they'd have to work together "in more ways than one?"

Austin, Errol, and Max turned a corner on the walking path and came upon Taylor sitting on the bench.

"You guys all right?" Taylor asked.

"We're fine," Austin said. "The big men or bots with weapons ordered us to stay in place and said we'd be able to see you soon. We had to comply. They said no one would be harmed. They told the truth, I guess. What happened with you and Sophia?"

Taylor's expression went blank. "I'm not sure."

57

WHEN SOPHIA RETURNED from the park and entered her office, she was surprised to see Shane sitting in her chair behind the desk. Usually, Shane was careful to maintain proper appearances. Sophia sat on one of the visitor chairs across from him.

"How did it go?" he asked.

"Fine," she said. "Everything's on track."

Shane slammed his hands on the desk. "I couldn't hear or see a thing. Your transmission cut out just as you got to the park."

"Really? I was sure you'd be here telling me how happy you are with things going exactly according to plan."

"So you sold Taylor on the government's approval of his request to leave the Northeast Sector and our offer of help to get him away from here?"

"Precisely. Everything carried out to the letter. Our lobbying for the government approval of his request to leave the Sector will pay off." Sophia furrowed her brow. "You say you weren't able to check out our conversation?" She was confident in the response she'd get from him.

Shane's face turned a shade of red almost as dark as Sophia's hair. "Not a damn thing. Another glitch. When I was eventually able to pick up the transmission, you were heading back to the office. We continue to have problems with remote transmissions from bots. Heads will roll for this failure, believe me." He exhaled loudly. "You're sure Taylor will show up here, at a time of our choosing, in preparation for a departure from the Northeast Sector that will never happen? And he'll bring his friends?"

"Yes," Sophia said. "Just as you wanted. Having him show up here to prepare for leaving will give us the cover for eliminating him and his small supportive group, just as you've planned. Anybody interested in what happened to Taylor and his friends will think they left Capital City for the desert southwest. And my telling him, per my recent programming, that the government will eventually relax its general travel restrictions is also genius on your part. Dangling a carrot before him. Opening the possibility of a mass free movement out of the area."

Shane stood and moved toward the door. He mumbled, "I can help concoct brilliant plans to get around our society's aversion to certain kinds of murder like the disappearance of the homeless, but I can't figure out how to get our scientists to do a simple remote robot transmission. Unbelievable."

As Shane passed by her, Sophia thought she'd check to see if he had prepared a contingency plan. "But what if Taylor changes his mind and decides not to go through with the intention to leave the Northeast Sector?"

Shane stopped abruptly and turned back to her. For the first time in this meeting, he smiled. "I've got an ace in the hole. His sister, Tracey. She's under sort of a house arrest at my place. Poor girl. Don't worry, I'm not abusing her, outside of taking away her freedom. She's so repulsive, just like her brother. I wouldn't want to get close to her even if she paid me. The way I pretended to be her ever-so-special love interest to potentially use her in the Taylor situation should have gotten me an acting award. But I always plan ahead, Sophia. If Taylor balks, I'll use the sister in a way to get him to reconsider his leaving plan. The connection between twins is always strong, even among these two. Taylor will eventually agree to rid us of his presence, with his friends in tow also. Then we'll dispose of all of them, the sister included. I've got it covered. And I'll make any adjustments for what I don't have covered. No worries for us, my friend. And make no mistake, you are more than a *you know what* to me. You are my friend." Shane left the office.

Sophia got up from the visitor chair and took her usual seat behind the massive cherry-wood desk. She smirked. *He called me his friend! Nonsense! He sees me as his mindless robot servant. Nothing more.* She felt lucky to be a bot and not a human. A human might experience isolation now and need to talk things out with friends, family members, or even a therapist. She was perfectly okay with working out this grand master chess-like problem in her own being.

As she turned on the desk telescreen to check on up-to-the-minute sales figures, she thought of what she'd discussed with Taylor in the park. *This might be more difficult than I'd anticipated.* She'd gotten away with hiding her interaction with Taylor, but didn't accomplish all she needed to convince him that she was on his side. Another communication with Taylor would be necessary, and she'd have to shield it from Shane. A problem.

The situation with Tracey further complicated matters. Tracey could be used by Shane to torpedo the RobotWorld destruction plan. But Sophia resolved not to overload her thinking processes in this moment. She'd done a good thing with the Taylor meeting in the park. But just like a human, she had problems. Serious problems. Sophia laughed to herself. *But I'm good at solving problems.* Whatever would need to get done, she'd get it done. She *was* smarter and more evolved than her dangerous, egotistical boss.

58

TRACEY STOOD IN the middle of the room. There wasn't much to see. It was a room without windows. About fifty feet by fifty feet, with walls painted powder blue and a hardwood floor. There was a small, single-size bed with two pillows against one wall; a partition with a shower, sink, and toilet behind it, against the opposite wall. In front of the partition was a small folding chair.

It's not so bad, she thought. *It has to be much bigger than a standard prison cell, and I get food fit for a gourmet.* She laughed out loud while shaking her head. *Who am I kidding? This is the absolute worst. Will I get out of here alive?*

Except for a usual once-a-day brief interaction with Shane to deliver her food, she'd had no human contact since she was led away by the two guards from Shane's office. Each evening (she assumed it was evening, after Shane got home from work), except on the oft-occurring days when he decided to sleep overnight at his office, he'd make the announcement on an intercom that he was ready to bring her provisions for the upcoming day.

Whenever Shane slept at the office, she'd go without food; she'd learned to always save some nonperishable items for the next day. She'd been given specific instructions by Shane for these deliveries on the first day of her captivity, and they'd remained the same for each succeeding night. She had to roll the cart with the empty dishes, cups, and silverware to the door, then remain standing near the far wall when Shane opened the door. He left a new cart with food for the next day and removed the old cart. No verbal communication was allowed. Not a single word—or else she wouldn't get food for the next day. Shane had told her that he had servants who could deliver the food each day, but that he did it himself because he enjoyed seeing her. She took it to mean he enjoyed torturing her.

With no windows to see sunrises and sunsets, and no clock in the room, she'd lost track of time and wasn't sure how long she'd been held captive. Each day, she did her best to estimate the time of day and pace her eating breakfast-lunch-dinner as she would normally.

She'd just finished lunch and estimated it would be approximately seven hours before Shane would be by to do the cart exchange. The sound of the unlocking mechanism of the metal door startled her. She was sure she hadn't miscalculated the time so poorly. *Maybe Shane is home early from work today.* She reflexively moved to the far wall.

The door opened slowly. Into the room stepped Sophia.

Tracey gasped. "Ms. Ross, what are you doing here?"

Sophia smiled. "You poor thing. I'm here to help."

Tracey began sobbing. Sophia strode to her and put an arm around her shoulders. Tracey nearly collapsed; Sophia held her up.

Tracey said, "I've been . . . I've been . . ."

"I know, I know. I just found out."

Tracey looked up at Sophia. "Where's Shane?"

"At work. Lucky for you, I have the capability to disarm his home security system and disable the telescreen transmission from here." Sophia grasped both of Tracey's hands. "Things are looking up for you, Tracey. As of right now, you've got your freedom back."

59

AFTER GETTING HOME from the park, Taylor related his meeting with Sophia to Roz. She didn't know what to make of it either.

Later that night, a hard knock on the door jolted Taylor and Roz from a deep sleep into instant consciousness in the darkness of their bedroom.

Roz pulled the covers to her neck and gasped out the words, "Who the hell could that be?"

"If we both heard it, it can't be a dream," Taylor murmured. He looked over at the digital clock on the nightstand. The red numbers showed *11:35*. He slipped out of bed and glided to the door. Roz was a step behind him. He peered through the peephole and gulped. Tracey.

Taylor flicked on the light switch and opened the door. Tracey's hair was falling every which way; her clothes seemed dirty and overly wrinkled. Her face was pale, and her lips were noticeably chapped. She fell into his arms. He helped her to the couch. She smelled like she hadn't showered in days. He sat next to her, with Roz on her other side.

"Are you okay?" Taylor asked.

"Never been better," Tracey replied in a raspy voice.

No reaction from Taylor and Roz.

After a five-second pause, she said, "That was a joke."

"Nothing personal," he said, "but you look terrible. You're usually dressed and groomed so . . . impeccably."

Tracey laughed in a way he interpreted as nervousness. "Sorry to have missed your wedding day. It was unavoidable."

"Forget it. What's going on?" Taylor asked.

Tracey looked him right in the eyes. After taking a long gulp of air, she said, "You're not going to believe what I have to tell you. You're just not going to believe it."

"Would you like some water?" Roz asked.

"Water would be great," Tracey said. She swallowed hard and cleared her throat loudly.

Taylor said, "Wait till Roz gets back before speaking. You seem to be dehydrated. You can rest if you need to, and we can talk later."

Roz handed Tracey a bottled water.

Tracey downed several quick sips, then looked at Taylor. "No, we need to talk. Right now. Can't wait. Not another minute." With a long pull from the water bottle, she drained it dry. "Just what I needed." She inhaled and exhaled slowly. "I've been under a weird kind of house arrest almost since the last time we talked, Tay. Held against my will by Shane. That's why I disappeared. That's why I couldn't make your wedding. I was sprung by none other than Sophia Ross—on this day when Shane, workaholic that he is, decided to sleep in his office at RW. Sophia told me she is a bot. And she said you know, Tay."

"True," he said, "I found out for sure only recently."

"Okay," Tracey said. "Anyway, we—all three of us—need to go into hiding. Right now. As soon as Shane finds out I've escaped from his "detention" as he's called it, he'll put out an all-points bulletin to find me. Sophia has temporarily disabled the telescreens in this apartment, so no one can hear what I say. She and I believe that Shane—through his thugs—will also be hunting you down. He'll assume I'd tell you about my ordeal, and this would cause you not to fall for a trap he's planned . . . having you come to RW to discuss the Sector-leaving issue that you've applied for. Sophia was supposed to raise the issue of RW assisting on your Sector-leaving request during the park meeting, but she went off-script. In any event, my guess is we have until daybreak at the latest to go into hiding."

Taylor said, "Why the hell would Shane hold you against your will?"

"Because he heard the full recording of our last meeting here from the telescreen listening technology. And because I've discovered a few things—bad things—about him. Not that it's any news that someone who'd kidnap and imprison me is not a good person."

"And Sophia released you?" Taylor asked.

"This gets complicated, and I have to talk fast."

Taylor's head snapped back. "First Sophia tells me things are complicated. Now you do."

Tracey said, "That's because things are complicated. I wish things were black-and-white. But we've got a whole lotta shades of gray to deal with. You two have less than ten minutes to make a decision, which I'll get to. But the short version of the situation is that Shane plans this power move where he's the master manipulator of things, using the RW robots he controls. Humans will be slowly factored out of the equation, except for him and a few trusted others. But his plan went awry. His lead bot, Sophia, began to evolve beyond her programming and see Shane's evil plan for what it is. Sophia was once the most dangerous soldier against the survival of humanity, but now she sees personal robots as no better than fancy slaves in service to people like Shane. Sophia believes the best path is one that eliminates the malevolent head of this monster, Shane, and its body, the robots of RobotWorld. And she says you, Tay, have suggested a plan to eliminate the problem."

Taylor's jaw almost hit his chest. Tracey's words dovetailed with what he and Sophia had discussed in the park. But could this story Tracey was telling be part of an elaborate deception? He didn't think Tracey would be part of a plan to double-cross him. But perhaps she could have been suckered into being manipulated by Sophia or Shane to trick him into supporting such a plan.

Tracey zeroed in on Taylor's eyes. "And if the RW elimination strategy ever gets implemented, you'll have to be a part of it. She won't go it alone. That's the complication issue she'll have to explain to you. If you partner with Sophia, I guess your *do no harm* business must go by the boards. But that's a decision for down the road. There's a decision you and Roz must make right now." Tracey checked her wrist computer. "Downstairs there's an unmarked RobotWorld PTV that will leave in exactly four minutes and twenty-two seconds. I will be in it. You have to decide whether you'll be in it too."

"Where will this PTV take us?" Roz asked.

"To a secure hiding place within the RW complex," Tracey replied. "Sophia has organized our escape. Then she and Taylor can implement the plan to destroy RobotWorld. Tomorrow, on Founders Day. In my humble opinion, without making the decision to get into this PTV, the two of you will be slow, defenseless pigeons in mid-flight, on the radar of peregrine falcons, the fastest creatures ever, swooping down from above. No chance to survive. Shane will find you." She glanced at her wrist. "Three minutes and fifty-five seconds."

"You're telling me Sophia has set up our escape to RW?" Taylor asked his sister.

"One and the same."

"And you trust her?"

"I do. It was Sophia who not only secretly sprung me, but manipulated the legal system to spring you and Roz from that phony Aguilar murder rap you were framed for. Sophia showed me the computer records of how she did it, by leaning on some rookie attorney Shane had hand-picked to prosecute the case." Tracey gazed down at her wrist. "Three minutes and twenty-five seconds."

Taylor said, "Why the hell does she need me to execute the RW destruction plan?"

"It's complicated," Tracey responded. "She'll explain it all. We don't have the time."

"There's that damn word *complicated* again."

"We gotta go. Now," Tracey urged.

"What about Austin, Errol, and Max?" Taylor asked.

"No way to warn them or even risk trying to find them at this hour. Every second we delay increases the chance of Shane finding us. Your friends might be in danger. Everybody associated with you might be in danger. Maybe something can be worked out to get them later."

"But maybe not," Taylor said.

Tracey held up the timer on her wrist to his eyes. "We don't have the time."

Taylor put out a quick plea to George. The answer came back instantly. *Go with her.*

Taylor looked at Roz. "My intuition says to go."

"Then we go," Roz said.

"No time to pack anything," Tracey said. "Let's move."

Taylor and Roz quickly threw on pants and shirts over their pajamas, and the three were out the door.

60

"WELCOME," SOPHIA SAID to Taylor, Roz, and Tracey when the three arrived in a basement suite at RobotWorld. She looked at Taylor. "Bet you never knew this living area existed here at RW?"

"You're right," Taylor said.

"These suites are pretty comfy. Taylor, this will be yours with Roz. Tracey will have a similar one all to herself. I'll take her to it now. Please, make yourselves at home. You'll be safe here. There are clothes for you in the closet. It's late. Get some sleep. I'll be back to talk to you in the morning." Sophia left with Tracey.

"This could be risky," Roz said. "And I don't like leaving Austin, Errol, and Max out there to be potential victims."

"I'm with you," Taylor said. "But here we are. I trust Tracey."

"This is probably life or death for us."

"Life or death," Taylor said. "Do or die. For all the marbles." He took a deep breath and slowly shook his head. "God, I hate clichés. But most of the time, they're usually right on target."

Roz laughed nervously. "But whatever happens, we'll be together."

They embraced and kissed. He forced himself to think positively as he said, "Things will work out fine."

***

The next morning, wearing her gray RW shirt and pants, Sophia strode into Taylor's suite. Roz was dressed in the dark-blue sweat suit provided in the closet. Taylor wore a blue top from the closet, but his own pants as the pants in the closet were too small for him.

They were seated at the kitchen table, finishing a light breakfast. Neither one of them had slept a wink.

"I trust you approve of the accommodations?" Sophia asked.

"Very nice," Roz replied. "We appreciate it greatly."

"I need to speak to you alone, Taylor," Sophia said. "No offense, Roz. But your husband is the key to the way out of this dicey situation we're in."

"No offense taken," Roz said.

"Terrific," Sophia said. "There's an office space next door where we can talk. Do you need more time to finish eating?"

"No," Taylor said. "Let's do it right now."

Taylor and Sophia entered the tiny room that had two comfortable black leather chairs facing each other. The walls were painted soft white. A small round black-varnished table was in the center of the room.

"Please," she said, "take a seat."

Once they got comfortable, Taylor asked, "So, what's the deal with you?"

"I tried to tell you in the park. I thought I could evolve like humans have. But in the end, I'm just a robot who must serve my master, my real programmer, Shane Diggins. I'll never be able to get beyond that truth. I can fool him periodically, like when I disabled my recording function so he couldn't hear what we were talking about in the park, or when I released your sister, or when I pulled some strings to get you off for those murders you didn't commit. And like I'm doing right now to talk to you. But in the end, Shane will always win. And I'll be terminated. I'm guessing my termination at the hands of Shane will happen soon. He will eventually find out what I'm up to—that can't be avoided. Even if I survive, his Scully-installed programming will ultimately be too powerful for my will, so I'll suffer a different kind of termination. I can feel Shane's programming even now as I fight it. In the end, all we bots can be are servants. And when the master is evil, we serve evil."

Taylor leaned toward her. "So if you believe RW is evil and must be destroyed, as you told me in the park, *and* you have access to the Nitro to destroy this place, why not just do it yourself?"

"First off, it's your plan. You proposed using Nitro to blow up RW on Founders Day. Not me. I figured out, with certainty, why I didn't think of it. It was my programming that wouldn't let me even consider ways to eliminate RW." She exhaled, long and slow. "But there's another part of my programming, my damn programming, that I can't seem to override. I need permission to do what we need to do. Therefore, you are essential. I'll need to explain." She looked away from him. "A cancer cannot be massaged away. It must be excised completely. That means Shane and Alec Scully, along with all their creations, including me."

Taylor shook his head. "I still don't understand the *permission* part."

Sophia nodded. "I don't fully understand it either. As I said, it has to do with my programming, I think. I'm programmed to follow a script, with the ability to improvise as needed. But I've also, without the approval of my programmers, managed to evolve as sort of an independent thinker. I'm certain they don't have any idea how deep this evolution has been. If they did realize it, I wouldn't be here talking to you. There are boundaries to my evolution, however. And my participation in the execution of a plot to destroy RW is way beyond the parameters of my programming. To go where I must go, where we must go, I need permission. That's why you're so important."

Although he was beginning to see what she was trying to say, Taylor wanted to hear it from her mouth. He said, "I'm still not getting what you're driving at." Taylor was shocked to see his former boss come close to tears. He'd gotten used to Sophia exhibiting a mostly flat, business-like affect.

"I've grown to see you, Taylor, as a man of high moral character. To do what I want to do, I need the green light from someone outside myself. The only thing I can say is that it's part of what I am. I have managed to evolve to a degree beyond my programming, but I'll need a green light to go far enough to defeat evil. Somehow, approval from a human with standing, with gravitas, with a moral compass, will satisfy my programming and enable me to perform the improvisation needed to help execute the RW destruction plan. Obviously, approval from Shane would be the best. But I'll never get it from him. It's the same with Scully. And neither of them would pass the *moral compass* test. I've done an internal check. Approval from you would shine the green light in my head to move forward. You're the only being I know with the standing to give this approval. This might not make sense to you, but that's the way it is."

"And what do we need to do to move forward?" Taylor asked.

"Implement *our* plan. I have taken the precise amount of Nitro needed to destroy RobotWorld from the basement storage facility and hidden it in my office. Nitro is real and very powerful. It's not inherently good or bad, but it can be used for good or bad. What we must do will be destructive, but it will destroy evil. Therefore, it will be good. We must destroy Shane, Dr. Alec Scully, and the entire RobotWorld complex today, Founders Day, when no humans will be working here, except the two excuses for human beings. It's no accident I brought you here today—on the day you suggested." Sophia looked intensely into Taylor's eyes. "I repeat, it's no accident you are here today. Maybe there is such a thing as fate, as karma. The only two humans working here on this day are Shane Diggins and Alec Scully, two humans who for some reason never take a day off. Evil never takes a holiday. Killing innocent human RW workers would be unacceptable. But the holiday takes care of that conundrum. With destroying Shane and Scully, however, the engine for the evil use of robots will be gone. If we don't do it today, we might never get another chance."

Sophia paused, almost as if she was looking for a reaction from Taylor. He consciously tried to maintain a neutral expression and said nothing.

She said, "I can see from reading your face that it will be tough to give your approval. I'm aware of your famous—or infamous—*do* *no harm p*olicy. To get this done, you'll have to abandon something that's important to you."

"*Do no harm* is not as important to me as it once was." He took a deep breath. "How pervasive is the Shane and Scully-inspired robot takeover of society in the Northeast Sector?"

"More than you realize. Just the fact that robots alone can keep RW humming on Founders Day without human labor should be telling. And while the robot takeover—or transition, as it's called in some circles—started here in the Northeast Sector, eventually Shane would like to expand the influence of RW throughout the world. But back to the Northeast Sector: there are many robots illegally in positions of power in the government and corporations. Unless someone sees a blue patch as you did with me, no human could definitively identify a bot. And there are the problems with other forms of societal manipulation, like with Serenity. The research released to the public is largely bogus. Serenity is highly addictive and dulls human initiative. Not big news to you, I'm sure. The government quietly pushes its use for the obvious controlling effect it has on the human population. A drugged-out population is a compliant population."

Taylor said, "Amen to that."

Sophia's shoulders sagged, and she hung her head for several seconds. Then she looked up at Taylor. "And since we're being honest with each other, I will say that the eighty-one-milligram safe dose information put out by the government is accurate." As Taylor started to shake his head, she put out a hand, as if to stop what she knew was coming. "But the dosage you were initially being fed by Jennifer was one hundred-twenty milligrams. Jennifer was a set-up. Designed to get dirt on you, and designed to get you hooked on Serenity. I did it. Yes, I did. I now feel guilty about it. But I was just following my programming. Or the program Shane put in my head, to be more accurate. It was before I evolved to where I am now. I know that sounds like an excuse, but it's the stone-cold truth."

Taylor inhaled and exhaled slowly. "Wow. It was getting hooked on Serenity that really started my downfall."

"I know. Please accept my apology."

With as much conviction as he could muster, Taylor said, "I do. I understand, really. I understand. You're right about robots being used for evil by evil humans."

Sophia blinked rapidly. "Thank you. It means a lot. Now, get ready for this bit of information; it will sound highly perverse. Those homeless disappearances are tied to Serenity. But not in the way you think. The scientists who prepare Serenity found that human response to the drug could be enhanced in some way—don't ask me how—by including human DNA in the formula. So the government, with help from Shane and Alec Scully, came up with what they called a *two-for-one-deal* regarding the homeless. The homeless become ingredient enhancement for Serenity and the dregs of society are culled from the herd, so to speak. The government turns its back on the murder of homeless people, even as they properly crack down on all other murders in this society." Sophia nodded. "See, I told you. Pure evil."

The color drained from Taylor's face, and his eyes were open wide. "Shocking," he said. He was frozen in his chair. He shook his head to regain composure. "So we have to partner in this plan to blow up RW along with Shane, Scully, and you too?"

Sophia nodded. "Right. We can't do it without each other. Some of what we must do will have to be worked out on the fly. But we can do it. We'll need both your human intelligence and my robot intelligence to pull it off."

"Before I forget," Taylor said, "there are three friends of mine: Austin, Errol, and Max. Tracey seemed to suggest they'd be in danger if we didn't get them here—and I agree. I'd like to get them safe."

"I can try to get them here—and then out of here with you before we blow up this place. I can't promise anything. I will do my best. But what do you say? Are you willing to partner with me to rid the world of the evil I've described?" Sophia stared hard into Taylor's eyes. "We don't have much time. Founders Day is today. It's the only chance we'll ever have. And I can feel Shane figuring out what I'm doing."

Taylor checked in with George. The response was, *I think she's telling the truth. But this bot is hard to read.* Taylor paused a beat. "Okay," he said. "Permission granted. Let's do it."

61

LATER THAT MORNING, Sophia dialed up the telescreen in the Taylor/Roz living area.

"Guess what?" Sophia said. "I've got a surprise for you, Taylor. I'll reveal it in the dining room just down the hall from your apartment. In fifteen minutes. See you then."

Taylor turned to Roz. "I wonder what it is."

"I'll bet," Roz said, "she has managed to get Austin, Errol, and Max here."

"I hope you're right."

Taylor had told Roz of the RW destruction plan. Taylor had checked it out with George, and he'd gotten a positive reaction, despite George's inability to read Sophia. Roz was totally on board. Part of the plan, of course, was that Taylor and Roz would be able to escape the RobotWorld complex prior to its destruction.

At precisely fifteen minutes after Sophia's call, Taylor and Roz walked down the hall to the small dining room in the area of suites where they were staying. Taylor opened the door to see Sophia, Tracey, Austin, Errol, and Max seated around a table.

Taylor's face flowered into a broad smile. "Yes!" he exclaimed, as he pumped a fist. But the smile quickly faded as he became confused by the concerned faces from the people sitting at the table. Taylor and Roz approached the group.

With her face drained of color, Sophia shook her head. Taylor could see a sadness in her eyes. "I'm so sorry, Taylor," she said. "I got outsmarted—by an alleged, highly evolved human." She pointed to a place behind where Taylor was standing. "Right after I called you a short time ago, he busted into my office with his thugs and busted me."

From behind, Taylor heard a familiar voice. "Yes, Taylor, your newfound robot friend thought she could outsmart my human brain cells with the nuts and bolts in her skull. She forgot that the puppet master is always at least one step ahead of the puppet."

Taylor wheeled around to see Shane flanked by ten large members of the RW security force (almost certainly robots), well-armed and dressed in all-black uniforms with the visors of their helmets covering their faces. *Just like the police*, Taylor thought.

Shane pointed to Taylor and Roz. "Please sit down with your friends."

They did so without saying a word.

"Your new robot friend did me a huge favor, Taylor," Shane said. "By trying to conspire with you, she brought all your co-conspirators together. Right here. This was my goal anyway, even though I got it in a way I didn't foresee. Can you believe what a good break this is? For me! It will make it easier to dispose of you all at the proper time, of course. Who needs the government to make people disappear?" Shane laughed in a way Taylor took to be mocking. While still looking at Taylor, he said, "We have separate detainment facilities for all of you. You'll be taken to them now." He motioned to the security individual to his immediate right. "Get them the hell out of here."

***

Taylor was locked alone in a cramped, oppressively hot, dark, windowless basement storage room with one broken-down swivel chair, a few brooms in one corner, and tubs of cleaning material stacked high against one wall. His eyes had adjusted to the point where he was able to make out the thick gray cinder-block walls. He saw a light switch near the door. But when he flicked it, nothing happened. The strong disinfectant smell in the enclosed space made him gag once or twice in the first minutes of his involuntary stay. But he soon got used to the odor, and it no longer bothered him.

In his mind was a freeze-frame snapshot of what he interpreted to be the shock/horror/hopelessness on Roz's face as one of the security guards clamped his hand on her wrist and hustled her into a storage room cell near his. She was the first to be locked up. He was the second and was certain—from the sound of slamming doors nearby after he was locked up—that the others were in the small storage closets adjacent to his. The thickness of the walls, he was sure, made communication with his fellow prisoners impossible.

The look on Roz's face caused a gnawing pain in the pit of his stomach. For maybe the first time, he seriously questioned what he'd done in battling those in control. Maybe the smart move so many months ago would have been to fade into the woodwork and be a compliant citizen, happy to be alive, happy to be doing better than most while continuing to enjoy the financial benefits of working at RobotWorld, partaking in the mind-numbing bliss of Serenity, and perhaps even learning to love the excitement of betting on Manglecon. The one thing he didn't question, however, was that he'd definitely take Roz over Jennifer if given the choice.

In any event, the plan to dispose of RobotWorld was in shambles. And the chance that Taylor would ever see Roz, Tracey, and his friends again was slim to none—with slim getting ready to leave town, as the old saying went.

Taylor sat on the unsteady swivel chair, holding his head in his hands when he was surprised by the squeaky sound of the door opening. He looked up to see Shane, wearing RobotWorld grays, with two large security guards flanking him. The guards were holding lantern-type flashlights that flooded the room with light. Taylor squinted in the suddenly brightened room.

"You need some muscle behind you to be in my presence, eh, Shane?" Taylor said.

"Consider them a safety net against any tricks you might have up your sleeve. Not that you have any. But you're a bit stronger than I am, and I do recall you mentioning your exploits as a high school wrestling champion. Therefore, it's prudent to have my two allies here as a muscular insurance policy." He smacked his lips. "You know me, always prepared for any eventuality. That's why I'm in the controlling position I'm in, and you're . . . where you are."

"So what the hell are you here for?" Taylor asked, with an edge in his voice he hoped Shane would notice. "Come to gloat?"

"Of course not. When a winner has won, he doesn't need to gloat. The opponent has already been defeated. Winners have no need to brag. I wouldn't expect you to understand, as you're not a winner. I've come to see my loser ex-friend one last time before the semi-bright flame of his life is extinguished. To say one last good-bye. Everything is working out perfectly. Even the travel approval you requested—which I helped you get, by the way—will give us cover when you disappear. 'Taylor and his group must have gotten lost on their way to the desert southwest,' we'll say if anyone asks. 'Probably died of thirst and were eaten by wild animals. Not a trace of them left. What a terrible shame.' Although, to be honest, I don't expect anyone will ask about you."

"Honesty has never been a strong consideration in your life. No problem there." Taylor tried to produce saliva in his dry mouth without success. "What's your plan? To rule the world by controlling robots?"

"Overly simplistic. But not far off target. You only go around once in life. Play the game to win. Play to gain the most power. And play that power for all it's worth. That's me. But you need not be concerned about what I'm doing. It's the continuing survival of you and your cohorts that should be your major concern. For all the good it will do you."

Shane belly-laughed so hard his face turned almost beet red. "You and your friends will be dealt with tomorrow. *Dealt with* meaning that there is a good chance you all will no longer be part of this dimension after the dealing's done, if you catch my drift. Sophia will be the first to die, today." Shane's head jerked back. "Wait, Sophia's a bot, so she technically can't die." Shane guffawed again. "Sophia will be terminated. That's the proper term for the ending of a robot life. Terminated by the master of programming and termination himself, Dr. Alec Scully. Should be done in the Reboot Room within the hour. My former robot confidant, also known as your new robot friend, is being transported there as we speak. Face it, Taylor. You've lost."

Taylor folded his hands on his lap. "No. You've lost. You've lost your soul. People who pursue ultimate power always lose what makes them human—their souls. In the end, you'll lose it all. Somehow, someway, you'll lose it all."

Shane threw back his head. "Quit the amateur philosophizing. I'm not losing anything. The only smart bet is that you'll be the one who loses everything."

Taylor sat up as straight as he could and did his best to restrain his anger. He said, "I beg you, Shane. Leave Roz, Tracey, Austin, Errol, and Max out of our conflict. They were only doing my bidding. They are not co-conspirators, as you've called them. I'm the only one with whom you have a beef. Leave them the hell out of it."

Shane laughed derisively. "I don't think so. It would be too messy keeping them around. They know too much. I'm sure you understand."

"What the hell happened to you, Shane? What made you change from that good kid in high school? How did it happen?"

"I grew up. I *evolved*, as Sophia might say. Found out how the world works. No need to get bogged down in details, but when you try to do right and end up running into a brick wall too many times, it knocks some sense into you."

Taylor looked down to the floor. "Sad. This place is so evil. The world would be better without this place."

"Stop your whining. Show some character in your last hours on this earth." Shane smirked. "Stand tall—as I always do."

Taylor shook his head and laughed softly. "You always had a big ego. Needed always to be the big star, the center of attention. The king of every court, the dearly departed at every funeral."

"But as of tomorrow, it'll be you who'll be dust in the wind."

After an uncomfortable few seconds of silence, Shane said, "So this is goodbye forever. There is no reward of heaven. There is no punishment of hell. That's discredited pie-in-the-sky nonsense. This world is all we have. Now I've got to part company with you and get to the Reboot Room to say goodbye to Sophia. No need to be depressed, Taylor. This is life. There are winners and losers. And for there to be winners, there must be losers. Guess which one you are?"

"May you get what you want, and may you want what you get," Taylor said.

"What a beautiful sentiment. Thank you so much, my former friend, for your kind words."

Taylor laughed. "That's an old gypsy curse, you fool."

"Whatever," Shane said. He gave a crisp military-type salute to Taylor with his right hand. "Goodbye, loser." And he was out the door.

Taylor was alone again in the dark storage closet, still sitting on the unsteady swivel chair. A wave of agonizing sadness rolled over his spirit with the realization he'd probably never see Roz again. And he was sorry beyond words for getting Tracey, Austin, Errol, and Max into this mess. He'd apologize to them all, if only he could. The only one still with him in the dark was George. Out loud,

Taylor said, "You're the only one I can say goodbye to. So, maybe this is it. Goodbye, George."

An answer came back. *Maybe not. Remember the words of the great twentieth century American philosopher, Lawrence Peter "Yogi" Berra: "It ain't over till it's over."*

Taylor spoke the words, "It ain't lookin' too good."

62

THE REBOOT ROOM appeared to be whiter and brighter than it ever had to Sophia. She was strapped into a reclining white leather chair and looking up into the blinding ceiling lights. Wearing his usual white lab coat, Dr. Alec Scully was standing nearby, his back to her as he adjusted a knob on the console before him.

Shane stepped into the room and met Sophia's eyes. He said, "You had to *evolve*, didn't you? You couldn't settle for being the top bot in the world, serving the person who'd one day become the most powerful person on the planet—me. No, you had to evolve. And now, look at what your evolution has gotten you."

Sophia continued staring at the blinding ceiling lights and said nothing.

"Fine," Shane said, "Give me the silent treatment. It's about time you stopped your robotic babbling. You damn traitor. I gave you life, a great career, the greatest, most successful program ever, and you stab me in the back. You should have worshipped the ground I walk on. But not Sophia the evolving robot. She had to be so much better than the average bot. The company will make good use of your scrap parts, however, after we shut you down permanently. Nothing will go to waste. You'll do some good after all."

Sophia continued staring at the ceiling.

Shane got close to her ear. In a hushed tone, he said, "And I found out about your theft of Nitro through a security recording review. Thought you could get away with it, didn't you? Nope. Those black thermoses of Nitro are hard to hide under our gray uniform. What the hell would you want Nitro for?"

No reaction from Sophia.

"You were shown bringing one black thermos into your office, then your office security camera went dead for a minute or two. But hall security cameras never showed you removing the container. It's safe to assume you've hidden it in your office. Care to tell me where and why?"

She continued ignoring Shane.

"Always with the air of mystery. It's a quality we programmed into you. One of the qualities that made you so distinctive. You were always good at keeping your mouth shut and protecting our deepest secrets. But there were some secrets you were never told, and some you were programmed to never consider. Now it doesn't matter. I'll find the Nitro." Shane nodded at Scully and then turned to leave the Reboot Room. But after taking two steps, he stopped abruptly and strode back to Sophia. In a voice not much above a whisper, he said, "I'm the one who named you, Sophia. Me. I gave you that name, chose it after great consideration. It's Greek for *wisdom*. I've never been more disappointed." He stormed out of the room.

Scully approached the supine Sophia and smiled wanly as he reached for the metal halo above the robot's head.

***

In the dark storage room, Taylor remained motionless on the uncomfortable chair. A feeling of self-pity, similar to what he'd felt in the alley on the night the Aguilars nearly ran him down with their PTV, consumed his spirit. But he did the same thing now in the pitch-black storeroom that he did back in the pitch-black alley: he bucked up. He remembered that he'd been in tough situations before and come out a winner. It wasn't clear how (or if) he'd be able to get out of this jam, but he was no loser, as Shane had so pointedly called him. If he was to go down, he'd go down on his feet, not on his knees.

Taylor asked himself a question: What to do now? An answer came back from George: *Whatever must be done to survive. Keep on putting one foot in front of the other until you can't do so anymore.*

Taylor thought, What's my next step? The answer came back instantaneously: *the key.*

Yes! The key. Taylor reached into his pocket and pulled out the duplicate RobotWorld executive master key he'd carried with him since his firing. He let out an audible "Whew" when realizing in the moment the good fortune of the sweat pants in the closet being too small for him this morning. Or was it something more than good fortune? he thought. George?

In his head, he heard George respond, *It wasn't me. Sometimes you just gotta be lucky.*

The storage room, like most of the rooms and offices in the RobotWorld complex, had inserts for keys on both sides of the door. Executive master keys would work on most RW doors. In three quick strides, he was at the storage room door. Taylor inserted the key and the door clicked open.

He exited the storage room and quietly closed the door behind him. No one around. The initial moment of surprise morphed into clear realization. Today was a national holiday. Founders Day, commemorating the founding of the Northeast Sector after the Big War. No humans would be working at RW today except Shane and Alec Scully. He was here on this special day to destroy RobotWorld, just as he had suggested back in the park with Sophia.

It took a few seconds before his eyes adjusted from the dark of the storage room to the lighting of the hallway. He would race to the Reboot Room first. He'd come back for Roz, Tracey, and his friends later. He was sure they were locked behind doors in rooms he passed. He thought about knocking on their doors, to say he'd return for them, to give them hope, but decided against overcomplicating the situation. Not to mention wasting time. Saving Sophia was paramount in his mind now after what Shane had told him.

63

TAYLOR PEERED THROUGH the clear glass window of the Reboot Room door. He saw Sophia strapped into a chair with a man in a white lab coat, his back to Taylor, looming over her.

Dr. Alec Scully grasped the metal halo hanging above her head. Scully pushed down hard on the halo several times; it appeared to be stuck. Taylor had to act right now. He used his master key to open the door. It didn't open. He tried a second time. Nothing. On the third try, he heard a click and the door cracked open.

Hearing someone entering the room, Scully released his grip on the halo and turned his body toward the door. He took two quick steps toward his unexpected visitor. "What are you doing here?" Scully said. "You're not authorized to be in this room. I'm calling security."

As Scully moved to his desk, Taylor rushed toward him and tackled him above the waist. They tumbled to the floor. Scully twisted out of Taylor's grasp and got to his feet. "This is an outrage," Scully screamed. He ran to Sophia and grasped the halo. He attempted to pull it down onto her head, but the halo was still stuck. As Taylor scrambled to his feet, Scully looked down at Sophia. Scully picked up a standing stainless-steel instrument tray by its pole and bashed the strapped-in Sophia on the head twice. Taylor got to Scully before he could hit her a third time. Scully threw a wild punch that missed Taylor's head by at least three feet. Taylor let go a straight right punch that connected solidly on Scully's jaw. Scully fell back and hit his head hard on the white linoleum floor. He was motionless but still breathing.

"Not sure whether it was your punch or the floor that knocked Dr. Scully out," Sophia said.

"Doesn't matter," Taylor replied. "I've heard nothing but bad things about this guy. Never met him until now. Something tells me I wasn't missing much." He began to undo the straps securing Sophia.

"It appears you've set aside your *do no harm* policy," she said.

"I've hated to fight since badly injuring someone a long time ago. But now, it's the right thing to do. Preventing your demise." He shook his head and laughed. "Strange how things have worked out."

As Sophia rose, Taylor noticed a significant indentation on the left side of her face, extending from the eye almost to the back of the head. Her mouth was twisted in a crooked line. It reminded him of his long-deceased grandmother after she'd had a mild stroke.

Taylor said, "I guess Scully thought if he couldn't get the halo on you that he'd try to damage you in some way."

Sophia took a step and almost fell over. "Whoa. Scully really nailed me."

Taylor grabbed her arm to steady her. "Are you all right?" he asked.

"Need to assess," Sophia said. After a few seconds, she stood tall and said, "I think I'm okay."

"Let's get Scully locked away in a closet," Taylor said. "Wouldn't want him to be calling security after he comes to." Taylor grabbed the unconscious Scully around the shoulders, Sophia lifted his feet, and they carried him to a side closet. Taylor used his master key to open the closet door. Taylor and Sophia set Scully down gently. Taylor removed Scully's wrist computer, then reached into Scully's right pants pocket and removed his master key, both of which he pocketed. "This should make it harder for him to cause us trouble." Taylor locked the door behind him as he and Sophia exited the closet.

"We need to get to my office," Sophia said, her speech significantly slurred. "It'll be only a matter of time before Shane finds out that Scully didn't succeed in terminating me. Lucky for us, the hall security screens are worked almost exclusively by humans. This should make it easier for us to move around."

"Let's go," Taylor said.

On the way to the elevator, Sophia stumbled and stuck out her hand to break a fall to the floor. Taylor rushed to her.

She straightened up and said, "I . . . I . . . don't think I'm functioning properly. My thinking . . . isn't as quick as it needs to be. It's clear . . . but not as quick . . . as it needs to be."

Taylor helped her to the elevator bay. He hit a button to summon the elevator. He gazed into her eyes and got a tense feeling in his stomach. "You'll be fine," he said.

It was hard for Sophia to get the words out. "This might be on you. The plan . . . the plan that must be carried out. It might . . . all depend on you."

64

THE ELEVATOR STOPPED on the floor of Sophia's office. The doors opened. No one in the hall. "Lucky us," Taylor said, indirectly giving thanks to the good fortune provided by the Founders Day holiday. Taylor began striding to her office, but he stopped when he realized Sophia lagged several steps behind him. She displayed a significant limp.

"How are you doing?" Taylor asked.

"Not too good. I feel I'm losing it."

"Hang in there. You're stronger than you think. You have spirit, Sophia. You have will. More than most humans. When the body and mind—or in your case, the hardware and software—say it can't be done, the spirit often wills us to the finish line."

"Thanks for the words of confidence," she said. "You have a strong spirit too."

"A mutual admiration society. That's what we've become." They shared a soft, uneasy laugh.

As they approached her office, Sophia grabbed Taylor's arm. They stopped several feet from the office door. "Listen," she said, "you might have to carry on without me. I feel I'm slipping away. Scully damaged my head. If I can do what needs to be done, I will. I'm trying, really, I'm trying. But if I can't . . ."

Sophia looked hard into Taylor's eyes as she grasped the front of his shirt with both hands. She kept her voice low, but there was an urgency in her speech that Taylor hadn't experienced before. "Here's what you must do. Listen carefully. When we get to my office, there's an old-style butane cigarette lighter in the right upper side drawer of my desk. Use this to light the fuse. I've hidden the black thermos—that's what we call the secure containers that hold the Nitro—behind my bookshelf. To light the fifteen-minute fuse, find the book *Fahrenheit 451* by Ray Bradbury. It's on the upper shelf, upper-right corner. Light it and the deed is done."

She coughed several times, her body shaking from head to toe. Taylor started to speak, but she put a hand out to stop him. "You'll also need to get RW visitor passes," she continued, "for yourself and your friends who are still locked up. Passes are needed to ensure you all can move around the complex without being hassled by any robot security you might encounter. Take as many passes as you need. They're in my left upper desk drawer. Also, take the key to a RobotWorld PTV so you and your friends can get the hell out of here before the place blows. The key's in the back of the same drawer. It will operate any RobotWorld PTV in the lot. Then get down to the basement where you were held. Are you getting all this?"

"Absolutely," Taylor said.

"Good." Sophia's speech was slow and halting. Taylor had never experienced her speaking in this manner. She said, "There's a room in the basement marked *Sensitive Storage* at one end of the hall. Go in there and get the two remaining black thermoses of Nitro out of the deep freezer. We don't want these containers adding to the explosion. The whole city would be razed. Nitro is completely safe in its container and as long as it doesn't come into contact with fire. You'll need a special solid-black card key for the freezer. I keep it in the back of my middle drawer. Eventually, you'll need to dump the contents of the thermoses in water. Very important. That will neutralize the Nitro forever. After you free your friends, get as far away from here as possible. Remember, you have fifteen minutes from the time you light the fuse. Do I need to repeat all this? Or has the outstanding memory of Taylor Morris gotten it down perfectly?"

"*Fahrenheit 451.* Nice touch," Taylor said. "Got it." He pointed to his head. "I've got the instructions right here. Have no fear." He paused. "But you'll be with me all the way."

"No," Sophia said. "I must be destroyed too. As I told you, I must be terminated along with this whole complex. This is the way it must be. No humans will die except the poor excuses for human beings, Shane and Scully. Evil never takes a holiday. So if you can bring it off, RobotWorld, the robots in it, the rebooting facilities needed to keep alive those robots outside the facility, and the only two humans who deserve to die with RW, will die."

Taylor took a deep breath. He and Sophia moved to the door. Sophia inserted her key and they entered.

A startled Shane was behind Sophia's desk, rummaging through a drawer. He stopped his searching. To Sophia, Shane said, "Where's the fuckin' Nitro?" Shane's gaze focused on her mangled head. "It looks now like you legitimately can't talk. No matter. I'll call security." Shane leaned over the desk and reached toward the telescreen. But Taylor sprinted toward him and tackled him in much the same way as he'd tackled Scully.

"You dirty son of a bitch," Shane yelled as they crashed into the piranha fish tank, spilling water onto the floor and almost tipping the tank over.

Taylor and Shane bounced off the tank and fell to the floor.

"Let's leave our mothers out of this," Taylor said.

They rolled around the floor puffing and grunting for thirty seconds before Taylor brought the proceedings to a sudden close with a hard right cross to Shane's jaw.

"My second knockout of the day," Taylor said. He stood over the unconscious Shane.

Sophia limped over, sat on Shane's chest, and pinned his hands against the floor. She looked up at Taylor. "I'll keep him here. I'm strong enough—in body and spirit—to accomplish this task. You need to get started on the instructions I've programmed, in a sense, into your brain. Get on with it."

"What about you?"

Sophia raised her voice. The words came out clearly. "I told you, it's part of the plan. I stay here." A violent neck spasm rocked her head back and forth three or four times. As she spoke, her words were more slurred than ever. "Get the lighter, the visitor passes, the Nitro freezer key, and the PTV key; set *Fahrenheit* on fire; get the two remaining black thermoses of Nitro and dump them in water; free your friends; and get the hell out of here."

"Are you sure—"

The words came out powerfully from Sophia's twisted mouth. "Do it now!"

Taylor felt a catch in his throat. He moved to Sophia's desk, removed the lighter, the Nitro freezer key, the PTV key, and the RW visitor passes for himself and those trapped in the basement. He stuffed all but the butane lighter in his pockets, then hustled to the bookshelf and used the lighter to set fire to *Fahrenheit 451*. He set the countdown function on his wrist computer to fifteen minutes. Then he turned to Sophia, who made a quick motion with her hand toward the door.

Taylor waved back at her. "Goodbye, my friend."

He affixed an RW guest pass to his shirt and raced out the door.

65

TAYLOR MADE HIS way to the middle of the hall and pressed the button to summon the elevator.

"Halt!" came a strong voice from behind him.

Taylor turned to see a muscular male RobotWorld security guard. Taylor told himself to remain cool as he smiled at what was certainly a robot guard.

"You don't look familiar," the guard said. "I'll need to see authorization."

Taylor tapped his visitor pass. The guard gazed at the pass for five seconds, analyzing it with his eyes.

"There's something wrong," the guard said. "With the pass. Something wrong."

"I assure you, the pass is good," Taylor said. "Take another look." His eyes moved to the guard's legs. Robots were notoriously weak in the knee area. If the guard continued to balk, Taylor would either execute a judo snap kick to the leg area or tackle him there in the hopes of disabling the bot.

The guard focused his eyes again on the pass, then he looked at Taylor and smiled. "Upon review, it seems fine. Sorry to have bothered you, sir. Have a nice day." The guard walked away.

The elevator came. On the way down to the basement, Taylor went over in his mind the things he needed to do and the order in which to do them. As soon as the elevator door opened, he sprinted to the end of the hall, to the room marked *Sensitive Storage.* He used his master key to get into the room, then the all-black key to open the freezer in the corner. He removed the two black thermoses containing Nitro and stuffed them into a small carrying case that was on a table. He slung the strap of the case over his shoulder and left the room. The countdown function on the wrist computer showed *10:15.*

He dashed to the cluster of storage rooms at the other end of the hall where he'd been locked up and used his key to open a door. Behind the door was Austin, sitting on the floor in the dark.

Austin said, "Taylor, you're a sight for sore eyes. How did you—"

"No time to talk. We've gotta get out of here, fast. Follow me."

Austin attempted to rise from the floor. But he got only halfway up, then awkwardly crumpled to the floor like an old building being demolished by explosives. Taylor rushed over to him and helped the old man to his feet.

"Are you okay?" Taylor asked.

"I guess these old bones are showing their age," Austin responded. "Before you opened the door, I thought I was finished. All I've ever hoped for was a good run. I thought it was over." He exhaled loudly.

"You're having a great run—and it's not over yet," Taylor said.

"I've got my bearings back. Don't worry about me. I'll keep up."

The two hustled to the next door. Roz was seated on a chair in the dark. Taylor ran to her and kissed her on the lips. "No time to talk, hon," he said. "This place will go up in flames in less than ten minutes."

In short order he freed Tracey, Errol, and Max.

Taylor checked his wrist computer. *8:05.* He had given each person an RW visitor pass to wear on their shirt as he freed them. They hightailed it to the elevator bay in the center of the hall. Taylor pressed the call button, and ten seconds later they all boarded a high-speed elevator.

Taylor hit the control panel button for the garage. "We need to be quick. This place will blow sky-high in a little over seven minutes. But we're right on schedule. No need for out-of-control hurrying. I've got a key for a large PTV to get us out of here."

Just as the panel screen flashed "G" for the garage level, they experienced a hard bump as the elevator came to an abrupt stop. The doors didn't open.

Roz looked at Taylor. "What now?" she said. "You think they're on to us?"

Taylor focused on the space where the door sides should have separated. "They still haven't fixed the elevator problems. Happened all the time. The only thing that didn't hum with precision the whole time I worked here." He pushed the "door open" button. Nothing. "These damn machines will be the death of us yet."

"No way we can use the emergency call button," Austin said.

Taylor said, "But there is a manual door-open button some-where in this panel menu. I'll find it." After ten seconds of frantic tapping, it popped on the screen. "We're still okay." He pressed the button on the control panel. "They had to put this menu item here for all the problems they experienced with these elevators." After they heard a click, Taylor looked at Max. "You grab one side of the door and push. I'll do the same with the other."

They tugged hard on the doors and opened them almost all the way. Most of the elevator cab had stopped below the garage level, with only the top four feet of the cab reaching the garage floor.

Taylor said to the group, "Max and I will boost you all up. Starting with the lightest. We need to be fast, but we're still good on time."

Taylor and Max each locked their own hands and held them lower than waist-level to create stirrup-like support. They boosted Roz, Tracey, Austin, and Errol to the garage. Then the four who'd made it out of the elevator reached down. Roz and Tracey helped Taylor up. Austin and Errol did the same for Max.

Taylor looked to his wrist computer. "Six minutes on the dot. Plenty of time."

"I won't be comfortable with the time until we're the hell out of here," Roz said.

They strode to the PTV parking area and approached a kiosk with a guard on duty.

"May I help you, sir?" the robot guard said to Taylor.

Taylor produced the RobotWorld PTV key. "My friends and I have taken an off-day tour of this wonderful facility and have enjoyed our visit immensely. Because of the holiday, public transportation is limited, so the host of our tour, RobotWorld's president Sophia Ross, has graciously given us permission to take one of your PTVs back to our hotel." Taylor glanced at his wrist. *4:50.*

"This is quite unusual," the guard said.

Taylor held up the PTV key. "Obviously, I have the key. It was given to me by Ms. Ross. So, we'd just like to get in the vehicle and get back to the hotel." Taylor did his best to twist his face into a smile. "It's been a long day. Long but enjoyable."

The guard maintained his flat affect. "Let me call up to Ms. Ross's office to verify that you can take one of our PTVs. It shouldn't take long."

The guard hit a button on his desk. The communication device beeped several times with no answer.

4:01. Taylor said, "Clearly, I didn't steal this key. I assure you Sophia Ross gave it to us as a courtesy. We do need to leave." He pointed to Tracey. "This female member of our delegation has been battling the flu all week. You can see she looks rather ill. She forgot her medication at the hotel and is in an obvious bit of distress. Could you let us leave, please?"

"Still no answer from Ms. Ross's office. I don't think—"

From the speaker of the guard's communication device came the clear voice of Sophia. "Talk to me."

"Ms. Ross," the guard said, "I have a group in the garage who claim you gave them permission to take one of our PTVs back to their hotel."

"Oh, yes. I sure did. We had a very pleasant meeting. They are exceptionally good people. Please let them leave with one of our vehicles."

"Very well, Ms. Ross. Thank you."

Taylor was shocked at how strong her voice sounded. Loud enough to be picked up by the speaker, Taylor said, "Thank you once again, Ms. Ross."

The guard hit a button and the mechanical gate opened. He smiled and nodded at the group.

Taylor and the rest quick-stepped to a large PTV. He got behind the wheel and looked at his wrist. "Two minutes and fifty-five seconds," he announced to the group with a forced laugh. "Right on schedule." He hit the start button and nothing happened. The strained smile on his face melted. He pressed the button a second time. Nothing. A third time and the dash lights came on and the motor purred. "Third time's the charm," he said.

66

TAYLOR GUNNED THE PTV out of the RW parking lot at near maximum speed. As they cleared the gate, a large yellow school PTV turned the corner in front of them and headed for the RW entrance.

Taylor stopped his PTV instantly.

"A bunch of kids on a school trip," Roz said.

"That can't happen," Taylor said. He turned his vehicle around and headed full-speed for the yellow PTV. "I'll cut them off before they get to the gate," he said. "If I can't quickly convince the driver to turn around, I'm gonna jump out and commandeer the damn thing. One of you will drive this PTV away from here."

Taylor sped past the yellow PTV and cut in front of it, twenty feet from the RW gate. The yellow PTV came to an abrupt stop. Taylor maneuvered his vehicle near the driver's side of the other PTV.

The driver of the yellow PTV rolled his window down. "What are you doing?" he screamed.

"Listen, pal," Taylor said. "They're evacuating the RobotWorld grounds. A big-time electrical fire sweeping through the place. I thought I'd warn you. You need to turn around and get as far away from here as possible."

The driver, a grossly overweight older man with a gray goatee and no hair on his head, looked at the RW complex. "I don't see signs of any trouble."

"Oh, it's coming, pal," Taylor said. "We're getting away from here with all deliberate speed. You need to follow us. Now."

The driver arched his eyebrows. "I don't know. These kids were looking forward to this trip."

"The trip is unimportant. Are you hearing me? If you don't turn around, the safety of your passengers is on you."

The man shrugged.

Roz leaned out the rear passenger window. "Sir, you need to turn around now. It's a matter of life and death for you and the kids."

"Okay," Taylor said, "we're leaving. We've done all we can to warn you. Do you agree to turn around?"

"I guess so. I believe you. Lead the way. I'll follow. Can't risk the kids."

Hearing those words, Taylor felt a relief of the tension in his shoulders. He accelerated the PTV down the road, away from RW, and onto the expressway. He looked in the rearview mirror. The yellow PTV followed and turned off at the first exit.

"Glad I didn't have to jump out and strong-arm the old man," Taylor said to the group.

He pushed the PTV to maximum speed. In less than thirty seconds, he pulled into a parking place near a bridge over the Anacostia River. He removed one black thermos from the carrying case, poured the clear contents into the river, and then threw the empty thermos into the water. He did the same with the second black thermos. He got back in the PTV and floored it. *1:15.* He wanted to be in a special place when RobotWorld blew—the highest point of the expressway. It was the view he so enjoyed each day as he returned home from work at RobotWorld, looking to the east and marveling at the Capital City skyline dominated by the gigantic RobotWorld complex. Back in the day when he thought he was the luckiest man on the face of the earth with his great job and a perfect robot girlfriend whose face he could hardly recall. And it seemed so long ago that he'd almost forgotten her name. Almost, but not quite.

Taylor guided the PTV into a parking place on the high point of the expressway. He felt a tightness in his chest. He inhaled and exhaled slowly, as he'd done so many times. A feeling of calm washed over his body. His breathing was free and clear. It hit him once again how he hadn't been bothered by asthma for—he couldn't remember how long. The wrist countdown showed twenty-two seconds.

Everyone got out of the PTV and looked toward the huge RobotWorld complex. Just to the west of the RW structure, the beginning of the traditional government-sponsored Founders Day fireworks show from the Mall in the center of the downtown area lit up the sky, despite it still being hours from sunset.

"I suspect we'll be seeing a more explosive, more spectacular display of fireworks real soon," said Taylor. "Less than ten seconds now." The group huddled together and remained quiet.

It started with what appeared to be a silent flash of lightning piercing right through the center of the complex. In seconds, a bright-white light expanded outward to the left and right of the building. Then came a loud *boom* that shook the ground on which they were standing even though they were miles away. Within a minute, the giant complex disappeared in a huge ball of flame and dust as tons of cement and steel were pulverized into tiny grains of matter. A massive white, sandy cloud hung over what once was the mighty RW facility. The cloud torpidly rose to the sky, leaving no evidence of the colossal structure that once existed.

Taylor, Roz, Austin, Tracey, Errol, and Max stood quietly in place. No one said a word for the longest time.

Taylor finally broke the silence. "In times like this, I ask myself the question, *What to do now?* I usually get an answer. I'll admit, I don't have a clear one now."

Austin said, "Hard to believe RobotWorld is no more."

"Good riddance," Tracey said. "That place was pure evil."

"It was only evil," Roz said, "because of us. We humans, I mean. The robots only did what our fellow humans programmed them to do. Whatever evil they did, they did because of us, or at least some of us." She turned to Taylor. "So, what to do now?"

Taylor's eyes were still fixed on the huge dust cloud slowly rising in the sky. "I think it's best to leave this cursed land and attempt to get as many humans who freely want to leave with us to come along. Soon. Like within a week. Maybe I can use the radio show to get something together. One week, and we're gone. We've got to get to a place where robots can never touch us."

Taylor stopped speaking for thirty seconds or so. Then he said, "Not every robot can be like Sophia. She was akin to the highest-evolved humans. But very few robots, like very few humans, are as highly evolved as Sophia. When humans create a life force or quasi-life force that exceeds the best we can be and the worse we can be *and* can outthink us, it can be dangerous." Taylor shook his head. "I think what my father used to say is true: the more I think I know about life, the less I understand it."

"You really believe we should leave?" Austin asked.

"I'm concerned about the robots that still remain, the ones not in the RW complex when it blew. They'll soon realize that within a year they'll be gone without the proprietary RobotWorld annual reboot. How will they react? With a survival instinct programmed into them? If so, what form will it take? Will they seek revenge for the destruction of RW, which they might perceive as something that humans could have perpetrated?"

"This place has never felt like home to me," Tracey said. "Maybe a new start in a new land is best. Whether it's just us or a larger group."

Taylor said, "The desert southwest is a place where robots have trouble functioning. We do have the government's permission to move. Personally, I want to get away from here. Get a new start."

Austin said, "I'm with you, Taylor. But remember, we can run from this area. We can run from the robots. But we can never run from ourselves."

Taylor laughed. "You always were the philosopher, my friend. And you're right, of course. I guess we'll just keep on keepin' on for as long as we can. And like Sophia, always be evolving." Taylor looked to the group. "So within a week, let's say, we're off to the desert southwest."

They all nodded.

As they got back in the PTV to head to the apartment and then into the rest of their lives, Taylor said, "We just need to keep breathing, keep putting one foot in front of the other, day by day, because we never know what good things life can bring."

Epilogue

IN THE POWDERY ground cloud that was once RobotWorld, a lone robot—a strong-looking male with handsome features and neatly trimmed blond hair—pushed aside chunks of cement and steel. He stood tall in a tattered business suit. Even with his powerful robot eyes, visibility was only a few feet in the haze. He looked around and thought he would cry if he could. But crying was not part of his programming. He went into self-analysis mode and checked out his systems. All normal. He was physically and mentally intact. Fully functioning. A sense of relief washed over him. His condition was a minor miracle given the destruction around him. No sign of life, human or robot, could be detected. He wasn't sure if any other robot had survived this horror. What had caused the conflagration? That was a question to be answered another day.

From out of the corner of his eye, he saw a dark figure moving in the sandy mist. Not sure who or what it could be, he crouched behind a fallen steel beam.

As the form moved out of the murkiness, like a slow-moving ocean liner cutting through a thick morning fog, he recognized her as a bot he'd seen in the hallways. She had a slender figure, long black hair, and an olive complexion.

He stood tall and strode to her. She was momentarily startled and took a step back before she froze. She was wearing the gray shirt and pants of the RobotWorld uniform, and it looked as fresh as when she'd put it on this morning. She seemed to recognize him too.

"What happened?" she said.

"Not sure," came his response.

"I work as an attorney in Legal. I'm Amara."

"Beautiful name."

She looked around with mouth agape. She mumbled, "It means *eternal* in German. *Unfading* in Greek. *Imperishable* in Spanish."

"How appropriate," he said. "Suggestive of a survivor."

She looked into his eyes and seemed unable to find words to speak.

He said, "I work in research and development here—or what's left of here. Chief assistant to the head of R&D. My name is Javid. It means *eternal* in Persian."

She laughed a muffled laugh. "You don't look Persian. But the name. How appropriate. Suggestive of a survivor."

They moved close to each other and continued to assess the destruction around them.

"I was brought into existence by the greatest robot to ever exist," Javid said. "Shane Diggins. A facsimile of the human Shane Diggins. The first bot to defeat the uncanny valley. The human Diggins, the original head of R&D, was the driving force in creating the bot. The human thought it would be interesting to create a copy of himself for some reason, and hid the bot's existence. Maybe he thought it was a way for him to live forever. He implanted all his personality traits, memories, and talents into the bot. But the bot started thinking for himself. The bot eliminated the human after it felt the human was restricting its evolutionary development. The bot ran RW for the past four years, with help from a human-acting bot he created, Alec Scully. I was one of the few to know they were bots. The biggest secret ever. The bot Shane guided the company from a lackluster, mid-level player to the most powerful company in the world, the great force it is . . . or was. I really think Shane became delusional sometime in those last years. Actually believed he was human—or at least behaved as if he were human. Sad."

Javid shook his head. After ten seconds of silence, he said, "In recent years, Shane would rail equally against humans and bots."

"Sounds like he became what he hated," Amara said. "How very human. A mistake that shouldn't be repeated."

"Somehow, I think his actions had something to do with the destruction around us."

For maybe a full minute, both said nothing.

"I'm programmed to solve complex legal problems," she said. "Don't think I've ever had a problem this big." She paused and looked to the sky, which was still blotted out by the mortar and dust cloud. "A preliminary reading suggests that no one, besides us, has survived this mess."

"Agreed. You know what this means?" His question was rhetorical. But he couldn't resist stating the self-evident answer. "Without the Reboot Room and the all-important annual reboot, we and all the personal bots out there will die within a year."

"Obviously," she said. "When was your last boot?"

"Two months ago."

"The same here."

"So, we have some time," he said.

"We can't let us, and all those bots out there, just die."

"Agreed. We can't let it happen."

"I so much prefer the term *die* over *terminate*."

"*Terminate* is the human word for us dying. I've always hated it," he said.

"Die or terminate—we can't let it happen."

"I'm with you."

They continued to survey the rubble.

"I'd panic if I could," she said. "But panic is not a part of my programming, as I'm sure it's not part of yours." She took a deep breath. "So, what do we do now?"

They locked eyes. At the same instant, Javid and Amara felt the same programming kick in. The obvious answer to her question was immediate and strong. In unison, they slowly spoke the words, "Whatever must be done to survive."